Launched in 1990 with her debut novel, *Darker Days Than Usual*, Suzannah Dunn wrote a further five critically acclaimed contemporary novels, and a short story collection, published by Flamingo, before writing her first historical novel, *The Queen of Subtleties*, which was published in 2004. She went on to write *The Sixth Wife*, *The Queen's Sorrow*, *The Confession of Katherine Howard* (a Richard & Judy pick in 2011), *The May Bride*, *The Lady of Misrule* and *The Testimony of Alys Twist*.

Praise for *Levitation for Beginners*

'Brilliantly articulated and often piercingly sad, Dunn's characters find themselves caught up in what may today be termed quarter-life crises . . . if this subtle book has a message, it is how alien and yet how relatable the past remains'
Guardian, Book of the Day

'A glorious writer . . . witty, well-observed and full of heart . . . this is a wonderful, accessible story full of love, memory and the truth'
Irish Independent

'Powerful and unsettling, Dunn's distinctive voice and knack for observation transported me straight back to my teenage years and had me gripped to the very end'
Carly Reagon

'A bittersweet, nostalgia-tinged adventure'
Daily Mail

'A deceptively clever, un
about the secrets and li
community that feels incr
Katherine

'Packed with period detail, this is a story that is alternately affectionate, nostalgic, chilling and mysterious'
Julie Ma

By Suzannah Dunn

Levitation
for
Beginners

Suzannah Dunn

abacus
books

ABACUS

First published in Great Britain in 2024 by Abacus
This paperback edition published in 2025

3 5 7 9 10 8 6 4 2

A CIP catalogue record for this book is available from the British Library.

ISBN: 978-0-3491-4135-0

Typeset in Plantin by M Rules
Printed and bound in Great Britain by
Clays Ltd, Elcograf S.p.A.

Papers used by Abacus are from well-managed forests
and other responsible sources.

Abacus
An imprint of
Little, Brown Book Group
Carmelite House
50 Victoria Embankment
London EC4Y 0DZ

The authorised representative
in the EEA is
Hachette Ireland
8 Castlecourt Centre
Dublin 15, D15 XTP3, Ireland
(email: info@hbgi.ie)

An Hachette UK Company
www.hachette.co.uk

www.hachette.co.uk

In memory of my best schoolfriend,
Katy Rensten (1963–2021)

1

Whenever I think of what happened all those decades ago, what comes to mind is something I know for a fact had nothing to do with it. What I picture is the injured, abraded face of my teacher's son. A bloodied and bruised twelve- or thirteen-year-old, unfit that day to attend his own school, and installed instead in a chair beside his father's desk to stare glumly back at awestruck nine- and ten-year-olds. And even though I know better, even though I know there was no connection with what was to happen a year or so later, to me it's as if his accident was the start of it.

As to the circumstances, I don't recall exactly what we were told, but we did know he had been hit by a car. Or *run over* as we would have said amongst ourselves, and certainly a nine-year-old looking at that mess of scabs could persuade herself of tyre tracks. My adult eye, looking back, sees that the damage – shocking though undoubtedly it was – was superficial. He had glanced off that car and there were no other apparent injuries.

No bandages or splints, and he sat on that chair with no obvious physical discomfort, the chief insult to his tender twelve- or thirteen-year-old pride.

And it's possible that almost half a century later he bears few if any scars from the incident and – who knows? – might not even remember it, or not as often as, inexplicably, I do. It's possible too that he might already have had, or have gone on to have, a lot of scrapes. But me, at nine years old: I had never come across a wounding so spectacular, and I was astounded that anyone could be so damaged and still standing, or sitting. It looked to me to have been a terrifyingly close-run thing.

If I close my eyes it is as if it were yesterday, but now, thinking about it, I wonder if it wasn't the spectacle of that poor face – the cuts and scrapes – that made the impression, but the fury in the eyes of a boy who, I imagine, miscalculated in a moment of high spirits and was brought down to earth with a bump. Then brought so low as to be stuck in that chair at the side of his dad's desk, staring down a class of nine-year-olds and daring us to pity him.

The seventies: butterscotch Angel Delight and Raleigh chopper bikes, and Clunk Click, and *Crackerjack* and *Jackanory*, 'Layla' and the Bee Gees, flares and ponchos, and the long hot summer of '76. But then again: Vietnam, Pinochet, Watergate, Bloody Sunday, the IRA and ETA and the Baader–Meinhof and Black September and the Red Brigade and the Angry Brigade. And little girl after little girl lifted in broad daylight from lanes and pavements and bundled into a van; bike dropped, wheels still spinning, for friends to find. A thirteen-year-old boy delivering a newspaper to a farmhouse shot in the head at close range.

In 1972, we had almost all the seventies still to come. We were a year shy of the Wombles and *Man About the House*, to say nothing of *M*A*S*H* and For Mash Get Smash, with several more years before *Starsky & Hutch* and *Charlie's Angels* and *The Good Life*. In June of that year, we had yet to marvel at the Olympian feats of Olga Korbut and Mark Spitz. And still training as if their lives depended on it were those athletes who would be massacred in Munich that September.

Forget, too, any long hot summer, because the summer of 1972 in England was one of the worst on record, with the Wimbledon men's final rained off for the first time in ninety-five years. And this summer that was no summer followed two national states of emergency and the three-day weeks during a winter in which we often spent our evenings in our coats by candlelight. And – remember – there were no smoke alarms in our homes in 1972. And a lot of unguarded hearths for us to gather around in our flammable nightwear. Upstairs on our mothers' bedside tables were bottles of barbiturates with no child safety caps; and beneath the beds, plastic bags for pulling playfully over our heads. Outside, in the garden shed, boxes of fireworks that on Bonfire Night would blow up in our faces. And all this was for those of us lucky enough to have a home because – as we all now know – God help you if you were taken into care. Our neighbours' gardens glittered darkly with laburnum seeds, and in the alley behind the fence were abandoned fridges perfect for our games of hide-and-seek. At the end of the street idled the ice cream van from behind which, brandishing our Mivvis, we could bolt into the path of a driver – un-clunked, un-clicked – who'd had one more for the road. I'm only half joking when I say I'm surprised that any of us lived to tell the tale.

At least at school we were relatively safe, if you turned a blind eye to points of compasses and held your breath against asbestos; we, snug in our two-classroomed Home Counties village school, were thriving. My cohort, tail end of the boomers, was going out with a bang: we were numerous compared to the handful of pupils in other year groups. In another way, too, we were a blip, in that our year was top heavy with girls: we were six strong; the boys – just two of them – mere bystanders. And if each of us girls was more friendly with some than others, we were all friendly enough. We got along, more or less, give or take, most of the time. At the start of June 1972, we were beginning our final half term there. And so we were almost done, nearly gone, when Sarah-Jayne turned up.

I was the first to encounter her. At break time I nipped back in from the playground to fetch my cardigan and, dashing into our classroom, intent on getting back to play, crossed paths in the doorway with our teacher – our headmaster, Mr Hadleigh – who was beating a retreat in his slippers and a haze of nicotine.

'Ah! Deborah' – his relief was audible – 'this is Sarah-Jayne, she's new.' With that one deft move she was sprung on me, left for me to deal with.

Mr Hadleigh would have been busy thinking of the cubbyhole squeezed next to the kitchen that counted in our school as the staff room, longing for a cup of tea and a cigarette and a plateful of digestives, and perhaps

4

a natter with young Miss Drake, the only other teacher, the infants' teacher, if she wasn't detained in her own classroom, the modern extension, consoling one of her little charges or mopping some spillage. And anyway, to give him his due, I was a good bet, safe hands, a sensible sort, and always did as I was told.

There across the classroom, luminous in the glow from the high Victorian windows, was blonde, blue-eyed Sarah-Jayne in a pillar-box-red trouser suit that was broad-belted and bright-buttoned, flared and wide-lapelled. What did she see when she looked over at the scrap who, back then, was me? Like my friends in the playground I probably couldn't have said, even in that moment, what I was wearing. Because what did it matter? – that's what my mum would have said. For God's sake, who's looking? We girls dressed in what we were given – hand-me-downs and jumble-sale finds and home-made affairs, pretty enough and soft with wear. Now, though, someone *was* looking, someone who was dressed to the nines, and fifty years later, those extraordinary eyes of hers are as vivid for me as they were at first glance: too blue and somehow diamond-cut. She dispensed that bright gaze warily, inclining her head as if to deflect it. She kept her eyes narrowed, which, along with the tilt of the head, gave her an air of appraising me although at the same time she seemed to wince, as if pained: *This hurts me more than it hurts you.*

Which, as everyone knows, is never true.

Rooted to the spot, I smiled back at her but my hackles rose. She got my back up even as she stood there nice as pie and butter-wouldn't-melt, with what should by rights have been a winsome tilt of the head. I knew then and there, right from the start, that she was trouble, and something inside me – everything inside me – rose up so that there I was, standing my ground, standing a little taller, digging in my heels, determined not to fall for it.

Still, I did what had to be done, took her back with me to the playground, and there, where I had left them, were Susan and Mandy. Susan, my best friend, was as usual a-flitter with chatter, her knobbly knees bobbing, with sunlight – such as there was, that grey day – rolling in her dark curls and sparking off her gold-encircled baby-bangled wrist. Her socks were slack, having given up the ghost, and around her waist her cardy was hanging on for dear life. Buck-toothed, bug-eyed Mandy was sunk back against the fence, pale blue T-bar shoes slotted side by side and her tummy making a bell tent of her skirt, as she sucked on the clot of elastic band at the end of her plait.

I took Sarah-Jayne towards them and in her splendour she could have been *The Golden Shot*'s Maid of the Month. Mandy's eyes bulged and her lips slackened around that strangulated tuft of hair, as Susan's face broke into a smile as broad as those on the infants' drawings. When I said, 'This is Sarah-Jayne,' Susan cooed, 'New girl,' just as she once had for me. But then Beverly came striding over and shouldered her way in. Drifting in her wake was doe-eyed Caroline, her ample self wrapped softly in her own arms. 'Mutt and Jeff' was how Mum mysteriously referred to the pair of them. Beverly planted herself squarely in front of the new girl and filed one flank then the other of her long, straight, centre-parted hair behind her ears, ready for business.

6

'You're new,' she said. She could always be relied upon to state the obvious. And from Caroline, who never said much but could be relied upon to back up Beverly, came a joyful bleat.

Then came the two girls from the year below us, Tracy and Virginia. Outside school, Tracy hung around with the village boys stranded in the no-man's-land of puberty, thriving on their contempt and derision, enjoying slanging matches in the park and the village hall car park, aflame with indignation. In school, she devoted herself to shepherding Virginia, who was large and unsteady on her feet and couldn't see very well. Poor Virginia, to have survived a brain tumour only to be left at the mercy of Tracy. We owed her for keeping Tracy occupied and away from us. But had we tried to intervene, Saint Tracy would have beaten us off with a stick, because Virginia was hers, an important job. And now here she was, swinging by, nosy, chewing vigorously, escorting Virginia by the elbow, to make herself known to the new girl and bestow her blessing.

'Hi, I'm Tracy. And this is Virginia.' She always spoke for the both of them. Virginia nodded politely to affirm it, her eyes huge in her lenses.

Sarah-Jayne was the picture of politeness and – I watched for it – she didn't flinch from Virginia.

Tracy said, 'Welcome,' with an absurd little bow, and Sarah-Jayne said thank you, and then, thankfully, Tracy was off ('Come on, Virginia, let's get you some fresh air'), and as they moved from earshot, Beverly said briskly, 'Virginia had a growth cut out of her brain when she was five; she can't help being like that.'

We all looked suitably grave, then Sarah-Jayne

7

said – with a wit that I recognise only now in the retelling – 'Remind me, which one's Virginia?'

It had been four or five years since I had been the new girl but in all that time in my group of friends there had been no one newer, so I had always felt that distinction remained mine. In class later that day while Mr Hadleigh taught us how to measure volume, I wondered: if I was no longer the new girl, then who or what would I be? If I had to be different, then better the new girl than the girl with the dead dad. It occurred to me that Sarah-Jayne knew nothing of this: in her ears, it would become news all over again that I had only a mum.

Not that Mum herself cared what anyone thought of her, or so she always said (*Who cares what folk think?*). She believed it was good to be different. Otherwise, you were just the same as everyone else and would disappear into the crowd. Don't follow, don't fall in with the crowd, she was always telling me: stand up for yourself, speak up, stand out, be strong. Take no one's word for anything. Make up your own mind. *If they all went jumping off a bridge, would you, too?*

And she certainly was different, although not to my mind at that time because she was a widow, but rather because she was Scottish. (Scottish widow! – but the Scottish Widow was still years away from our screens.) The only Scot I knew of back then, if you didn't count Ronnie Corbett, was *Dad's Army*'s dour, doom-prophesying Frazer.

Or *Scotch*, according to a lot of people around our way, at which Mum would roll her eyes to me and say, *Aye, like the mist*. She did say aye. Even och aye. And wee. She really did. And pal, and blether; and the way she put it, people – or folk – 'stayed' in places, rather than lived there, as if everyone kept a bag packed by the door. Mercifully, she never said we were doomed. But, unsettlingly, even when she spoke normally, she didn't, because every what or where or which or when came hooted, owl-like, or so it seemed to me – *h-what, h-which*.

She called me *Dayborah*; and I was always the full Deborah, never Debbie or Deb. *You've got a proper name, make sure you use it.* She didn't often use her own full name, though, which was Sandra. *Sand-ra*, as she said, like on *The Liver Birds*, but everyone else around our way said *Sarndra*, which she'd mimic for me in a deep, booming voice: *Sarndra Daaaarke*, as if she were being summoned. She preferred Sandy, which sidestepped the problem because no one was going to say *Sarndy*.

'Sandy Darke, short and sweet,' she'd say. 'Just like its owner. Pair-fect.'

Other times she complained it was an odd name: *Sandy Darke what? Sounds like something's missing.* (But she did always sound to me as if she was complaining – that querulous tone, that arched eyebrow of a voice.) Sandy Darke *what?* We never considered Shaw, probably because that was already so publicly taken. I did once say Beach, but Mum knocked that back, claiming that beaches weren't dark.

Well, half the time they are, I thought: at night, they are.

But no, dark wasn't what you thought of, she said, when you thought of a beach. Cove, though, apparently, was different: she could imagine a sandy cove under cover of darkness. But was that a name – Cove? If not, she said, it should be; and she said it as if she were trying

9

it on for size: Missus Cove. She'd just have to marry a Mister Cove, she said.

I was surprised, I remember, to hear that. I was perhaps seven or eight years old at the time and had never considered that she might marry. By which I mean, of course, *re*marry. Thinking back, now, it's a surprise that she hadn't. She had been widowed at twenty-four. But because she was my mum, I never thought of her as young, although I suppose I knew that others did and I suppose I knew she was younger than the mums of my friends. Everyone always said she and I could be sisters: *peas in a pod*. We had the same waist-length hair, but that was because we were both went to – as she put it – the Sandy Darke Salon, which was in our kitchen and offered just the one style, a snipping straight across the bottom with the household scissors.

I was aware that widows could remarry, and – true – she had cried when Pete Duel from *Alias Smith and Jones* shot himself, but then so had everybody because he was lovely and it was sad; it wasn't that she had actually properly loved him and she certainly wouldn't have married him. And anyway she was always saying how it was just the two of us: *You and me, eh? We do just fine by ourselves.*

My dad, unbelievably, had been Ray Darke: a name to conjure with, Mum would say, her eyebrows rising as if he had had only himself to blame, although usually she also said, *You wonder what the old girl was thinking when she chose that, except she never did think any further than the next drink.* Which was why we didn't have anything to do with her. Well, and because by the time I was in school she too, Mum said, was dead. Not to speak ill of the dead, Mum would say, but good riddance to the awfy auld besom. I still had a grandad on that side, or last Mum had heard; but he wasn't interested, she said. Only interested in the horses – which to me, obsessed with the annual WH Smith Win a Pony competition, was a significant point in his favour. That was a man I would've liked to have got to know.

Of her own family she only ever said she was best off out of it. She'd left them for London and lived for a wee h-while with her sister and her husband *but if you choose to believe a man like that over your own flesh and blood*, and they'd had a row and blood isn't thicker than water and good riddance to bad rubbish, then she married my dad and became a Darke and had me. We didn't need anyone else, she said: we were fine by ourselves, just the pair of us.

Darke was a poor fit for Mum and me: we were in fact both fair, Darke sitting on us like a joke – a rebuke, even – and a particular failing on my part, seeing as unlike Mum I was Darke by birth. 'Och, you Darkes never do what's expected of you,' she said. (My dad, she said, when I asked, had been 'mouse'.) Mum had had a different surname before she was married. A maiden name, she called it, which sounded to me like something from a fairy tale. And anyone who found Sandy Darke to be a bit funny didn't know the half of it because as a girl she had been a Gilhooly, which I judged best kept under wraps. Frazer's doom was enough of a threat; I didn't want Mandy getting hold of Mum's maiden name and following me around with *Och GilHOOOOly*. And that was to say nothing of her having grown up somewhere called Pee-balls.

I rather liked the poor fit of my surname because

I felt as if I were undercover. Anyone looking for a Darke wouldn't give me a second glance. But it was my first name of which I was proud. Deborah, I felt back then, was a name to be said with an eyebrow-lift of a different kind from my mum's habitual, derisive kind. A Deborah – it had seemed to me – might come from somewhere other than a village like ours and would know a thing or two about the world. 'Yours is a name with a history,' Mum would tell me, 'but it's also up to the minute.' No better position to be in, she said. Pairfect. It was a proper name, whereas some other names, those of girls at school – Lisa, say, or Karen – she dismissed as made up.

Deborah was a proper name, but there was also that business of my being a Deborah proper, Mum insisting against my being reduced like every other Deborah to Debbie, Debs, Deb, mere winks and nods towards the name. (Stand up, stand out, don't go jumping off bridges and disappearing.) It goes without saying that Debra was out of the question – not that I needed to be told, because *De-bra* wasn't one for the school playground. All that said, there was a brief time – the year before Sarah-Jayne came – when Marc Bolan's *deboree-deb* made me the toast of the school.

Sarah-Jayne, I decided on her first day, had a made-up name. Not the component parts – good solid names, both of them – but the conjoining of them. It was bright and shiny, it seemed to me, and somehow pleased with itself, having me think of the twin fake-brass fastenings on the bib of my hotpants.

Something that it's not, I learned over the years, is a name to conjure with. I've searched on and off but

12

turned up no trace of this particular Sarah-Jayne Todd. Presumably she has slipped like the rest of the girls under a married name (or two, or perhaps more, in her case). Unlike me: I soldier on as who I always was, if in name only. That year, 1972, was the year Tutankhamun came to town – to the British Museum – and I lapped up our lessons on the ancient Egyptians, priding myself on knowing everything there was to know about them. For them, the worst possible punishment was a change of name: worse than death, a deeper kind of death than death itself.

With my schoolfriends, it is as if I looked away and then when I turned back around, by which I mean turned to the internet, they were gone as if they'd never been. As if fallen prey to a Pied Piper. But I doubt most of them went far. They were local girls – from local families – as I never was. My own move away came seven years later than Sarah-Jayne's but was set in motion when I first took the school coach out of the village to the grammar school while the others caught the bus in the opposite direction to the comp. I don't remember anything more than the odd, awkward hello among us after that September day when we started at our new schools. I don't suppose any of us had intended it that way, but that was how it happened.

And then not long after I left home, Mum moved into a flat in town, so our link with the village was gone. The school closed decades ago, transformed first into a Montessori nursery school and then, after Miss Drake's 1960s extension was demolished, becoming a dance studio (that polished wooden floor put to good use) and 'wellness centre'. In my mind's eye my friends from the school remain their bright, shiny little ten- and eleven-year-old selves, in their tank tops, on their Chopper bikes, which suits me fine because why would I want to picture them now at sixty? (What would have become of Susan's mass of dark curls?) I'm happy to leave them be. To me, it's as if they are still living their lives somewhere but in miniature, under glass, so that all I have to do to be able to see them is lean in and look down, as I did so often in later years at our local museum's model railway with my son when he was small. He and I would peer through our own rapt reflections at the trains puffing and tooting along their tracks and the passengers in trilby hats, and we could have tapped on that glass all we liked but, thrillingly, to those tiny, busy, well-groomed people, we were the ones who didn't exist.

My mother died last week. The day before she died, she spoke just the once from her hospice bed, breathlessly, semi-consciously and barely comprehensibly. By which I mean barely comprehensibly to the nurse, who glanced at me, probably startled by her speaking up at all, but perhaps also at what sounded like something from a joke, a punchline (actress, bishop), because what she had said was *odd business, up at the vicarage*. I held my breath and gave no indication that I had heard.

The last word Sarah-Jayne ever said to me was *Go*. I never saw her again. Fifty years on, who's to say she's even still alive? People do die young, as I more than most, with my poor dead dad, should know. And anyway – I have to remind myself – we're no longer young. She could already have gone the way of several of my grammar school friends and fellow students (car accident, breast cancer, ovarian cancer and – hushed up though it was, back then – suicide). I have a strong sense, though, that she persists. I picture her at a school gate, picking up her kids, although here I have to correct myself because any children she had would be well past school age. She could be at a school gate as a grandmother if she was an early starter, which she probably was.

It might not merely be Todd from which she has slipped free but also Sarah-Jayne: perhaps she's now a simple Sarah or Jayne, even an elegantly understated Jane. I can picture her home from the school gate – the school gate to which she almost certainly won't have been – with a woman she has invited back for coffee. I see a gleaming kitchen island, posh biscuits on a plate, milk in a jug, and hear a good-natured moan or two about their respective menfolk along with some chatter about raffle tickets or a cake bake in aid of their own local hospice. She's pleasant company for a weekday morning, and there's no suggestion of anything ever having been amiss.

2

That first day of hers at our school, when Miss Drake rang the handbell and we trooped back into class, Sarah-Jayne was taken by Beverly to the table she shared with Caroline, and settled there between them. Our particular year group fell naturally into two groups – Beverly had never had any time for the potion-making that Susan, Mandy and I enjoyed, or our pretend Spanish-speaking, our play horse-riding – and it appeared that she and Caroline would be the group to take up this new girl. Just as well, I thought, because Susan, Mandy and I already made a trio; there was no room at our table. It was a relief to see the new girl flanked by that pair and know that we three could remain as we were, because it was bad enough having to deal with Mandy.

The first lesson after break was maths, always dreaded by everyone, including, it seemed, Mr Hadleigh. When it came to maths, a defiant look would steal over him, and he would order us to our workbooks. Every other subject – English, history, music, art and craft, the nature table, rounders – he taught in person, to all twenty or so of us in that classroom across the various year groups, with no need for any books. And in all those other lessons he would talk in accents and funny fake voices (workhouse supervisor, Egyptian slave driver), pitched to appeal as much to a seven-year-old boy as an eleven-year-old girl, joyfully bellowing instructions, firing questions, tapping time. He was within a few years of an early retirement on grounds of ill-health, though, and he ended up getting out before there was any requirement to teach science. I do wonder if even by our time he was tiring of tambourines.

Faced with maths, he retreated, to become quite unlike his usual avuncular self, avoiding catching anyone's eye, turning sharp and short-tempered, his sulkiness suggesting he felt betrayed by the stipulation from upon high that we should be numerate. His sending of us to our workbooks was a kind of throwing up of his hands and the petulance implied that we had only ourselves to blame, as if we'd asked for this. For us, too, though, there was this sense of having been led up the garden path, because in all our other classes we learned to talk our way out of anything. In English, I learned that if we just kept talking, we could bring anyone round, our stories taking on a life of their own. But persistence in maths, I found, only dug me deeper in. It seemed to have been invented to trip us up.

So, there we were, that day, all twenty or so of us in that classroom left to our own devices, having to do whatever our various books instructed us to do. We worked through the levels at our own pace, which in my case was that of a snail and a despondent one at that.

Only ever in maths was our classroom quiet, although it was noisy enough with self-pitying gasps, ashamed tuts, and vigorous, furious applications of erasers. During our daily half-hour of maths, despair descended in that tall Victorian room and in place of our exuberance the air was dense with dust motes and the fragrance of waxed floorboards.

Whenever we had completed a page, we had to take our book up for Mr Hadleigh to check and tick or correct and explain, and then – perhaps bolstered by our stupid mistakes and misunderstandings – he would attempt a jauntiness that fooled no one, and dispense largesse at the point of a nicotine-stained fingertip: *Ah well, but you see here* . . .

Sitting between Beverly and Caroline, her place squarely marked with an intriguingly denim pencil case, Sarah-Jayne worked throughout the lesson – this lesson that was no lesson – with head bowed and cocked as if teasing the maths. There were no self-recriminatory sighs or defeated exhalations from her, and during that deadly session she was up several times to Mr Hadleigh's desk with – it was clear from all the ticking – her correctly completed pages. Mr Hadleigh didn't look as pleased as we might have expected; in fact, he looked faintly disgruntled, as if she were betraying some fundamental principle by needing none of his bountiful *Ah well, but you see* . . . All he could say to her was what sounded to me like a slightly grudging *Very good, Sarah-Jayne*.

She looked nothing like trouble, that day, yet there was something that troubled me in how she left her chair for those treks across to Mr Hadleigh's desk. She made something of it. It was all done in the blink of an eye,

18

yet unmistakably there it was: a backwards shove with her bottom to send her chair sliding back from the table, then an emphatic placing of both hands flat on the table-top to lever herself to her feet with a playful reluctance: *Oh if you insist.*

And thus she made us watch, she made us wait for it, and then, with that wince of a smile, it was as if she had given in to us. She stalked across the classroom, over the sprung boards, as if she were wearing heels. She acted as if everyone were watching, which meant that – somehow, magically – everyone was.

By the end of that dispiriting half-hour, I knew the new girl was clever, or certainly at maths, which rang another alarm bell because in our year group I was supposed to be the clever one. Not that cleverness had much currency among us – no one wanted to be a clever clogs, too clever by half. It was an encumbrance, even, in a way, in that I couldn't go with Susan to the local secondary that coming September, but instead would have to travel much further to the grammar, wearing a stiff, scratchy blazer, the breast pocket emblazoned with a boar's head, and at the grammar – everyone said – the work would be so much harder. Still, clever was what I was, Mum said, and I should make the most of it, make something of myself, stand out and move on up in life, not settle like most people do.

But so far, it was only maths at which this girl had proved herself so capable. And Mr Hadleigh's offhand response to her workbook had been gratifying. I could hope that she wasn't imaginative, as Mr Hadleigh always said I was. Mum was less keen on imagination (*Shall we imagine I've paid the leccy bill?*) although once when

I was crying about maths she said, 'Och, anyone can push a few numbers around'; she, who'd had to learn to do exactly that so that she could be paid for doing Mr Watt's books and keep a roof over our heads.

After maths, that day, there was a spelling test and then for break time we all went together into the playground, in dutiful attendance on the new girl. Normal service suspended – no hopscotch or skipping. Even Wendy came spinning into our company; she didn't belong to either group and in class had to sit with the boys because Beverly refused to tolerate her. As we gathered by the fence she bounded up with a 'Wotcha!' which had Beverly rounding on her – 'Don't start' – but Wendy ignored the rebuff and cut across Beverly to ask Sarah-Jayne, 'Do you like horses?'

Sarah-Jayne looked ambushed and I too was puzzled because Wendy herself had no interest in horses. Anyway, Beverly was having none of it. 'Come on,' she said, escorting her charge nowhere in particular, just a few steps further along the fence, at a remove from Wendy. Caroline followed because she always did, which left Susan, Mandy and me to decide whether to fall in or take this as the opportunity to break away. It might be a matter of a mere few steps but if we took those steps then we'd be committed.

And what would be the point of that? I could tell this new girl, standing around trying so hard to look perfect, wasn't for me nor for my two friends, and anyway Beverly seemed to have the situation covered. It was on the tip of my tongue to suggest to Susan and Mandy that we go off and play as usual but I was worried that would be impolite. We were nice girls, we did our best, we knew to be welcoming and we certainly wouldn't have wanted to give offence. But for how much longer should we attend the trouser-suited spectacle? When could normal service respectfully resume? She didn't need us, she looked to be in good hands with Beverly, and I couldn't envisage her cantering about, not dressed like that.

She didn't look to me as if she would like horses but she did appear very much to like her clothes: at that moment, she was rearranging her lapels, splaying them even wider across her collarbones. I didn't know what to make of how she looked. Bright-blue-eyed and button-nosed, with softly feathered gold hair: all very lovely, yes, but her features were so regular as to be unremarkable. If she were in a magazine – and she could be – you would flip through without noticing her. She could turn heads but could just as easily be part of the background. She had nothing like Susan's little mole at the corner of her mouth, nor Mandy's buck teeth, nor the pale blue vein that fluttered on Beverly's temple. She was extraordinary but ordinary, stunning but bland, and I found as I stood there in the playground gawping at her that I could summon up first one version and then another but not both together. This made me think of a puzzle in an old annual I had at home, a line drawing that either looked to be of a vase or a pair of faces in profile facing each other. I would be able to see that figure in my book as either one or the other, but however much I tried, never both in the same instant. It was as if I had to choose, but at the same time it felt like no choice at all.

Wendy turned to the fence and began playing clap hands with it – *My auntie toe-elled her I kissed a sole-dier* – but managed between the sung phrases to bellow at the new girl, 'Where do you live?'

This Sarah-Jayne answered, although she spoke guardedly, as if merely humouring Wendy. 'The vicarage.'

Wendy shrieked, 'Your dad's a vicar!' although she knew full well that wouldn't be the case.

Nevertheless Mandy rose to it: 'No, *stupid*, because remember? There's no vicar in the vicarage.'

Because the vicarage was just a house, if a grand one. 'The vicar's gone, he's gone off to heaven!' Wendy sang out, nonsensically, still clapping. 'Popped his clogs! Cream crackered and popped his clogs!'

She always took things too far: the vicar hadn't died, he'd simply gone, or more accurately had never been there in the first place – not this particular one, anyway. The vicarage, which looked to me like a gigantic wedding cake, was too grand a residence for our shuffling, mumbling vicar.

Susan skipped over to Sarah-Jayne and shyly confided, 'A long time ago, a famous lady from the telly used to live there.' This we all knew: it was village lore, our claim to fame.

Naturally, the new girl's interest was piqued. 'Really? Who?'

Unfortunately, there she had us because although at various times we had been told the name, it had meant nothing to us and gone in one ear and out the other: just a name from way back, like Tony Curtis or Diana Dors. Someone from the war: someone in black and white. But surely she was missing the point, I thought, because the actual name was irrelevant; what mattered was the one-time vicarage resident had been a star. That was what was worthy of note.

'Not a lady from Benny Hill!' said Wendy. 'Not one of *those* telly ladies!' and then she was on to the Benny Hill theme tune and running around in a circle, throwing alarmed looks over her shoulder, flinching and feigning outrage as if someone were trying to pinch her bottom.

Ignoring her, Susan admitted regretfully, 'She was quite an olden-times actress.'

Sarah-Jayne accepted this with a nod, then said, 'Anyway, we're not going to stay there. We're looking for land.'

Which made them sound like pirates.

'To build somewhere,' she said.

All of us except Wendy and Caroline lived in council houses, and ours had been built ages ago and – it was obvious – by people who didn't really care. They were of the same brick as the school toilet block around the back, and the boiler room: a sour dim red, which looked like it needed a good wipe. Wendy lived with her mum (Deevorcee Dilys) and big brother (Weirdo Wayne) in a Tardis of a cottage in a lane behind the church. Caroline was the only one of us to live in a building that clearly had been designed: it lounged under a sidelong roof and was split-level, as my mum had a habit of whispering, awed, when we passed it. 'You wouldn't think it of that mother, would you,' she'd say, 'peely-wally as she is with her nerves.' Caroline's mum wore cardigans as capes over her bony shoulders and blinked a lot.

Two houses were being built across the lane from our school by Saint Tracy's dad. Well, not by the man himself – we had never glimpsed him up there on the scaffolding – but by his building firm, Gibb – or Glib, as Mum said every single time a van of his went by. It was Mum who told me that a few years back Tracy's dad had bought the orchard from the vicarage then cut the trees down and built Vicarage Close on it, keeping the biggest of those new houses for himself. The Gibb family home looked like a mansion, I thought, only smaller. As for the two houses opposite the school, they were still skeletons, forlorn under tatty tarpaulins, but Mum said they were going to be quite something: a balcony each, and a flat roof, and what she wouldn't give, she always said, for a flat roof.

Sarah-Jayne told us, 'We've just come back from abroad,' gazing into middle distance, her arms folded, as if this revelation were nothing, but from all around came an intake of breath. We did of course know abroad existed – Mr and Mrs Hadleigh had been to Sweden with the Volvo Owners Club and Caroline had been to France three times. My mum said toilets in France were holes in the ground but whenever I had tried to raise this with Caroline she laughed – that bleat of hers – which I didn't know whether to take as confirmation or refutation, and I didn't push it because somehow we all knew not to push Caroline.

'Where?' Susan was thrilled.

'Germany.'

'Germany?' Mandy voiced our disappointment.

Predictably, Wendy broke into *Vee Vill!* and I didn't have to look over at her to know she was goosestepping.

Wide-eyed, Susan probed: 'But why Germany? Why not somewhere else?' Such as Spain, I knew she meant. Susan and I were fans of Spain: that was where we wanted to go on holiday. That was our ambition, and in preparation we often spoke Spanish to each other – we made sounds that we felt sounded like Spanish and pretended to understand each other, and we did sound fluent. Mum and I never went away on holiday – *Does money grow on trees?* – but each school summer holiday we made a kind of holiday at home by having variety packs of cereal so that we started each day in a special and luxurious way.

'My dad was working there,' was Sarah-Jayne's answer.

All this was too much for Beverly; she lost interest if she had ever had any in the first place and called time on the discussion by cutting in with a purely practical concern: 'Let me show you the bogs.' My mum said never to say bogs: it was common, coarse, and people who talked like that really didn't help themselves.

Sarah-Jayne snapped to it, turning to the school building. 'I'll get my bag.'

Bag?

'Your bag?' This from Susan.

'Hairbrush,' Sarah-Jayne enlightened her, gesturing at her own head, at hair that looked to be in no need of any attention.

'Oh.' Susan never brushed her hair – she couldn't, there really was nothing anyone could do with it. Which, in my opinion, was its glory.

Beverly put paid to any prospect of what my mum called titivation. 'There's no mirrors,' she told Sarah-Jayne, matter of fact, 'just bogs.' She reconsidered: 'Well, and a sink.'

That cavernous sink with its sibilant tap and streak of discoloration like rot in a bone was at least as alarming to me as the toilets with the tarnished chains hung from precariously elevated thunderous cisterns.

The new girl accepted it, turned her attention instead to Caroline, who was resting against the fence and rocking a signet ring contemplatively back and forth over her knuckle.

'What's on that?' she asked.

Caroline's dark eyes rose from her reverie. She was probably as surprised at having been addressed as by the question itself.

'There,' persisted Sarah-Jayne, indicating the engraved face of the ring.

And now Caroline wasn't fazed; it was as if she realised that she had in fact been waiting to be asked, and tipping it to catch the light she said, 'Just a design,' in that husky, rarely used voice of hers.

Sarah-Jayne considered, then pronounced, 'Pretty.' She added, 'Sometimes people have their initials.' And with a small smile, 'Or someone else's.'

Caroline raised her hand and regarded it anew.

Wendy bounced over. 'Yes, but what's *that*?' pointing at Sarah-Jayne's own left hand. Somehow I had missed it: a felt-tip squiggle or scrawl of some kind.

Sarah-Jayne contemplated it, and answered Wendy relatively kindly, as if she were a teacher explaining to a pupil: 'It says "David".'

'David?' squealed Wendy.

'Cassidy,' she elucidated, as she started off with Beverly towards the toilets.

'Oh, David Cassidy,' agreed Mandy, quickly, unsurely, covering for us. Because we did all know who he was – we listened to the charts – but why write his name on

26

your hand? We only ever wrote on our hands if we were in danger of forgetting something and why might she forget David Cassidy or even need to remember him in the first place?

Wendy was just as quick to collect herself and boomed after Sarah-Jayne a rendition of the chorus from the hit single but in a deep voice, much deeper than David Cassidy's own: 'How can I how can I how can I how can I ...' *How can I be sure.*

Sarah-Jayne paused in her tracks, turning back to us all with a smile that didn't illuminate those cut-glass eyes, and said lightly, knowingly, as a kind of joke if not for Wendy then for the rest of us, 'Oh, he can be sure of me.'

3

Sarah-Jayne wasn't the only new person to turn up in my life that week. At home, a couple of evenings before, I was watching *Star Trek* – the Vulcan ambassador and his wife, visiting the starship *Enterprise*, had just revealed themselves to be Spock's parents – when our doorbell screeched. Mum wondered aloud from the kitchen who it could possibly be, and from the settee I saw her go to the door and open it to what Mr Hadleigh would probably call a 'youth': no longer a boy but not a proper grown-up. Gangly, he looked as if he'd made a dash through a pile of clothes and got entangled in them, although a pair of bicycle clips had him firmly by the ankles. His face was tanned despite the weather we'd been having, which made his eyes as pale as glass, and he stood there blinking in the doorway as if it was we who had startled him. But all this was eclipsed by his holding aloft a tortoise. 'This fella yours?'

As my heart went out to the creature, Mum recoiled. 'God, no.'

The boy said, 'Found him by your gate.'

'The Porters', I bet,' said Mum; and called to me, 'This the Porters'?'

I didn't know, but was drawn from the settee to the living room doorway.

'Porters,' he repeated, emptily, looking lost. I'd never seen him before; he wasn't from around here.

'A right zoo over there,' Mum said with a dark glance over his shoulder and up the road. She said this, about their house being a zoo, because they had hens: Letty, Hetty and Betty. A tortoise, though? And she must have been thinking the same because she said, 'Although what they'd want with that, God knows. I mean, they can't eat its eggs, can they.'

He raised it, peered expectantly underneath. I couldn't tell if he was joking.

I came up behind her and peeped around her, because you didn't get to see a tortoise every day. We had no pets: Mum said she had enough to deal with. I had high hopes every year of the WH Smith Win a Pony competition. If – when! – I did win, she'd have to concede and anyway she wouldn't have to do anything because I'd do it all and probably Smith's would help. Each year, I knew the answers to the quiz, because I'd read all the books in the library on horses, but the tiebreaker was the problem; that tiebreaker was the bane of my life, it was so unfair, because it left it all to chance. Mum said I had every chance but I knew that my slip fluttering amid all the others in that barrel meant that was exactly what I didn't have. At the same time, though, I couldn't quite believe that the sheer force of my longing for that pony wouldn't be enough to nudge my slip towards Mr Smith's delving fingertips.

Would a tortoise do for now, though, instead? If he wasn't the Porters', could we adopt him? In a flash I saw our future together, me coming home from school every day and going straight to see him: there he'd be in the garden waiting for me and then I could feed him – what would I feed him? – and talk to him.

'Go and ask the Porters,' Mum told me. 'Take it with you.'

It.

I had to take him from that boy and for a heartbeat I didn't know how I was going to do that, but then he just plonked him into my hands and it was easy. The tortoise had a pleasing solidity. The boy stepped aside on the doorstep – the smell of cigarettes dispensed in puffs as he vigorously gnashed some gum – and I set off in my slippers.

Behind me he was saying of the tortoise, 'Getting frisky now it's summer. Looking for a lady friend.'

Mum hooted derisively. 'Some summer!' She was right, it was June and the summer hadn't yet started. I was cold without my coat and the path was wet. I'd be in trouble with Mum for heading off in my slippers – I should have thought, and I was surprised she hadn't noticed. She lowered her voice but I could still hear her: 'Aye, and I'd be hibernating if I lived over there. No heaters, just the old fireplace. And bare boards – can you believe that, this day and age? The way some people bring up their kids!' She didn't mean they were common, though: they were, she said, arty types; they had ideas, she said, as if ideas were like nits.

Our house was a council house on a lane of council houses and Mum often said she had never thought she'd

30

find herself back in a council house: that wasn't part of the plan, she'd say, although she never specified what the plan had been. 'But life chucks rubbish at you and you do the best you can, eh?' A roof over our heads, she always said, and a nice enough roof, not so bad as roofs go. I had my own room, in which I could hear the church bells on Sundays and on their practice night and ringing for weddings, and the discos at the parties afterwards at the new village hall. We kept our house nice, Mum said, which not everyone in our road did, because some people kept their dustbins where you could see them, and we were here because of circumstances, unlike them. Our next-door neighbours – old Bert and Lil, who had budgies called Wilson and Pike – had been in their house all their married life, she said. Don't settle, Mum was always saying to me, which meant all kinds of things but one was living in a council house. Don't just settle, in life. Bert and Lil must have settled. It worried me, the word settle. As if Bert and Lil were muck at the bottom of a pool, the water closed over their heads.

The Porters didn't keep their house nice but that was because they grew vegetables in the front garden. Scratching about growing tatties like my auld grandpa in the war, Mum said. Then again, the Porters were different, it occurred to me as I let myself – and the tortoise – through the gate, and didn't Mum always say different was good? Once when I had gone to them with a sponsorship form Mrs Porter had asked me in, and on their kitchen table they had candles burning, but not like when there was a power cut: the candles were stuck into the tops of tall bottles down which the wax melted in folds, like fairy-tale ball gowns. I had made the mistake of telling Mum about those candles. I did try telling her they did also have light switches and in fact there had been a lamp on, too, but she wasn't listening, busy saying how it was like Victorian times over there.

That evening was when Mrs Porter gave me the pull-out pages from the newspaper: all about Tutankhamun. You might like this, Deborah, she said. I knew he had arrived in the country: he had been flown over ('Pity they didn't bring some of his weather with him,' Mum said) and we had done him at school but what Mrs Porter gave me was a treasure of its own. 'Just look at this,' she'd said, flexing the picture of his golden mask into the candlelight. 'You have it,' she insisted, so I took it home and sellotaped it onto my bedroom wall.

Now once again on their doorstep I paused to take a last long look at the tortoise, willing him not to be theirs. I would call him Sammy, I decided: that seemed right, I didn't know why but it did, it was somehow a tortoise name. 'Sammy,' I whispered to him, to try to gauge his response, but it was hard to guess what he was thinking. I spent much of my time coming up with names for the pony that with any luck I would soon win (and Lucky was the front runner); but then here I was, caught on the hop by a tortoise. I rather liked that I'd had to think on my feet, though, and was pleased with my choice. We were shaping up, I felt, to make a good team.

Mrs Porter came to the door, so very pregnant that it was as if she were acting a part, and threw up her hands. 'Oh crikey! Where did you find him?'

My heart fell, but perhaps I could visit now I knew he was there. And I could work on Mum for a tortoise maybe when I was eleven and at grammar school.

'By our gate.' I didn't mention the boy, and how could I? I didn't know who he was. And for a moment it was as if I had imagined him. Anyway, he'd be gone by the time I got back across the road, and I would never see him again.

'Oh Deborah,' she was saying, 'thank you so much, you are a wonder!' But it was she who was a wonder: I loved her long, loose bushy hair and her freckles. I was hoping I might be rewarded with one of her home-made biscuits – they were odd, not really biscuits, but I liked them, the raisins in them burnt and chewy. She held the tortoise aloft and admonished him to his reptilian face, 'You *scamp*!' but then, summoned by the wailing of her little boy, she was – with more gales of thanks – gone.

I trudged back down the path, soggy-slippered and empty-handed. Mum said Mrs Porter was too old to be having babies – she must be in her thirties, she said. Any older and you probably had to adopt, as had Mr and Mrs Hadleigh. Mind you, she'd say, my poor old Granny Gilhooly had her last at forty-two and thank God those days are behind us and there's no need for that.

The new baby would be Mrs Porter's second. Little Willem was two or three. All those books in that house, Mum said – we could see the walls of bookshelves from the road – but they can't spell William. She had asked me what the new one was to be called and when I said what Mrs Porter had told me, Eloise or Rafe, she said Louise is normal although a bit Plain Jane if you ask me and I suppose Ralph is normal too but what kind of name is that for a wee 'un?

When I got back, that lanky boy was still on our doorstep.

'Yes?' Mum enquired of me, and I confirmed it: yes, the Porters'.

To neither of us in particular she said, 'Honestly, you'd think she had enough to do with that snotty nosed wee 'un and another on the way without running around after tortoises.'

'You're Scotch,' said the boy.

I'd squeezed past by then but I could practically hear the roll of Mum's eyes. She didn't say *like the mist*, though; she just said, 'Aye, and you're the pearly king.'

He laughed that off and said he was from Rainham.

She said, 'What are you doing around here, then?' No one ever came down here unless they lived here. She made it sound like a joke, but I could tell she wanted to know.

He said he was lodging at the Gibbs', was going to cut back across the fields to their house. 'Know 'em?'

Fur coat, nae knickers was what Mum said to me about Mrs Gibb; I fervently hoped she wasn't going to say that now.

'Och, who doesn't know the Gibbs?' she said, 'And missy here's at school with their lass.' Bit of a madam, was what she tended to say about Tracy. 'The Gibbs, though? Since when have they taken *lodgers*?'

My dad had been a lodger when my mum had met him; that much I knew. They'd both been in London at the start of their grown-up lives, him in lodgings – or 'digs', as she more usually said, which to me made him sound like a badger – and her in a hostel full of girls because she had moved down to stay at her sister's but that had gone wrong and they didn't speak because *if you choose to believe the word of your waste-of-space husband over your own flesh and blood . . .*

34

The boy was saying he was working for Mr Gibb – Gibbsy, he called him; he said he was learning the trade. 'Him and my old man go way back and he owes him one, so for now I'm one of the family.'

Mum asked if he was working on the houses opposite the school.

'About to,' he said: he'd been at a site behind the fire station in town but was starting next week on those houses.

'Nice-looking, those,' Mum said. She thought flat roofs romantic because you could lie up there catching the sun, if there was any.

Then she called down the hallway to me, making me jump: 'Francis of Assisi here is staying at your friend Tracy's house.'

She knew very well that Tracy wasn't my friend.

He said, 'Sunny,' and inexplicably she said, 'As in share,' before introducing us: 'I'm Sandy and that there' – a jerk of her head – 'is Deborah.' Then she was asking him what it was like at the Gibbs' and he said he couldn't complain; he had a room of his own and was free to come and go. 'Which I do,' he said, 'as soon as it's *Crossroads*,' and he sang some of the twangy theme tune.

Mum always said *Crossroads* was hardly *Peyton Place*, and who wants to watch people rattling around a motel? Or – her little joke about the rickety sets – a motel rattling around people.

'Once that cobblers comes on,' he said, 'and they're cosying up in front of the box, I'm off. On my bike. Get some air.'

'Aye, and you'll be getting more than air if you cut across Farmer Giles's fields,' she said. 'He's a one for taking pot shots.' Then she added, 'Only joking. He's called Farmer Taylor.'

After that, she fetched him a beaker of water, then he was off on his way.

4

For her second day at our school, Sarah-Jayne sported a completely different look: tie-dye T-shirt and jeans. Myself, I was dressed the same as the day before, down to the knickers and socks; I had a change of those only at midweek, because Mum had enough to do without endless laundry and anyway who's looking? I knew of jeans, but no one I knew actually had a pair and they belonged in my mind to the telly show *Follyfoot*, to the morose misfits in that dilapidated stable yard. I didn't have any kind of trousers because my mum didn't like them, either for me or for herself. *Troos* she called them, as if they were funny, but actually she didn't find them funny: 'They're not for wee gerils,' she'd say in a pitying way, as if girls who wore them were subjected to an imposition.

That second day, Sarah-Jayne's denim pencil case was partnered on their table by a smaller shiny red one, which, I gathered, had been brought along by Beverly. This was new, Beverly hadn't had a pencil case before – most of us didn't – and I guessed it had been begged, borrowed or stolen from her older sister, Spike (so nicknamed for the heavily mascaraed eyelashes). Quick work from Beverly, and a surprise, too, because she never bothered with accessories and she really wasn't someone to be swayed. Bullish Beverly: I'd have to say it for her that she was always herself, even if I'd never considered that to be much of a recommendation, yet here she was – Beverly, of all people – copycatting.

We didn't bother with pencil cases in our class because we just helped ourselves to pens and pencils from the collective drawers as and when we needed them, a scattering accruing on our tables throughout the day to be returned at tidy-up time. As it happened, I did have a pencil case of my own, but that was because it had ponies on it; it had been one of my birthday presents from my mum, along with other pony-themed items: a pony-shaped eraser, which of course I wouldn't use, for fear of mutilating his muzzle; a bookmark that I kept in my I Spy book of ponies, which itself had been a present on a previous birthday; and a handkerchief embroidered in one corner with the head of a winsome palomino although I wasn't to use it as an actual handkerchief because *Don't I have enough laundry to do?* Not that I would ever have considered getting snot on something so beautiful. My own case held a handful of felt-tips and crayons just for appearance's sake but it stayed beside me, not at the edge of the table as Sarah-Jayne's pertly was, and Beverly's now, too, ostentatiously partnering it.

Unlike Beverly's, Sarah-Jayne's pencil case was artfully scruffy, which was a new one on me. From where I was sitting, I couldn't quite see that it was written on; but this we learned from Wendy, who, passing on her way to the pens drawer, snatched it up and held it exaggeratedly aloft, beyond retrieval, and, as she took a dancing step or two backwards, pigtails bouncing, scrutinised it before hooting provocatively: 'Ooo ooo oooo!'

A savage '*Wendy!*' from Beverly was echoed by Mr Hadleigh's weary 'Wendy . . . ' *pipe down.*

Everyone was forever having a go at Wendy but she really didn't help herself.

She proclaimed what she had found written on the pencil case: 'Hearts! Look! Love hearts! Lerve hearts!'

Sarah-Jayne didn't seem worried: she held out her hand palm upwards in a parody of bored patience: *Give.* She didn't look particularly displeased; in fact, she looked as if she was in on the joke, had perhaps even initiated it.

Wendy hadn't quite finished, making a show of reciting for all to hear what she found written there – 'DC 4 SJT, DC for me' – and then with a change of tack that had me swallowing a laugh she looked around us all as if over a pair of imaginary half-moon specs to inform us, 'I love David.'

'Oh Gawd,' tittered Susan.

My mind was whirring: Sarah-Jayne *loved* David Cassidy? She must be a fan, then, I thought, a real proper fan: we heard about them on the radio and we saw them beaming from the covers of girls' magazines in Smith's, witnessed them jostling one another in the crowds on *Top of the Pops.* They were silly, Mum said, *running around after pop stars*; she said they'd be off after someone else in two minutes' time, and then came the usual talk of jumping off bridges.

But Sarah-Jayne didn't seem the type to run around screaming, quite the contrary. And as for us: Susan and I liked various pop stars but neither of us had thought of dedicating love hearts to them; that would be going a bit too far. Susan had a love heart on a chain that sometimes she wore around her neck but that was just because it was a pretty shape; it wasn't actually *for* anyone.

Mr Hadleigh laid aside his pen and with a tobacco-scented exhalation did as he was obliged as our teacher to do: 'Wendy . . .'

This did bring her to what might generously be described as her senses, although as ever she wasn't going to go quietly. In a final snipe, she said to Beverly, 'Don't get your knickers in a twist,' with a momentary loss of composure on 'knickers', then deposited the pencil case with a considerable flourish into its owner's open palm. Sarah-Jayne acknowledged receipt with a nod and no faltering of her smirk, and settled it back in its prime position on the desk, no harm done.

Wendy's parting shot was a stage-whispered 'Dayyy-vid Cassidy!' hissed like a curse as she swept on her way. Sarah-Jayne returned to her work, writing methodically in her book, and Beverly made a show of doing the same although it was obvious she was itching to kill Wendy, while Caroline leaned back in her chair and luxuriated in a stretch that moved the bosoms she was growing.

'Honestly,' Mandy muttered to my side, but it was unclear of what or whom, precisely, she disapproved.

Not until I left the classroom at break time, passing the other girls' table, did I get a chance to see for myself the biro scrawls on the pencil case: inscriptions within love hearts as curvaceous as blown kisses, each pierced by an arrow at a slant like a hand on a hip. When we were in the porch, at the shoe bench, changing our plimsolls for outdoor shoes, I said to Susan we should head for the end of the field and get practising our handstands; but as soon as she had fastened her sandals she was off after Sarah-Jayne, to intercept her in the doorway. 'So, you like David Cassidy,' she said, shyly, unable to bring herself to say 'love'. She was taking it upon herself, I knew, to try to make up for Wendy's goading and ridicule. Typical Susan, being sweet. (*Nothing like her bruiser of a mother*, my mum often said; *wouldn't want to come across her in a dark alley*, but luckily we didn't have any alleys in the village.) Mandy joined her, standing solemnly alongside, gnawing at her lip, lending weight to the endeavour. I hung back, kept to the shoe bench, waiting it out and ready to turn on my heel and be off as soon as we could into playtime.

Mistaking Susan's kindness for genuine interest, Sarah-Jayne answered mock-ruefully as if owning up to a foible, 'Oh, I'm just completely in love with him. He's so dishy.'

Susan was politely enthusiastic in the face of this self-confessed happy helplessness. 'Yes, he *does* have a really nice smile.'

And true, he did have a nice smile. Well, a smiley one, anyway.

Then, seemingly at a loss, she offered, 'Mandy' – *meet Mandy, here* – 'likes that one from Sweet.'

Mandy frowned, flushed: 'No, I don't.'

'Yes, you do, remember?' Susan addressed her patiently. 'You said you like his hair.'

Mandy reconsidered, 'Oh, his hair, yes,' although still

41

doubtful and I could see why, because didn't everyone like his hair? Wasn't that the whole point of him?

And Sarah-Jayne allowed, 'Well, yes, that hair is gorgeous,' adding with a playful roll of her eyes, 'Better than mine.' Her own hair was just like David Cassidy's, it occurred to me. She did look a lot like him: they could be brother and sister.

How much longer, I wondered, before Susan and Mandy and I could go off and play?

Beverly plodded over and pronounced, 'Slade's better.'

'Not for hair, though,' said Susan, not unreasonably.

Beverly shrugged: *Have it your way.*

Wendy had beaten us all to it and was already outside in the playground but now she reappeared in the stone arch of the doorway, juggling an apple and a packet of Twiglets. 'Do you know him? David Cassidy.' And even though she didn't take her eyes from the apple and the Twiglets we all knew the question was directed at Sarah-Jayne, who, wary of a trap, froze. Beverly stepped in to answer for her, brazening it out, 'Of course she doesn't know him,' before thinking to check, 'Do you?' because who, really, knew anything about this girl? This girl from abroad.

No response, just the glittering of her eyes, which somehow admitted that she didn't.

Wendy caught the apple then the Twiglets, snatching them down from their impressive trajectories, and wiped her nose on her sleeve. 'But how can you love someone you don't even know?' She asked it apparently guilelessly, as if she were enquiring about, say, the life cycle of a butterfly, but when Caroline took a step forward, broad-shouldered, square-jawed – no trace yet of the Rubenesque beauty she would become in just a few years' time – Wendy raised her hands in mock surrender: *I'm only saying.*

In a few years' time I'd be doodling the odd love heart, even if my own heart wouldn't be in it because I lacked the knack – mine being cramped and angular, nothing like those plump ones made from Sarah-Jayne's carefree curvy lines. It never helped that Mum said love was a fairy tale. Hadn't she and my dad, I wondered, been in love? They'd married, and they'd had me, and we all knew from school that babies happen when a man and woman love each other very much, unless there's something wrong, as for Mr and Mrs Hadleigh, and they have to adopt. I didn't dare ask. Back when the Porters' dog had died – by mistake, from someone else's rat poison – she had warned me never to mention him in their hearing. So I took similar care with her, avoided asking about my dad or our life before we came to the village in case she was too sad to be reminded, and indeed sometimes, suddenly, she seemed so sad that it was as if she had dropped over an edge, gone clean away and left me on my own in the house for a few days, although actually she was in fact still there, across rooms, in doorways. But even when she was fine, she didn't talk about him. Why dwell on the past? – that was what she said, and always crossly, as if anyone who did so was personally letting her down.

Little did she know that in the privacy of my own room I did a lot of dwelling on the past, because I was in love with a boy who had been dead for thousands of years. Mind you, he was looking good on it: the picture of him that Mrs Porter had given me was stunning, if admittedly of his death mask; but anyway the lustre of those eyes, the humourful cast to those gloriously full lips, that lift to his chin, although that might have been down to that handle thing (what was that?) beneath it. David Cassidy was nothing, compared.

Tutankhamun wasn't a name to fit inside a love heart nor even onto a pencil case, not that I would have wanted to make any such declaration. Susan would have laughed and enjoyed it in her own sweet way (You're mad! He's dead!); the problem was that she would tell Mandy, who would be baffled and make no bones about that, and I knew from experience how Mandy's reproachful expression could look a lot like disgust. And although I told myself it didn't matter what Mandy thought – what did she know about love? What did she know about anything? – I wasn't going to volunteer myself up for her disapproval.

What we had, Tutankhamun and I, was for keeping between the pair of us and would be all the stronger for it. Wendy had asked Sarah-Jayne how she could love someone she didn't know, but that didn't apply to me, because dead though Tutankhamun was, I felt I knew him very well. In class we had learned that for the ancient Egyptians to say the name of the dead was to make them live again, and I had found that I didn't even have to say his name but merely to think it, hard, into the silence of my bedroom, and I could detect him reaching back through the thousands of years of his loneliness towards me.

In the whole of history, he had only me. He'd had a wife – by my age he'd been married, which I presumed

44

was something that pharaohs did – and his wife was only a little older and had already had a baby and with her dad, which didn't seem quite right but that's what I'd read, although possibly someone had messed up the translation of the hieroglyphics. No one knew for sure what had happened to her but likely she'd had to go on to another marriage after he'd died; so in the afterlife she was the wife of someone else. She had gone on into a life without Tutankhamun, as had everyone else.

Those people who had worshipped him enough to bury so much treasure with him had only done so because he was a pharaoh, and once they'd sealed him up in there for eternity with all the gold and jewels they would move on to worship his successor, because that was how it was. And incredibly he had been covered up and lost under rubble and everyone forgot about him, and before too long no one knew he'd existed. But then, when he was discovered, it was all about the treasure. No one except me in the whole of history mourned him for the boy he had been. His being dead wasn't the misfortune for me that others might have thought, because he was always there for me. He was going nowhere, locked into his early death like an insect in amber.

What, I wondered, would my dad have been buried with, had that been normal then and had he been buried, which he hadn't because Mum said it was unhygienic. There was no grave for us to visit and nothing of him around our house; no photos, even, because, Mum said, that would be morbid. But, then, we had no photos at all except the professionally taken group portraits from school or Brownies, the price on the order form causing Mum a sharp intake of breath and likewise when it came

45

to counting the notes and coins into the small manila envelope that was attached for their receipt. I don't remember even particularly wanting those photos – all of us standing awkwardly to attention, only pictured there to prove our existence. But despite the cost and the dubious quality it seemed we did have to have them, each one propped on the mantelpiece until relegated to the top drawer of the sideboard – with my 'baby book', the official record of my weights and jabs – in favour of a newer version.

Mum had no photos of herself when she was young except for a strip of four taken in a booth with her friend – 'pal' – Jeannie when they were fifteen or sixteen, the pair of them squashed together like puppies in a basket. Thumbnail-sized and flash-bleached, Mum's face was nevertheless vivid with laughter, and it was clear even in black and white that Jeannie was boldly lipsticked. I was entranced by this glimpse of Mum before I came along and even before she met my dad. She kept the photos in her purse and I'd beg her to slide a fingernail into the slot and lever loose that strip, extract it and lay it flat between us. Then she'd enter the spirit, play the game, crowing with affection and astonishment – 'Look at us there, eh!' – and saying admiringly of Jeannie that she was a one and had been the life and soul. She always ended up sighing and wondering where Jeannie was now but it had the ring of something said for the sake of form, and the fondness in her tone suggested that Jeannie was so long ago to her, now, as if to be dead.

She had no other photos of herself growing up because, she said, she wouldn't have been packing them into her case when she was leaving for London. She said that's not what you're thinking of when you're heading out at seventeen. Whenever she mentioned that case of hers, I pictured my own little red satin-lined vanity case – my seventh birthday present – with the mirror inside and its clunk-click clasp, and I wondered what *I* would pack. She said she hadn't known, then, that she would never be going back. 'I'd yet to drop the match onto that particular bridge,' she said.

But if that made some sense to me, what struck me as odd was the absence from our house of any wedding photos. It was clear even from doorsteps that wedding photos were a prominent feature of my friends' homes, displayed on mantelpieces and coffee tables, shelves and windowsills. And surely Mum more than most had reason for commemoration. But she simply said she didn't know what kind of wedding I thought she'd had, as if only fancy weddings were photographed, which I suspected wasn't true, and anyway any old photo would have done me.

They had married at the registrar's office in a dinner break, and she'd worn a nice dress: that was all she ever told me, even though over the years I clamoured for more. Which nice dress? What kind of nice dress? How nice?

She couldn't remember, or so she said: just a dress. Just nice.

It's not entirely true that there were no photos at home, because one day when I was eight or nine I found, by accident, buried in the bottom kitchen drawer beneath the Green Shield Stamps book, a handful of one-pound Premium Bond certificates and Mum's Widowed Mother's Allowance book, a small black-and-white photo of a man.

There was nothing written on the back. He didn't look

particularly young to me but even then I realised that was because it was an old photo. He was wearing a suit; he looked old-fashioned; no one wore suits any more unless to a funeral. The photo being black-and-white, I couldn't tell if his hair was mousy, and anyway it was brutally short. No one I knew had hair like that and, shamefully, I was relieved that he was kept out of sight.

From then on, though, I took him out of the drawer, sometimes, when I was alone in the house. In the photo, he was standing not quite full square to the camera and facing the sun, with not so much as a smile, his features screwed against the glare. Myself, I'd squint or glance sideways at him, varying how I viewed him in the hope of bringing something more or different into focus. Try as I might, though, there was nothing, really, to see. A mere assemblage of light and dark. Someone who could be anyone. There was no way of looking at it that would yield what I wanted from it: the answer to the question of whether this was my dad. It was as if I lacked a key, a legend that would unlock it for me, have the various elements fall into place and declare themselves. I certainly couldn't see any of me in him or, when I peered into the bathroom mirror, of him in me.

Why was he hidden? As if it wasn't bad enough to be dead. At least I could retrieve him, bring him into the air, the light: that was the least I could do. It wasn't right of Mum to have done what she'd done, in hiding him away, and why had she? It wasn't his fault he'd died.

We should have some photos of him around the house, I thought, and we should also have one of them together – Mum and Dad – in the early days, before his leukaemia, in love, carefree, pleased with themselves, probably sitting on a beach, bare feet half buried in the sand, his shirtsleeves rolled up and his arm slung around her cardiganed shoulders, the pair of them in a pleasurable huddle against the breeze, their smiles so direct to the camera as to be almost a challenge: done and dusted, chosen and committed, together and let no man put asunder.

There should have been one of him with me, too, perhaps on that same beach, the pair of us braving the elements, stark and pallid in our swimwear, poised to scarper; he so skinny as to be almost concave, towering beside me, holding my hand; and me, tiny and knock-kneed but potbellied, my swimsuit with a frill around the hips like a misplaced gill.

5

That second day of Sarah-Jayne's at school, we spent our dinner break in the old school house. I had wanted to play outside but ended up trooping after the others because I couldn't risk being left with Tracy and Virginia or Wendy, although even then I didn't escape Wendy because she came bounding in behind me. The house it is, then, I thought, despondently, just for today. It had been a bad enough dinner time already because we'd had curry, which was just normal stew but dyed green and with sultanas thrown in.

The school house adjoined the school but with its own separate entrance and a proper front door because it was an actual house, built in Victorian times for the schoolmaster in the days when there were police houses and nurses' homes. Even by the time we were at school those days were long gone. Mr and Mrs Hadleigh, and the son who Mum said was a handful but when you adopt it's the luck of the draw, had a cheerful-looking bungalow on the road towards town. Ours was a village with a vicarage that wasn't a vicarage and a school house that wasn't a school house.

Unoccupied though the house was, it did still look the part, with picket fence and garden gate, garden path and front step. Inside, it retained the bare bones of a domestic residence – a kitchen and a bathroom of a kind, if with severed pipework – but although it wasn't in a bad state of repair, and looked to have been modernised at some point (to judge from that indoor bathroom), it was lifeless. Not spooky; spooky would at least have been interesting. Hollow was how it felt to me, and as we filed in that day I experienced the familiar sensation of being somewhere soundproofed, the silence somehow too close, pressing.

In the hallway, Sarah-Jayne asked if Mr Hadleigh had ever lived here. She didn't sound hopeful and we said we didn't think so.

Mandy wondered, 'Did *anyone* ever live here?'

'Did anyone ever *die* here?' said Susan, trying to jolly us up, but apart from a little hoot from Caroline it fell flat. The house simply didn't lend itself to intrigue.

Sarah-Jayne glanced up the stairs and asked, uneasily, 'What's up there?'

'Nothing,' Beverly said. 'Boxes. Deliveries.' Rolls of paper, packs of pens. The front room was the only one that was properly used: most days we came to watch an educational programme on telly – programmes about singing, mostly – and the room was furnished accord-ingly, with hard-wearing grey floor tiles, whitewashed walls, and a bevy of low grey stackable armchairs with-out arms, onto which we now clambered.

The telly, off duty, had been wheeled away on its tall

51

stand like a Dalek into a corner; for each programme it would be manoeuvred back into position to stare us down with its bulbous dark green screen on which we could glimpse our faint and distorted reflections before the blackout curtains were drawn across the window to cut any glare. Slumped in the gloom, we would watch jolly presenters and enthusiastic studio audiences sing and dance. Afterwards, the curtains would be mercilessly yanked back and, blinking and disoriented, we were shepherded back across the rainswept playground to our classroom.

Now we found ourselves by chance grouped around Sarah-Jayne like an audience. She wanted to know, 'We're allowed in here?' On our own, she meant: unsupervised.

'Why wouldn't we be?' Beverly said – no one was going to stop us, and although that was typical Beverly talk it was also the truth because at school, as far as we knew, nowhere was forbidden us. The infants were supervised at playtime in the playground by the dreaded Mrs Morgan – a tartar, according to Mum – who came to school every day specifically for that purpose and lolled against the fence, hefting her bosoms, lips pursed in anticipation of her next cigarette, but she was currently off having her veins stripped and anyway she wasn't bothered what we older ones got up to. And what harm could we come to in there? It was just a house, with nothing much in it.

Sarah-Jayne looked around, appraisingly, then asked, 'Who comes in here? Do the boys?'

Did she mean the boys in our year, Neil and Ali?

'Just us,' said Beverly.

Sarah-Jayne smiled politely. 'To do what?'

Nothing, really. Nothing much.

Susan tried to explain. 'Oh, we just . . . ' But then she ran aground and gave up with a heavy shrug. Be us, she probably meant. Be.

Wendy produced a pack of Polos from a pocket.

'We should watch telly,' Mandy offered, as a sort of joke. The only programmes during the day were the schools ones: we'd be trapped listening to folk songs.

'There's nothing on,' said Beverly, reclining, and Caroline leaned against her, shifting to tuck her rotund calves beneath her.

'No Benny Hill,' joked Susan to nervous laughter at the prospect of provoking Wendy but luckily she was engrossed in opening the tube of Polos.

Conversationally, as if we were all marking time at the bus stop, Susan remarked admiringly, 'Benny Hill is just so rude, isn't he.'

More nervous laughter; and Sarah-Jayne, head tipped to one side, said, 'My sister thinks he's inane.'

'In*sane*.' Wendy popped a Polo onto her tongue, then offered them around.

'But Max – that's her fiancé – says she's got no sense of humour.' *Fiancé*: we all took it in. Sarah-Jayne warmed to her theme: 'Max is just so funny.' She spoke of him, I felt, as if he were her friend.

'Your sister's getting married?' said Susan, diligently following up and probably relieved to be leaving behind the tricky business of the meaning of 'inane'.

Absently, Sarah-Jayne confirmed it – 'Mmm' – as if it were unworthy of further comment.

'Wish my sister would,' Beverly slurred around her Polo. 'Good riddance.' At which Caroline bleated.

Susan asked Sarah-Jayne, 'Is she older than you?' but my laugh had her realise what she'd just said and she rolled her eyes, good-naturedly corrected herself: 'I mean, is she *lots* older?'

'She's twenty-six.' Again said as if it were nothing. But twenty-six! – that was probably older than Miss Drake, whom my mum called a 'wee lassie'. Whenever we asked Miss Drake how old she was, she'd say with a laugh, 'Twenty-one,' but we'd become wise to that.

My mum had had me at twenty. She and my dad had met and married when they were both nineteen.

Sarah-Jayne added, 'And Max is thirty-five.'

Older, even, then, than my mum.

'Old-age pensioner,' said Beverly, to which Sarah-Jayne, with a playful grimace, said, 'Oh, anything but: he's been a bit of a man about town, I think, our Max.'

Susan cited, questioningly, our nearby town – with its swimming pool and library, its bakery and greengrocer, its toy shop and travel agency and doctor's surgery – whereas 'up town', two and a half hours away on two buses, was London. But the distinction seemed lost on Sarah-Jayne, who replied, breezily, 'No, he's from everywhere, from all over, I think.'

Like a gypsy, then.

'He's just what my sister needs, though. Calm her down, get her to grow up a bit,' and with a tilt of her head she added, 'She never even finished school – she was expelled.'

This was said casually but she must have known that we would all sit forward. Mr Hadleigh's boy had been expelled from a school – for setting fire to a bin, Mum had told me, although a rumour persisted that he'd eaten the class hamster – and a friend of Bev's sister had been expelled from the local comp for riding a motor-bike around the sports field. It was always boys who got expelled; what could a girl have done, to get expelled?

Susan asked, huge-eyed, urgently: 'Why? What did she do?' then, abashed, 'I mean, can you say?'

She could indeed: 'Levitation.'

Wasn't that hippies hovering cross-legged in the air? I had a vague memory of having seen something about it on *Nationwide*. Wendy said before I could: '*What?*'

Sarah-Jayne turned those eyes on her. '*Trying* it,' she specified. 'With some friends.'

Susan was tremulous. 'And did they manage?'

Sarah-Jayne shrugged. 'She never tells me anything.'

It was all rubbish, I knew. Mum always said, *The rubbish people believe!* Ghosts, curses, religions. Mandy said that tomatoes scream when they're sliced but only bats and dogs can hear it.

'We should try.' The Polo clanked against Wendy's teeth. 'Levitating.'

Susan gasped mintily: 'We can't . . . '

For once, Wendy had backup from Beverly: 'We can do what we like.'

Mum would say *Don't meddle*. Fortune-tellers and ouija boards: *that's looking for trouble*. The reason I didn't want to try levitating, though, was because I suspected I'd be as bad at it as at cartwheels and handstands.

Wendy threw it open to the room: 'What's the worst that can happen?'

Mandy grinned: 'The wind could change,' and we'd all stay stuck up in the air, she meant, because Mrs Morgan was forever telling us similar about pulling faces. This got a laugh but Susan was still worried: 'We might get expelled.'

'Grrrreat!' Wendy was up on her knees on her seat.

Beverly wasn't having it: 'Who's going to expel us? No one knows what we do in here. No one cares.'

True.

'Yes, but' – Susan again – 'why did Sarah-Jayne's sister's school expel her? What's wrong with levitation?'

Sarah-Jayne answered – or, rather, didn't – with another of her shrugs; but then said, 'It was a convent.'

Little Charlotte Biggs, from Brownies, who lived a few doors down from Caroline, went to a convent instead of our school. Every morning when we passed her house we'd see her getting into the car in a boater, and now I imagined that boater floating around in the air.

Wendy raised her arms like a high priestess. 'Levitation is devil worship!'

'Don't be stupid,' said Beverly.

'It's not, though, is it?' Susan was genuinely worried.

'It's *angels* who float about,' countered Mandy, and Caroline, looking soulful, added, 'True.'

Wendy had already assembled herself into the pose, straight-backed and cross-legged – she too must have seen *Nationwide* – with her skirt taut between her knees, on which her hands rested palms upwards. I couldn't tell if she was serious – or as serious as she was ever capable of being – or if she was making fun of it all. But in any case she was pitching herself into it as she did with everything. She had her eyes ostentatiously closed – face tipped skywards – and, I saw, Sarah-Jayne took the opportunity to give her a look. *Don't*, I thought. It was unfair. Wendy might be annoying but she was merely being game. She hadn't started this. And anyway she was ours to ridicule, not Sarah-Jayne's. And worse, that look of Sarah-Jayne's had been pointed, aimed with a wrinkle of her nose at what she considered the indelicacy of Wendy's pose, the skirt raised over parted thighs. But who was looking? Not us, I thought, crossly: cartwheelers and handstanders as we were.

I was wrong, though: the subject of levitation was dropped as if at a snap of her fingers, leaving Wendy stranded with her skirt hoicked as everyone's attention switched to Sarah-Jayne telling how her sister had met her fiancé in Germany. Wendy threw off her levitation pose and sprang to the window, craning after something that had caught her attention; it was impossible to know if she even noticed she had been left high and dry, let alone cared. I did, though, on her behalf, and was surprised how much.

'And is there anywhere around here,' Sarah-Jayne was asking, 'where people can meet?'

Room-wide bafflement was voiced by Mandy: 'Meet?'

Wendy went crashing from the room, then from the hallway into the playground.

'Where you can meet people,' Sarah-Jayne continued. 'Other people. In Germany we had this club, on the base.' She crossed her legs and I saw how she took pleasure in the alignment of the flare of her jeans with the length of her shoe. 'Thursday evenings. Couple of hours, till nine. You could meet your friends, hang around together, play records and dance.' Her eyes flashed: 'Get all the juicy gossip.'

Juicy . . . ?

But we met every day at school, and often again in

the evenings at the park; why would we need to meet anywhere else – other than the park – later?

Susan offered, 'We have Brownies on Wednesdays, at six until half-seven. We all go to that.'

'Worse luck,' said Beverly, which was just sour grapes because her six hadn't won the cup.

Brownies was off until the end of term because Brown Owl was having her bunions done.

Susan added, 'At the hall.'

Our Brown Owl was Mrs Peters, Peggy Peters to Mum, who said admiringly of her that she was *a cut above*. She wore her hair in a bun, which for me made her a wonder, like someone in a book. The hall, too, was really something: it had opened for business the previous summer and was a source of village-wide pride for its car park, its double doors, spacious lobby and proper stage with a complex arrangement of curtains, and the enormous kitchen, the vast serving hatch, cloakrooms and toilets with a whole row of cubicles. You name it, the hall had it. It buzzed and thumped every Saturday night with wedding parties and twenty-firsts.

Sarah-Jayne asked, 'Who goes to this "Brownies"?'

'We all do,' Susan repeated proudly.

'The boys?'

The only boys of our age were Neil and Ali and had she not seen them? What use were they to anyone? Constantly kicking a ball about. Susan said it wasn't for boys; boys had to go to Cubs, except there wasn't any.

'Or Scouts,' said Mandy.

Susan said, 'There isn't any Scouts.'

Mandy rolled her eyes. 'But if there was, that's where they'd have to go.' Just as we were going to have to go to

58

Guides next term because we'd be too old for Brownies, but there was no Guides. No one had come forward to run a pack. *Don't look at me*, Mum said if ever the subject came up at home, although I wouldn't have dreamt of it. She said she had enough to do. No time for do-gooding. And anyway she couldn't stand do-gooders. Presumably Peggy Peters was an exception or somehow didn't count.

Sarah-Jayne explained, 'I meant somewhere you can meet people and hang around playing records and dance.'

Mandy said, 'At Brownies we did our country dancing badge.'

Even Virginia had done it, although she'd needed to be led around.

Susan chirped up with: 'And we always sing this song, it's sooo good,' and she sang with gusto: '*Down among the dead men, pow wow, pow wow,*' no doubt intending us all to join in but none of us did.

Sarah-Jayne bestowed a smile on her for her effort, then clarified, 'Well, no, I meant dancing like ... ' she paused to consider, 'well, like Pan's People.'

We all loved Pan's People, but we would never dance like them. They were proper dancers, up there on the stage on *Top of the Pops*.

When no one said anything to that, she went on: 'I met my boyfriend at our club.'

Beverly's sister, Spike, had a boyfriend, who roared into the village on a scooter, but to hear this talk of boyfriends from Sarah-Jayne brought to mind someone else's sister: Caroline's toddler sister, who loved to clomp around in her mum's shoes.

'Is he nice?' Susan sounded slightly panicky, I thought, and was being polite. Mandy, beside her, was pop-eyed.

'Boyfriends are gits,' said Beverly, cheerfully, which earned her a playful, reproachful shove from Sarah-Jayne, who then replied sarcastically to Susan, 'Oh no, he was really awful.' My mum was often sarcastic – *full of the milk of human kindness*, she'd say of Mrs Cobb who ran the village shop – but that was when she was cross, whereas Sarah-Jayne looked a bit embarrassed, for us rather than for herself. 'Oh, he was *horrible*,' she quipped, before giving up on the sarcasm and levelling with us: 'He was actually really sweet.' She added, 'He was a bit older than me – twelve – but we still found we had loads in common.'

Twelve. Like Wendy's weirdo brother, Wayne, of whom I'd catch sight sometimes at the park on his bike, circling, going nowhere like a fish wallowing in the shallows. Poor Wendy was left at home with him on the nights when her mum was working shifts.

Sarah-Jayne said of her boyfriend, 'I'll have good memories of him.'

Memories: the implication sank in. Don't fall for it, I willed Susan, but of course she did, whispering, aghast, 'Oh no! You can't see him any more!' Tragedy.

Sarah-Jayne glittered. 'No, but not every love can last, can it, and that's what made it so special. We knew it couldn't be for ever.'

At which point, we were – literally – saved by the bell. Sarah-Jayne rose, so that it looked as if the rest of us were following her. 'It was nice while it lasted,' she said of the romance. 'And, as dear ol' Max says, there are plenty more fish in the sea.' She joke-grimaced, put-upon and tragic. 'Say lah vee,' she said incomprehensibly with her tight, joyless little smile.

My unease in the school house probably had something to do with what had recently happened there, which had its roots back in the spring when we had each been given a letter to take home. This letter, unusually, had been in a sealed envelope. Reading it, Mum told me, 'Birds and the bees. You'll be watching a telly programme about how babies are made.' She was going to have to sign a permission slip, she said, rolling her eyes because this was a rigmarole. I already knew, from her, about babies – eggs, seeds, tummies – and if none of it made complete sense, that was true of quite a bit of the grown-ups' world. Mr and Mrs Hadleigh had had something wrong and that was why they'd had to adopt Matthew, who, it seemed, had been some kind of leftover, which was probably why he didn't quite fit: *Square peg in a round hole, that one*, Mum said.

'You know it all already,' she told me, spooning gold-fish – peach slices – from a tin into our bowls for pudding and gesturing for me to pass her the tin of cream. 'You're lucky, no one's kept you in the dark.' And with a sigh she said to remind her to send me off with the signed slip in the morning.

At school the next day my form was deposited onto a pile of similar on Mr Hadleigh's desk to be swept away into his drawer, and I had forgotten about it when, one morning some weeks later, we settled in the school house and the curtains were drawn and what appeared on the telly was not a man with a tambourine encouraging us to sing along to 'La Cucaracha' but an indoor pool like the one to which we were taken each week for our swimming lessons. Just like at ours, gleeful shrieks were bouncing off the water, echoing from the girdered roof and great glass walls. Girls and boys of our age were thrashing exuberantly around in the pool, or scuttling up the chrome ladders and along the poolside, fighting off the chill and their own impatience to take a turn at divebombing.

So far, so normal, except – the realisation shot through me – *they were nude*. Each small body in that crowd was raw as if prised from a shell and then set back down to run around regardless. I was aghast: did they not know? Protest stuck in my throat as if I were fighting my way up from a dream. And we, too, I realised: we, like those hapless girls and boys, were acting as if nothing was amiss. We had been led in here and – the door shut on us and the curtains closed – abandoned with nowhere to look except at a veritable warehouse-load of stripped children. And it unspooled, relentless: up the chrome ladders those kids scampered, one after another, and for them the damage was already done, they were filmed and preserved there denuded in the dark green bubble of the telly screen. But for us? It was happening right now, in this room, yet here we sat, allowing it, even helping it happen, but unable to acknowledge it. Drawn fractionally away from one another, we held ourselves with exaggerated stillness as if in terror of giving ourselves away to a gunman.

And then worse: the commentator, off-screen, called cheerfully to one of the poolside girls; he singled her out, waylaid her, friendly as anything, and like a fool she obliged and came to him. Eager to please, she stood smiling, up close and in full view of the camera, her teeth chattering and her arms clamped around herself, each hand clutching the opposite shoulder. Holding herself there, shivering and dripping, she was clearly desperate to get back into the water but only, it seemed, because she was so cold.

The disembodied, determinedly cheerful and oh-so-proper voice remarked that she looked to be having a nice time and she politely agreed, making the effort to bring a shine to her eyes. I suspected she had been coached: *Aren't you lucky! Just think how lucky you are!* And as she agreed that she was having a great time, the gaze of the camera descended her body and lingered on the pudgy fold between her legs.

I closed my eyes and didn't open them – nor even my ears – until the programme had finished and we were being escorted back to our classroom, where, thank goodness, we were straight up to the hatch for Joan-the-cook to dish up rissoles and roasties. Everyone strenuously avoided mentioning the programme, the sole hint of any tension coming when the Bakewell was served and a skirmish broke out between the boys involving a splodge of skin pinched from someone's custard.

6

What had happened had put me off the school house, but
not the pool. Nothing could have put me off the pool.
We in the village might have our new hall but town had
gone much better and built a pool inside a magnificent
silvery hangar, and it was to this wondrous place, four or
five miles away, that our whole school was transported
by coach every Wednesday morning. Ten per cent of our
entire primary education was dedicated to learning how
to keep our heads above water.

Even though the whole enterprise was arduous, with
the journeys and the changing of clothes, the clamour
and chlorine, it was for me – who was, on land, a mere
dipper of toe in water – the highlight of each week. Me,
instantly tangled in any skipping rope and always chosen
last for any rounders team: I swam better than anyone
except Wendy. All week I hankered for that pool, the
very essence of me latching on to the whiff of distant
chlorine and straining towards it.

When we arrived at school on Wednesday mornings

the coach would already be idling outside, making itself felt inside as a hum in the floorboards and a scent of flat cola while Mr Hadleigh took the register. As we boarded, the unfortunates who were prone to travel sickness were detained at the front like lepers with Miss Drake and Mrs Hadleigh, who came along to help, and their bundle of sick bags and the surly driver with his unconscionable hairpiece. For the rest of us, the seating arrangements were a free-for-all, exploited to the full by the boys with their habit of whacking every seat they passed to produce a plume of dust. On Sarah-Jayne's first school swimming expedition, Beverly led the way, heading for the back seat, to sit her slap bang in the middle of it as queen of all she surveyed. Good luck to her, I thought; not for me the risk of being catapulted down the aisle.

The coach always took at least half an hour to cover that mere four or five miles, lumbering through the lanes between our village and town, and then creeping growling and grunting across town from junction to junction. We girls, lulled into a feverish drowsiness, sang songs and shared sweets and snacks according to complex rotas and arcane bartering systems while the boys marauded up and down the aisle, taunting and whacking. Miss Drake and Mrs Hadleigh, up front, between school and destination, abdicated their responsibilities and stared mesmerised through the immense windscreen.

Arrival brought an abrupt change of gear – *Chop-chop, everyone* – and a whirl of bags and clothing and towels and hats and goggles and, before we knew it, we were sloshing through the sickening foot bath and then there it was, the pool, pristine, faintly restless as it readied itself for the onslaught.

A roiling mass of frigid, acrid water was the last place on earth I'd have expected to thrive; but then again, being on land never did me any favours, knock-kneed and two left feet and all thumbs as I was. In that pool, when it came down simply to sink or swim, I'd strike out into the unfeasibly dense water, heading for the far wall, and I'd feel that I was flying; in water, I was everything that on land I could never be.

It had been so for as long as I could remember. I had never been a beginner but had been placed right from the start in the intermediate group. *Water baby*, Mum called me, *born swimmer*, but I knew there was no such thing and at some point I must have been taught, although not by her because she, herself, couldn't. My dad, then.

And now I was in the top group, which wasn't a group but a pair, just me and Wendy, in training for our Gold awards, with Wendy better than me because she could dive. *You'll get it*, she'd assure me, *and once you've got it, you've got it, and you never lose it*. It seemed to me that I just needed to trick myself into falling; or trick myself that if I kept going, head first, I wouldn't fall, it wouldn't be a fall. But I could never help saving myself, pulling up at the pivotal instant so that the dive became a jump and a poor one at that, a belly flop.

The two swimming teachers covered our three groups: Mrs Judge took care of the 'babies', while Mrs Baxter's attention was divided between the intermediates and the top group of Wendy and me. I imagined Sarah-Jayne would be in the middle group; she didn't look like much of a swimmer. She certainly hadn't shown any enthusiasm so far – she had been uncomfortable in the changing room, contorted by the towel she wrapped high and tight around herself, which somehow obliged us all to do likewise with ours, and then had taken for ever to pick her way through the appalling foot bath and emerge onto the poolside. Her peach-coloured costume was a vivid contrast to everyone else's shades of blue. She was sticking close to Beverly – Caroline was spectating, off swimming yet again with one of her headaches – who by comparison looked years younger in a costume jaunty with piping and a blister-textured cap.

Sarah-Jayne had yet to put her cap on: her hair was still loose, swishing over her shoulder blades and blazing under the powerful lights. Each week before we boarded the coach, Mr Hadleigh went on at us to remember our swim caps because, he said, our hair clogged the filters and drains and did we think anyone wanted to swim through girls' hair? Beverly had been sporting the scalped look as she'd left the changing room, as had the rest of us, but Sarah-Jayne was delaying putting on her cap until the last possible moment. She did the same with entering the water, perching on the poolside and only at Mrs Baxter's barked insistence lowering herself daintily to bob next to her friend. She was clearly middle-group material, I decided. No competition. During the session I caught glimpses of her alongside Beverly, doing precious little in a stilted style, smirking.

After the screech of Mrs Baxter's whistle to signal the session's end, we were crowding for the return slosh through the foot bath when Susan let out a wail: 'My love heart!' Stricken, stark-eyed, her hands were at her bare throat. She should never have been wearing that necklace – the rule was no jewellery in the pool – but must have forgotten to take it off. As one, we froze. She couldn't go to any grown-up because we had been specifically warned about this, and we knew too that we'd all cop for the telling-off – *You never listen, you girls, you can't be trusted, you have only yourselves to blame.* Susan was vibrating with anguish, her breath rasping and rapid. We turned as one to the culprit, the water, which gulped down our stares; but within seconds, miraculously, I'd spotted it – 'There! There!' – and then, before I knew it, Sarah-Jayne had tipped herself headlong into the blaringly blue depths, her dive so sharp that the water itself seemed taken unawares and barely shifted to close over her. There she was, below the spangled wavelets, pulsing with each stroke before rising like smoke to explode back through the surface, shiny-eyed from breath-holding, one arm raised in triumph and a gilt chain streaming from her fist as water clattered down around her like applause.

The return journey that day, as always, was much calmer than the outward, our energy spent and high spirits settled. Thanks to the vending machine in the lobby of the pool, we travelled in a haze of prawn cocktail flavouring, the stink of the lurid pink powder rivalling that of the chlorine. I wasn't allowed to buy crisps – *Does it grow on trees?* – but I did have a compensatory half of a Bar Six packed in my bag.

Again, Beverly had commandeered the back seat for her trio. Further down the coach, I had a double seat to myself, with Susan and Mandy behind and Saint Tracy and poor Virginia in front. Virginia wasn't allowed to swim but had to spectate along with a ragbag of verrucas and stitches, plaster casts and ear infections.

Across from me, Wendy too had a double seat, on which she sprawled askew, shoulder blades juddering on the window, legs outstretched and feet protruding into the aisle. Usually I was pacified and elated on the way back, as if after a good cry, but on this occasion I was unsettled. Because clearly Sarah-Jayne was a far better swimmer than it had suited her to let on. Mrs Baxter wouldn't care – she was after commitment and if you weren't prepared to give it, thrashing through the water with burning eyes, she wasn't interested. So, unless Sarah-Jayne decided she wanted saving from the middle group, she would be left to idle there. And didn't that suit me? It wasn't as if I wanted her with me and Wendy. Of course not. So, why did it rankle?

As the coach pulled away from the car park, Tracy, in front of me, said to Virginia, 'Give here, let me,' and from the scent I could tell she was peeling an orange for her; and then in the same conversational tone she told her, 'There's a pool at the vicarage, did you know that?'

The rubbish she must tell poor Virginia, I thought, and which Virginia bore with infinite patience, the lack of focus in her magnified eyes lending them a tenderness. Virginia, we all knew, was going to take the test next year for the grammar school. The part of her brain that had been removed wasn't the part for cleverness.

Tracy turned into the aisle and spoke down to the back seat, quite chummily: 'That's right, isn't it, Sarah-Jayne – there's a pool at the vicarage.'

Humouring her with an obliging, falsely bright voice, Sarah-Jayne said yes but that it was full of leaves.

So, a pond, then.

In a flash Wendy was up on her knees hollering indignantly over the headrests, 'Well, fish them out, then!' The leaves. 'Use a net!' Sacrilege, from her point of view, to have a pool and not use it.

Not that it was a pool. It was a pond. I peeled the paper off my Bar Six.

Mandy, behind me, was similarly sceptical. 'A pool? What, in the garden?'

Tracy got to her feet and blared over my head to Mandy, 'A pool, yes!' and flung her arms around in a depiction of crawl, a stroke she never in fact used; she could barely manage breaststroke. Virginia rose at her side and smiled benignly, as if Tracy were her precocious child.

Pond or pool wasn't a distinction that Tracy would make. Non-swimmer as she practically was, she would think people swam in ponds. And any house as grand as the vicarage was bound to have a pond, probably a big one, and perhaps in the olden days vicars had indeed swum in it.

Sarah-Jayne called politely back to Wendy, 'No' – *I mean* – 'it's empty.'

Perhaps not a pond, then. Because an empty pond wouldn't be a pond: no one would say it was a pond; it would just be a dip in the ground. This did now sound more like a pool. But how could – why would – a vicarage have a pool?

Despite myself, I too was craning around. Sarah-Jayne was intent on Caroline's hair, a kirby grip between her teeth; Caroline was holding still, submitting. On the other side of Sarah-Jayne, Beverly stared through the window, sort of off-duty. Neither she nor Caroline had any interest in any pool; they were content for the company of the new girl, and everything else rolled over them like music.

Did Sarah-Jayne perhaps mean a paddling pool? But then why would a vicarage have a paddling pool?

Wendy yelped: 'It's derelict?'

And that was something that a pool just shouldn't be: it was too heavy a word for a disused pool.

In answer, Sarah-Jayne, muted by the hairgrip, tilted her head, giving it consideration and, perhaps, cautious assent: *You could say that.*

Susan jumped to her feet, yanking my headrest as she did so. 'Is it big?'

Sarah-Jayne replied through her teeth. 'No ... '

'*How* big?' Mandy, all doubt and confusion.

'*Not* big,' Susan said, but Mandy came back with 'Yes, but ... ' *how* not-big? How *small*?

And I spoke up, because I just had to, I couldn't just sit there. 'A pool?' I had to get to the bottom of this. If there was a pool at the vicarage – derelict or not – right there in the middle of our village, I would have known. Mum would have known – she made out she didn't speak to anyone (*I can't be doing with coffee mornings*) but still she knew everything about the village, and she would have told me, because she told me everything.

Sarah-Jayne took the grip from between her teeth and answered me directly, almost as an aside beneath all the hubbub. 'It's probably just left over from—'

'Oh!' Susan interjected. 'The film star!'

The telly lady was elevated to a film star, and if she had had her own pool then perhaps that was what she had in

71

fact been. Sarah-Jayne slid the grip into Caroline's hair and raised her eyebrows as if to say maybe. I saw that it didn't really matter to her: a pool at her house was, for her, neither here nor there. And it was true that the vicarage wasn't really her house, moving onwards as she would be whenever her father sighted land. But I was trying hard, in my mind's eye, to picture it: a flaccid diving board, the dusty depths, the deep end collecting muck. Nevertheless, neglected though it sounded as if it was, and begrudge Sarah-Jayne though I did, I found that I did want it to be there, behind the vicarage's wall. Almost on our doorstep. Because what an extraordinary prospect, I thought: a piece of a different world washed up and lodged by mistake in ours, like a big dinosaur fossil.

But Wendy remained on the war path, and her concern was purely practical: 'You should fill it!'

And it was this that brought me to my senses: a pool in anyone's garden would be full of cold water. Not heated like in the public pool. Even if it were filled, it wouldn't be a shimmering light blue, but dense with the dead weight of stone-cold water.

Sarah-Jayne relinquished Caroline, who tentatively touched her hair and examined her reflection in the rain-streaked window. Turning her attention to her swim bag, delving, Sarah-Jayne offered, 'Maybe we'll fill it when the hot weather comes.'

Five weeks more of school, Mum had said to me only that morning, but summer seemed a world away. For a moment, I was lost in a reverie of school summer holidays at their best: meals on the hoof, or rarely any meals because we all lived on lollies, and days stretching late into the night.

Sarah-Jayne said, 'We had a proper pool at the house when we lived in Cyprus,' which sort of made me jump, and Wendy, too, who whipped back around and asked, 'You did?'

Sarah-Jayne looked up blankly from her bag and clarified, 'Yes, at the house in Cyprus.'

'Cyprus?' Susan asked. 'Where's that? Cornwall?'

Sarah-Jayne said no, it was abroad, 'And it's really hot, there.'

The house, I thought. Not *my* house. Not *at home*. Who was this girl who moved around, house to house? And why did it feel to me as if she had lied to us? I had to remind myself that she hadn't hidden from us that she had once had a proper pool: we hadn't asked her about previous houses. And, anyway, I supposed, she was telling us now: she couldn't say everything all at once and she was saying it now. So why did I feel that she had kept something from us, that she'd been underhand – that she'd been stringing us along? It had been good to have a pool there in Cyprus, she told us with no obvious enthusiasm, adding with more vim that they had had a pool buoy, or so I thought until she said, 'We called him Fred but that was just a joke, because his real name was something foreign.'

She smiled at the memory of him. 'Pool boys come and keep the pool clean,' she said to Wendy. 'They use the nets, and' – she shrugged, happily – 'it's really nice because you can just sit and talk with them while they work.' Beverly glanced admiringly at her, and then the pair of them were talking together about lifeguards and only then did I realise that as much as anyone else, and despite myself, I had been hanging on her every word.

★

73

When I got home, that day, Mum asked as she always did, 'Good swim?' She approved of school swimming lessons: we were learning something useful, unlike, say, in history. If ever I talked of what we'd learned in school about pyramids or the Romans' underfloor heating or the workhouse, she'd counter: 'What's the point of all that? They're dead and gone.' People who were alive, she said, were the ones we needed to worry about. We also did a lot of art at school and that too she didn't like because what was the point if you already had eyes? Why draw or paint something that anyone could simply see for themselves? Like bowls of fruit, she said, although actually we didn't have a bowl of fruit.

If history and art were unnecessary, religious studies was actively evil. Ours was a church school – there was no alternative in the village – so we were forever trooping up and down the lane to the church. All stories and lies, she said: 'The biggest lot of nonsense I ever heard and you wonder what they take us for, expecting us to believe any of that.' Never believe anything that anyone tells you, she always said. 'And I wouldn't mind' – which was itself a lie – 'but Mr Hadleigh doesn't even believe it, although of course he can't *say*, in his position; he's got to go through the motions because the auld vicar's breathing down his neck; and as for that vicar, that's a fine way to earn a living, preaching love and forgiveness but showing precious little of it, from what I've heard, for anyone parking in front of the lychgate.'

What she wanted us to do at school was the three Rs: two of them were pretty useful, although it had to be said that you didn't learn about life from books and they gave you ideas, but the third was crucial. And if she hadn't been good at maths at school, she could manage numbers well enough to be able to do Mr Watt's books – a different kind of books from the ones that gave people ideas – for her job, which she did at home. She had to have a job because my dad had died and the Widowed Mother's Allowance wasn't much. There was no one for her to run crying to, she said, when our cupboards were bare, which I thought made us sound like Goldilocks. 'That man's been good to us,' she'd say of Mr Watt. We even had an offcut of his carpet in our living room.

Mum did sometimes do another job, which was delivering leaflets in town, but because of me she mostly had to work at home. She couldn't have a job in the outside world as some of the other mums did – Mandy's mum was a receptionist at the doctor's and Beverly's worked in the greengrocer's in town and Wendy's mum, divorcee Dilys, poor Dilys, worked weekend nights at the local old people's home – because where would that leave me? We didn't even have a weirdo Wayne with whom I could be left.

When I was small she had taken a course that came at intervals in the post. I had vague memories of the big important-looking envelopes over which I found her crying, once, when I came back downstairs after bedtime with leg ache. She said I had to work hard and do well at school so I could get a good job. My dad had had a good job, in insurance, up in town. I too could work in town, as a secretary: *cheek*, Mum said of the secretaries up in town, *they're so cheek, those lassies, and with the world at their feet*. I wanted to be an archaeologist – the world at my feet in a different way – although I did have concerns about curses, seeing what had happened to Lord Carnarvon. Best not meddle was Mum's word on that.

We ate earlier after swimming, because I was hungrier than usual. Other evenings, we ate when children's telly ended and the six o clock news came on. But always when we had finished eating Mum would say, 'Well, what was the point of all that? Gone in two seconds.' Something she once let slip about my dad was that he hadn't believed in food; it was a waste of time, he'd said, and one day boffins would invent something better. 'Give them twenty years,' she explained to me, 'and they'll come up with a tablet we take every day. But it's fish fingers until they do.' No fish fingers, though, that particular Wednesday, but the whole kaboodle, the actual fish, be it in a bag of parsley sauce (I liked the sauce if not the parsley aspect). Sitting with our plates in front of *Blue Peter*, I asked her if she had known there was a pool at the vicarage.

She hadn't. 'That so? You sure? A pool?'

'The new girl said.'

'You've a new girl?' *You didn't say.* And I braced myself for *What's she like?* Because I wasn't sure I knew how to answer that. But she just said, 'At the vicarage?' and, 'Och, well, him who's renting the vicarage, Peggy Peters tells me he's ex-forces.'

Forces? Like powers?

'Raff,' she said. As in riff? 'They'll have lived all over.'

Well, she was right about that: Germany, Cyprus.

Taking my cleared plate off me, she said, 'They do their years,' which had it sound as if he had been in prison, 'and then they're out on civvy street on some big whack, and nicely set up to use their contacts.' Her tone implied this was suspect. 'For vicarage man,' she said, 'it's radars or something. Aye, clever man,' she allowed, sounding dubious.

None of this made much sense to me but I didn't let on and instead contributed, 'He's looking for land.'

'No doubt they'll move on,' she said over her shoulder on the way with our cleared plates to the kitchen. This was something I hadn't considered, and it gave me a dizzying shot of hope. From the kitchen, over the clattering of dishes in the sink, she called to me that she was surprised the new girl hadn't gone private.

Every morning when my friends and I trooped through the village, our raggle-taggle procession lengthening the closer we got to school, we passed the Biggses' bungalow at exactly the time when little Charlotte's mum, sporting electric-blue eyeshadow, shepherded her daughter from their glass lobby across the driveway to the car. Tiny Charlotte was a barely animated ensemble of collar-and-tie; she was blazer-bulked and half garrotted by boater elastic. Her mum always looked startled to see us all there in the lane, as if caught in the act, although that might have been an effect of the eyeshadow, and in an attempt to smile she would raise her top lip like a neighing horse.

Mum reappeared in the living room doorway to say, 'They'll be waiting for secondary for that, though, won't they.' To send Sarah-Jayne private, she meant. 'But I didn't know they'd a wee girl. Peggy Peters said there's a daughter about to get married.' *Marr-eed.*

For a change, I actually knew something: yes, I said, that was the other one – the big sister. The levitating one, I thought. 'She's twenty-six.'

'Is she, now.' A brisk wipe of her hands on the tea towel. 'Anyway, so what's she called, this new girl of yours?' and when I told her, she grimaced as I had known she would.

That evening, Susan, Mandy and I went to the park. I longed to talk to Susan alone about Sarah-Jayne but even if I had dared suggest meeting up without Mandy, and even if Susan agreed, Mandy's house was close by the park and we could never pass without being spotted.

Mandy came out chewing on a Curly Wurly. 'Want some?' She thrust it spit-wet to Susan first and then to me. Closing her door behind her, she joked, 'We should call for Sarah-Jayne.'

Susan exclaimed, 'Oh, my saviour!' and gave a little skip. 'And she's so *fashionable*, isn't she! It's like she's off the telly!' Then, of the vicarage, 'I wish *I* lived in that house! It's probably got . . . ' she considered, with a hum, 'a *ballroom*.'

I couldn't help but laugh: 'It's a *vicarage*; it won't have a *ballroom*.'

She was undeterred. 'Well, a . . . cellar, then,' and she waggled her eyebrows to intimate sinister thrills.

Mandy drew the Curly Wurly slurpingly from her mouth. 'My grandad's got a well.'

Susan enthused, 'Spook-y! Wonder what's down *that*!' Water?

Mandy said, 'You know what I'd have, if I had some great big house?' She stuck the Curly Wurly back into her mouth and bared her teeth around it so she could continue speaking: 'A telly room.'

At this, though, Susan turned sensible: 'That's a

living room.' Meaning Mandy already had one; we all already had one.

'No,' Mandy barged through the park gate ahead of us, 'a *special* telly room. *Especially* for telly. You go in, shut the door, and' – triumphantly – '*just watch telly.*'

Susan glimmered as she broke it to us: 'We actually *do*, we already have that . . . in the house.'

Then we were onto the swings, and Sarah-Jayne was forgotten. But later, idling my way back home, I saw the vicarage at the top of Church Lane and thought again of the pool that she had claimed was there.

Never misses a trick, this one, Mum was always saying of me, sounding proud but wary, as if it were me who needed watching. But a pool at the vicarage, it seemed to me, was one big trick to have missed. With no particular plan in mind, I turned on my heel and headed up the lane. I'd simply have a look at that vicarage, I told myself. A proper look. To see what I could see.

It kept itself to itself behind its railings. Despite its grandeur – shining white as it was, and standing tall – there wasn't much to see. I had no idea who'd lived there before Sarah-Jayne. Just people, any old people: the village was full of them going to whist drives – whatever they were – and dinner dances at the hall and doing flower-arranging at church.

This particular evening, it held no signs of life. The long windows, as yet unilluminated, swallowed the sky's dwindling light, shadows of clouds gliding across them as if the panes were bodies of water. How could Sarah-Jayne, in her jeans, with her tributes to David Cassidy biroed onto her hands, be living in there – amid cavernous fireplaces, I imagined, and framed portraits?

She didn't fit. Perhaps she was different when she was at home – perhaps she wore cardigans and knee socks. But somehow I doubted it.

The house looked back at me, all front, giving nothing away – but the pool, if it did exist, would be around the back, which might be less secure. It adjoined the churchyard. Dusk was deepening, but the graveyard didn't worry me so much as any passing nosy parker wanting to know what I was up to.

Having glanced around to check I hadn't been seen, I hurried through the lychgate; and moving swiftly up the path between the graves, I thought how if my dad had been buried, he wouldn't have been buried here because we'd come from somewhere else, which would be where he died. *Way off*, was all Mum ever said of where we'd lived back then: *Och, way off, closer in towards town*, by which she meant London. Big Ben and turn-again-Dick-Whittington. Before we'd left that place, I'd been old enough – just – to start school; I'd been at that school for a term, Mum said, but all I could remember was my coat peg, marked by a sticker of a hedgehog, and that there had been a girl called Clare, who might have been my friend. How could I remember a sticker of a hedgehog, but nothing of my dad?

The hedge between the church and the vicarage was behind the heap of grass cuttings and flowers cleared from graves, the slimy stems reeking of stagnant water. My footfall here was absorbed by needles dropped from trees that Mr Hadleigh said were here long before the church; there'd have been an old church before this one, he'd told us, although this version looked old enough to me. It certainly wasn't modern like the concrete triangle in town with its swirly stained-glass windows. The windows of this church showed beardy men in robes looking sorry for themselves.

The hedge was dense with the same dark green needles, effectively shielding the vicarage garden from view. Howard Carter wouldn't have been put off, I told myself as I paced back and forth, he wouldn't have given up; and eventually I did spot a gap at the bottom that was big enough at a push, I thought, to allow me, on all fours, to peer through.

My problem was that it gave on to a brick wall: a small building towards the back of the vicarage garden, which I was going to have to crawl around for a peek. I dragged myself all the way through the hedge, branches squealing on my anorak, then shuffled along on my hands and knees for a view across the lawn. The back of the house was quite unlike the front, its windows of various sizes and on different levels, one left open and catching the last of the daylight. Of the pool, I saw distantly a border of coping stones and the twin chrome arcs of a ladder.

7

The next day we all spent the break times on the field doing handstands – Sarah-Jayne was moderately good at them, although not so good as Caroline, who inadvertently displayed pad-thickened knickers – but on Friday we were back in the school house. When Mr Hadleigh had announced it was break time, we had as usual all risen as one and made for the porch, but instead of eddying and settling into our little groups of, variously, rose-petal-perfume-makers and pom-pom-knitters, everyone had headed together across the windswept playground and I had tagged along because to hang back would have been to be adrift, to be left literally in the cold.

This time, even Wendy came.

Perhaps I was easily led because I was slow to surface from the lesson we had just had, much of it adhering to me like a dream. We had been working solitarily and quietly, using our imaginations. Mr Hadleigh had had us writing a diary as if we were someone in Tutankhamun's household, because, he said, if you looked at bits of history from the sidelines then sometimes you could see more than if you were in the middle of it. In the porch, retrieving our outdoor shoes, I asked Susan who she'd been. A cook, she said, doing something with satsumas, and Mandy had been a cleaner, dusting the treasures, which we agreed was a good way to get to see them. Wendy piped up that she'd been a vet, but we weren't sure about that because in all the weeks we had spent on the ancient Egyptians there had been no mention of any vets. Plenty of mentions of cats, though, as Wendy reminded us: so, she said, where did they go when they were ill? Perhaps to a priest, said Susan: a special cat priest, which, given what we'd learned of the ancient Egyptians, didn't seem so far-fetched.

The discussion of vets occupied us as we crossed the playground and until we were at the front door of the house, which meant I was spared confessing who I'd chosen to be. It wasn't that I had broken the rules – I hadn't even bent them, really – but I knew deep down that what I had done hadn't quite been in the spirit of the exercise. Because I had been Tutankhamun's wife. Privately, I had been taking a stand, because I'd overheard Sarah-Jayne snarking to Beverly that no way would she have married a man who wore sandals. (But what was he supposed to wear? Lace-ups? Wellies?) In my imaginary diary extract, I hadn't been his actual wife. I hadn't imagined myself as her, but instead I'd been me and simply put myself back thousands of years. The problem with that, though, was that I knew, with the benefit of my thousands of years of hindsight, that my husband was going to die. At nineteen, too, which

Mum would call *in his prime*. I couldn't escape the fact of that, and it had rather overshadowed my morning.

What I didn't know was how; and no one did, not even all these centuries later or perhaps especially all these centuries later. We were in the dark, as Mr Hadleigh put it: cause of death could have been anything because, yes, there was that crack in the skull, he said, but that could have happened after he'd died. Which left me not knowing which way to look; I didn't know what to be on my guard against, couldn't tell from where the danger was coming and frankly all morning I had been a bag of nerves.

We crowded into the hallway of the house, our breathing sounding too loud to me; I had the feeling of being trapped underground. This time, Sarah-Jayne took the lead into the front room and was the first to flop down onto a chair, throwing herself back in it as if she had had an exhausting morning but could now revel in liberation. With the exception of Wendy, the others took hold of their chairs and dragged the dead weights of them bumping and shuddering across the coarse carpet to form a half-circle. Wendy just tipped herself backwards into a chair as it stood, sprawling across the seat and hooking her legs over the backrest, which meant that she was spared Sarah-Jayne's knowing glance at the hems of her trousers, a look which was then flashed around the rest of us, twinkling with amusement: there was something funny about those trousers, it seemed, which didn't need saying because, she seemed to think, we could see it for ourselves. In the next instant, she feigned catching herself and gave herself a little shake, ticking herself off for being picky, which had my skin crawl. All

I could see was that the trousers weren't flared – was that supposed to be the problem? That wouldn't be Wendy's fault. Sarah-Jayne wouldn't have known that they would originally have been Wendy's brother's: she had to wear his hand-me-downs because – Mum said – her dad was off with a trollop.

Who was Sarah-Jayne to judge us on our looks? I was too wary to sit; I took a chair but merely knelt up on the seat, back to front, and rested my arms on the top of the backrest. I wasn't staying, I reassured myself, although I didn't yet know how to make the break nor if anyone would come with me.

Glancing around, Sarah-Jayne said with that smile of hers that was no smile, 'We should have parties in here; this would be a great place for a party.'

This drab room was no place for a party, for a table covered with a bright tablecloth, for paper plates and balloons and a giant bowl of jelly. It was impossible to imagine in here the argy-bargy of musical chairs and a mound of tattered wrapping paper from pass the parcel. At Caroline's most recent party there had been a magician, with hankies and coins, oohs and aahs, as her mum bobbed in the background, close to tears.

'We could invite whoever we want,' Sarah-Jayne said.

Yes, but everyone was always invited – even Wendy – whenever any of us had a party: there weren't that many of us, so nobody could be left out. That was just how it was. I didn't have parties – Mum couldn't stretch to that – which meant that for my birthdays I had Susan and Mandy to tea, a nice tea with Mr Kipling's French Fancies with candles in them, and jelly and ice cream, but lately Mum had been saying that when I turned twelve it would be different: from next year I could take a friend to the pictures and then even perhaps to the Wimpy. Mum and I both knew that friend would be Susan – but where, I worried, did that leave Mandy? I didn't want Mandy – and it would be the perfect birthday present to have Susan to myself – but she'd know she'd been left out. I couldn't raise it with Mum, though; she wouldn't understand, she'd just say, *Och, Mandy*, which everyone except loyal Susan did when it came to Mandy, if everyone else said it minus the *och*.

Wendy enthused to the ceiling, 'We could stash a secret supply of fizzy in here.'

Susan leapt at the prospect, her eyes dewy: 'I love Coke!' It was one of the things she and I loved about Spain – we'd heard from a cousin of hers that in Spain you could drink Coke all the time, the hotels serving it all day long which meant that you could have it for breakfast if you wanted. Wendy flung her arms wide and sang in fake opera, '*I'd like to teach the world to sing, in perfect harmony,*' but none of us joined in, and instead Sarah-Jayne said, 'Coke's best with vodka.' She crossed her legs and leaned forward like Lesley Judd on *Blue Peter*.

'Vo-ka?' Mandy frowned.

Was that something like lemon, or ice?

Wendy whirled around, righted herself in her chair. 'Uh-oh, no! That's like Jew-bonny, it's for grown-up parties, and those drinks *stink*.'

Mum had stayed with her sister and brother-in-law when she had first arrived in London and they had wine at their Sunday lunches and, she said, it was like vinegar. And they didn't eat their tea until eight every evening, by which time she had such a thumping headache she never knew what she was eating.

Sarah-Jayne addressed herself for no obvious reason to Caroline. 'Vodka doesn't smell, doesn't even really taste.'

Wendy protested, 'But if you can't taste it, why drink it?'

And now Sarah-Jayne acknowledged her, with an understanding smile. 'Because it makes you feel . . . ' she considered, dreamily, with a private smile, 'floaty.'

To which Caroline contributed a long, sweet sigh.

Mandy was puzzled, 'Did your mum and dad give it to you?' and Sarah-Jayne shot her a look that Beverly voiced for her: 'Not on your nelly.'

Chastened, Mandy offered, 'My favourite drink is milkshake,' which we all knew – well, all of us apart from Sarah-Jayne. Nesquik, Mandy meant. I had once asked my mum if we could get a tin of it but she'd said she wasn't made of money and we weren't buying that muck. 'Strawberry,' specified Mandy, which we also all – except Sarah-Jayne – knew, although that hadn't stopped Mandy saying it hotly, defensively, as if for any of us to think otherwise would be a slur on her character.

Beverly said, 'That strawberry flavour sticks in my throat like sick,' but Caroline roused herself to add, 'It's not so bad if you swirl some golden syrup in it,' and I imagined her gliding through that house, over the split level and past the breakfast bar, her frail mum asleep upstairs, to lick golden syrup off the spoon.

Businesslike, Wendy said, 'Grown-up drinks make you feel sexy, you start kissing everyone, and once when I was little my mum and dad had this party for New Year and I woke up and this man and lady were in my room kissing loads like on telly,' but then, talking over her, Susan was confiding in Sarah-Jayne: 'Just before you came, we saw this programme in here.' Oh no, I thought, please no, but on she went, blithely, 'About the birds and the bees,' awkwardly waggling her eyebrows.

Sarah-Jayne said nothing, just tipped her head to one side in encouragement, but Beverly butted in, attempting to cut the scandal down to size: 'Kids at some pool, in the nudd.'

Mandy, though, was grave: 'All of them, the whole class of them.' A swipe of her hand, *pff*.

My mum said, *There are gerils – stupid gerils – who believe anything any man says to them, and then that's it for them – pff! That's all it takes. That's it. You must never, ever let any man near you, you understand me? Are you listening to me? Do you hear me?*

Pff – like a plug pulled?

And then withering to nothing, like the lady in that old film, turning in front of your eyes to dust.

You never get your life back after that.

'But,' offered Susan, brightly, 'it was so we could see. So we could learn. We were supposed to be learning.'

'It was stupid,' said Beverly, and for once she was right.

Wendy said, 'Yes, but some people do go around bare. Playing tennis, going off camping.'

Susan was astonished: 'No, they *don't*.' And then, more kindly, and concerned, to the extent of patting Wendy's forearm: 'Wendy, no one plays tennis in the nuddie.'

Wendy insisted, 'They go to special camps for it! It's so they can get fresh air all over them. They don't believe in clothes except when they go to places like the post office.'

This was horrible.

Beverly announced, 'I am never taking my clothes off for anyone,' but Susan rued, 'You have to, when you get married.'

Mandy countered, 'You could wear your nightie,' and Susan reconsidered: 'If your husband is nice, maybe he won't look.'

That was when Sarah-Jayne spoke up. 'They have to,' she told us, matter-of-fact. 'It's part of it. They have to see you all over.' She looked around us. 'It's about trust.' She tipped her head and said, softly, as if casting a spell, 'You entrust yourself.'

As luck would have it, at that moment Miss Drake looked in on us: into the doorway came her mop of red-gold hair and the grin of horse-sized teeth. *Soap-and-water lass*, Mum always said of her.

'Hello, girls!' Her greeting of us was always celebratory, whereas other grown-ups only ever addressed us en masse to put us in our place ('Pipe down, girls'). 'Sorry to interrupt your pow-wow, but I'm in here next with my little ones.' She said she'd come to get the room ready and switch on the telly to warm up, which had us all leaping to assist in her energetic efforts, whumping the chairs back into place in a semicircle around the telly to the accompaniment of her cheerful thanks: *That's so kind, thanks so much, girls, bless you.* Then, 'And if I could trouble you to vacate in the next few minutes, just as soon as you're ready . . . ' before she was off to retrieve her pupils, my mind eye's following her racing across the playground, teeth-first and Scholls clacking in her wake.

Susan was moved to voice our collective enthusiasm for her, 'Isn't she just so lovely?' and Sarah-Jayne's eyes glittered as she concurred: 'She does seem nice.' Then, though, she winced, apologetically. 'If only she'd just' – and with a wrinkle of her nose, she flapped a hand floorwards – '*shave those legs.*'

Back in our classroom, I thought over how none of us had said a word to that, which gave the impression that we agreed, that Sarah-Jayne had told us something we already knew. But I, for one, had never given a moment's thought to Miss Drake's legs and was dismayed that anyone would. To anything of Miss Drake's, in fact: it had never occurred to me to take her apart like that and hold pieces of her up to scrutiny. She was just so perfectly herself, made of herself all the way through like a tree trunk with its rings. That she shave her legs or do anything else to titivate could no more be required of her, I felt, than of a pebble.

She spent her days on the go in the service of her small charges, picking up and putting right, swabbing and wiping, tying and buttoning, sticking and glueing. She whizzed around, clog-shod and well scrubbed, chap-lipped and bare-legged, in many ways not so different from her charges; just bigger, but not by all that much. She shouldn't have to be thinking about her legs. Nor, for that matter, I knew, should I. Yet, that afternoon, I could do nothing but. For the rest of that day, however hard I tried to resist, her little legs loomed large for me. Whenever she clattered into our classroom in search of supplies and tripped away clutching recorders or the giant papier-mâché bumblebee, I stole surreptitious glances while at the same time attempting to gauge the interest or otherwise of my friends. Were they, too, looking? Or had they known of this alleged hairiness all along? But if it was common knowledge, then why hadn't

I heard about it? Perhaps, I thought, it had been kept from me; perhaps it was considered indelicate to raise such a subject in front of me.

Back in the half-term holiday, before we'd given up on the arrival of better weather, Mum had retrieved my summer dresses from the bottom of her wardrobe and had me try them on to see if, in her words, we could squeeze another year out of them. With the first one, she'd grimaced and said I'd shot up; and stepping forward to tug it down, then back again to appraise, she caught my eye and added with a nod towards my shins, 'Och, and that's nothing, no need to worry yourself about that.'

My heart tripped, because what was nothing? But I knew. I did know what she was looking at, because that was where I too now was looking and presumably what I could see was what she had seen: my hairy legs.

'You're just downy,' she said, passing me the next dress. 'Down is all that is.' She shook the dress free of creases. 'Lucky you're fair.'

And, yes, the hair was light and fine but that brought its own problems because it was fluffy and made a haze, a kind of halo. It seemed to have grown over the winter. As I had shot up, it had shot out. During the endlessly cold winter, shut away beneath my tights, it had incubated. Just as Bert next door forced his rhubarb.

'No one's looking,' she said, although that was precisely what we both were doing.

The poor weather had been convenient because so far this half term I had been able to hide my downiness under socks. And in the changing rooms at the pool each week I was swift, and hoped for the best. What was clear to me from the changing room was that no one else was afflicted as I was. Mandy's legs were probably the hairiest, but even those hairs were short and like dashes made with a soft pencil. Caroline's legs – like polished wood, her calves shaped like maracas – were, as far as I could see, entirely hairless.

What made my problem even worse was that Mum was dead against shaving. *Once you start*, she warned me, *that's you*. Doomed, was how she made it sound. The hair grows back thicker and darker, she said, which sounded like something from a fairy tale although what she had actually said was the Forth Road Bridge. It was what had happened to her, she said: this was the trap into which she had fallen. Brandishing her Ladyshave, she warned, *Don't you ever start this palaver, or you'll end up like me*. Conned was the implication, hoodwinked, led up the garden path.

The Ladyshave had been a Christmas present to herself, the only one I'd ever known her give herself. I presumed she had started shaving back in the days of Jeannie, because she no longer believed in titivating or what she otherwise called primping and preening; she didn't care what she wore, nor did she do her hair or wear make-up or pluck her eyebrows. (*What's good enough for Liz* . . . which, I later learned, meant Elizabeth Taylor.) Any attention paid to appearance, with the exception of legs, was 'pandering'.

Don't dwell, don't meddle, don't pander.

I'd find no refuge in trousers even if I could persuade her to allow them; Wendy had shown me what a minefield they would be. Mum railed against anything that was unnecessary and no doubt that would include excess fabric. Flaring would, in her view, I suspected, be a kind of pandering. And anyway she called trousers troos, a word holding little hope of any flare.

So, what was I going to do? I knew I was going to have to do something. Usually at weekends, Mum had lie-ins while I hung around in my nightie, holding out too long against getting dressed but ending up chilled to the bone; but that particular Saturday, I was still working through my toast, half listening to *Junior Choice*, when from upstairs came the telltale whine of the Ladyshave and I knew, then, that the time had come. Bull, I told myself, horns. Up I went and from the landing I saw that she too, sitting on her bed, was still in her nightie. She was contorted to concentrate on one leg, drawing the buzzing implement fastidiously to and fro on her shin like a cat lapping at its fur.

I made sure to look as if I were merely stopping by at her room on the way to my own. I must give no sign, I knew, that what I was about to say mattered to me. It should seem a passing remark, off the cuff. There should be no opportunity for her to shoot me down. All I needed for now was to slip it past her and get the nod.

So, striving to sound world-weary and woman-to-woman, with a grimace directed at the Ladyshave, I said, 'One day soon, I'm going to have to start all that.'

My hope was for a ruefully raised eyebrow, but she paused and held aloft the agitated Ladyshave, which had me braced for the usual *Och, away with you! Who on air-th is looking?* What she said, though, with a frown, was: 'Who's been putting ideas into your head?'

A smile sprang up and stayed smarting there on my

93

face. Because she was joking, surely. Ideas into my head? No one put ideas into my head. Which she knew. She, surely, more than anyone, knew. Because it was all she ever asked of me: that I follow no one's lead, that I jump off no bridges. That I stand up for myself, stand apart from the crowd. *It's me*, I had the urge to insist, to plead. *It's me you're talking to, here at your door.* But she was already back to the buzzing: it hadn't been an actual question; she wasn't waiting for an answer. For me, it took a beat or two longer. Standing there, stunned, in that doorway, I wasn't sure she even knew, really, what she'd just said. Primping and preening and pandering as she was, there on her bed, she had spoken to me as if I were just anyone else.

8

It was too wet and windy that Saturday for our usual trip on the bus into town, the highlight of which would have been a big warm bloomer from the baker's. We would have stuffed ourselves with doughy handfuls and then skipped dinner and remained out of sorts, if not entirely unpleasurably, for the rest of the day. Not this Saturday, though, and the weather was too poor, even, for me to go to the park. Mum decided to clear out the cupboard under the stairs and told me to go and amuse myself.

Up in my room, I had dolls for company, a motley crew assembled over the years, but although I did wish I could feel more generously towards them, in truth they were no more to me than lumps of plastic. The array of scales was confounding: some were small, slender and long-limbed, their stalk-like bodies topped with a shock of bright blonde hair so that they resembled daffodils, while others were almost life-sized pudgy babies, one with a repugnant plastic-moulded kiss curl. In all cases, what did for them was how lifelike they were, how spectacularly they were failed by the blankness of their sightless blue eyes.

So, I never played with them, and my neglect was shamefully obvious: the grubbiness of their pink limbs, and the disarray of their clothing, disastrously mixed and matched as if they had fallen victim to some disaster. I felt bad, because at one time or another they would have cost Mum what she called Good Money and we had precious little of that. But whenever I was left to my own devices I abandoned them and went next door to Mum's bedroom, to the drawer of her raw-brown dressing table, which held a treasure trove of make-up bottles and compacts, remnants from the days when, presumably, she was a titivator, a primper and preener.

In that drawer were a dozen or so cartons and compacts, bottles of nail varnish, palettes and lipsticks, and – sounding more suited to the kitchen – panstick. They had a dignity lacking in those grubby, dishevelled dolls who made big (if blank) eyes at me, begging to be played with, crying out for attention. Although these bottles and cartons might be scuffed and smudged, their peach-coloured contents variously gloopy and desiccated, the swirly gilt script of their labels spoke to me of a certain confidence and grace. They were enticingly hand-sized, too, and those that weren't dimpled or faceted were pebble-smooth, and some were satisfyingly pebble-heavy. Some were slender, but others ample-bellied, dimpled, wide-hipped, full-skirted. Some, it seemed to me, were cheeky, but others aloof and superior; some were cheerfully brisk, even blunt, while others were shy and retiring. The top of one nail varnish bottle tapered like a wimple; others had lids that popped on and off like hats. I did my very best by them in terms of names – Annette, Lynette, Stephanie, Tabitha, Belinda, Juliette – and as the three-leafed mirror looked askance, I slid them around on the surface of the dressing table, listening in on their various squabbles, and adjudicating.

And so the Saturday afternoon passed, but then the evening stretched ahead with nothing much on telly because this was – supposedly – summer. Back at the bank holiday we'd been treated to a *Generation Game* special, but since then it had been slim pickings. All in all, it was a dismal weekend to cap a week that, due to the new girl, had already been bad enough. 'Wet weekends,' Mum said glumly of the pair of us at teatime but in my case she didn't know the half of it, nor would I tell her because if she got to know about Sarah-Jayne I knew what she'd say: *What are you? Sheep?*

And I really didn't need to hear that, because I was just as baffled. Sarah-Jayne, of all people, to command attention and wield influence. She brought to mind those cut-out figures in my Christmas annuals that came complete with outfits to be attached by the simple folding of tabs over shoulders and behind the waist. At first, they seemed such a good idea, held such promise on the page – stylish and adaptable and so easy to make – and every year I cut carefully and hopefully along the outlines only to be left with bits of paper because they were never more than the sum of their paper-thin parts.

Not that I had actually ever for a moment thought that Sarah-Jayne was a good idea. No, not me, I thought as I stared out of my window into the rain. I knew that school hadn't been perfect before she'd come. We had, at best, rubbed along. Mandy had been friends with

Susan before I came and there was no getting around that, and Wendy was maddening, and as for Beverly, well, the day I walked out of that school for good would be with any luck the last time she and I had anything to do with each other. But the point was, I thought, that before Sarah-Jayne had arrived we had for good or bad been ourselves. And now they all seemed to be forgetting themselves, falling in line behind this cruel-eyed new girl whose head was stuffed full of magazines, giving themselves over to her.

On Sunday, the rain cleared, but too late for that to be of any use: the weekend was over. We'd eaten our special Sunday tea of rarebit – Mum's made with Slimcea and Outline – and it was time for our weekly bath and hair-wash. Mum went upstairs to run the bath, but then in no time she was back in the doorway, wide-eyed, wordlessly conveying a warning.

I managed to ask, 'What?' even as I shrank from knowing. It was clear that bad news was about to land on me and I would have to bear up.

She said with an eerie evenness as if anxious to conceal her whereabouts, 'There's a spider in the bath.'

In my mind's eye, I saw it: black blotch on bone-bright enamel, beady body filled with God only knew what, both hard and soft, squishable yet indestructible.

'And it won't go down the plughole.'

So, she had already tried. I hoped she'd used the rubber shower attachment – a fierce directed flow – rather than merely run the bath so that the spider rose triumphantly on the tide on its parachute of splayed legs.

I hardly dared to check: 'Has it drowned, though?'

She looked away, bleakly, into nowhere. 'They don't,

do they,' she said, 'because they're made for rain. They just' – she shrugged, helpless – 'fold up and then ...' *unfold again.*

My breath scrabbled at my lungs. That spider would be like a billiard ball in the bath, ricocheting, outrunning us even as it had no place to hide.

'It's too big,' she admitted, 'to go down.'

The torrent-battered body in the plughole, its legs at nasty angles. *You didn't try hard enough.* I'd mash it, I thought, desperately: yes, I'd mash it with something and force it through that grate. Or, 'Use hot water,' I said. Kill it with that. *None of your 'rain'.*

'Deborah,' she winced, and she was right, because for a fraction of a second it was me crouched there inside those sheer and blindingly bright walls under the pitiless scream and slam of the water.

I said, 'We can go next door,' but my voice sounded small, pathetic and pleading. 'Or over the road. Get someone.'

She dipped her face into her hands and whispered through her fingers, 'I should never have passed this on to you.'

This terror of spiders, she meant, and I fought down my pique because she spoke as if it were irrational, whereas we were right to fear them, because they inhabited the dark recesses of our house, scuttling along the rafters or seeping behind the skirting boards. There was good reason to be afraid.

I tried again: 'We can go over the road.' I had no one specific in mind to ask for help; anyone would do. But she was tight-lipped and said, as I dreaded she would, 'I'm not a charity case.'

But this wasn't about charity. This was a spider in the bath. This was an entirely proper situation in which to ask for help. We needed a kindly man with a glass and a piece of card – I knew how it was done, how he'd hold it up to have us recoil and squeal as he enjoyed telling us it was more scared of us than we were of it. 'Mum,' I said, 'please,' trying to keep from my voice any trace of what I burned to say: *Don't be stupid, stop being stubborn.*

Why, I thought for one thunderous, treacherous heart-beat, was I saddled with a mum like this? We sat here in this house under defunct light bulbs because she would never ask for help. She didn't want anyone in our house. Because no one should know our business. She didn't want anything to do with anyone. *Women, all chummy*, she often complained of coffee mornings, with a shudder: *I don't want to be one of those women.* And sometimes she said an Englishman's home was his castle. But she wasn't English nor a man.

I thought of how we smiled and chatted with the neighbours and kept our house nice and tidied the bins away, but all that effort was wasted because she couldn't even ask those neighbours for help with a spider. And for one dizzying moment it was we who were going down the plughole and not only was the water rising around us but just then it was as if she were holding my head below the surface.

But then she said, 'That Sonny, the cycling boy: go and get him.'

Who?

'The tortoise-rescuer.'

What, from the Gibbs'? I pictured their mansion's brass-knockered front door, on which I had never knocked and I wasn't going to start now. And anyway, what? Bring him here, that lanky, twangy-voiced boy? I wasn't so sure that I wouldn't prefer the company of the spider.

She was warming to her idea. 'Go on up there,' she said with a nod in the direction of the main road. 'See if he comes by. Cycling. Because he does, remember? You heard him: evenings, out on his bike. Go up there, and if he comes by, nab him, tell him we need him.' And then as if it was all his fault: 'Francis of A-bloody-ssisi, *he* can deal with this.'

I managed a mere 'Me? Up at the road?'

She bit my head off: 'Well, *I* can't, can I! I can't stand there on the edge of the road all night, can I! But' – and it flew at me like an accusation – '*you* can.'

So, that was how I came to be squatting on the verge, that Sunday evening, among the clods and hummocks, the blistering of dandelions and litter of lolly sticks, determined to catch no one's eye should anyone pass, be it on foot or in a car. I hoped I was far enough away from the bus stop not to risk the bus pulling over and then the driver tutting at my having wasted his time. Susan's dad was a bus driver but thankfully not on this route. I scanned the road in both directions, longing for the boy to appear so that I could leave my post and so we could be spider-free, but at the same time dreading sight of him. I kept busy by bargaining with myself as to how long to give it, which was pointless because I had no idea how much time was passing.

And then, after ages, there he was, pedalling furiously, yellow hair rising and falling rhythmically around his head like wings, and my problem became how to stop him mid flight. If I failed, though, and he went whistling past me, I would escape by a whisker, I could return home alone, feigning dismay and indignation that I had tried my best. But then we'd still have that beast gloating in our bath, growing ever meatier. There was nothing else for it: I stood up purposefully and fixed my sights on him, took a definite step forward and halted meaningfully at the kerb, but made sure to look disdainful so that any witness might think me about to take him to task – *Oi! Watch your speed, this is a dangerous stretch* – or send him on some errand – *You! Going past the farm? We need a pint of milk, pronto.*

He was slowing down, although even from my distance I could see he was puzzled. He wasn't committed to stopping until suddenly he did, gliding level with me but evidently with no recollection of who I was. Then, though, came a spark of recognition and over an embarrassingly fart-like piping of his brakes he yelped, 'Hiya, kid!'

He balanced on tiptoe astride the stationary bike, and being at a standstill gave him the opportunity to sniff some snot raucously back up his nose. My own nose buzzed with the scent of him, which was like hay. He looked quite brown but it was impossible to tell what was sunburn from what was grime. Contriving to look somewhere over his shoulder, I informed him, officiously, as if more or less quoting:

'Mum says can you come to ours, we've got a spider.'

Done, I congratulated myself even as my face was burning. Home stretch, I told myself.

His own weasely face broke wide open into a smile. 'Spider?'

Yes, well, I thought, he'd be laughing on the other side of that weaselly face when he saw how big it was. Not that I could vouch personally for its dimensions.

'Big bugger, is he?'

Bugger. Mum always said 'bee': *He's a right bee.*

And jovially, 'So, where is he?'

I told him.

'Ah well,' he said, knowingly, 'let's see what we can do,' and swung himself off the bike, led it ticking into our road.

As he propped the bike against our hedge, I took the lead into the house, yelling for Mum, desperate for her to appear but trying to sound casual as if I were in some telly programme and it was all good fun.

'Ah!' She appeared, acting businesslike, as if he were a tradesman come to do something, but then faltered and dropped the act, confiding in a low voice, 'I am *so* sorry about this.' *Sue sorry.*

'Naaaah!' He flung his skinny arms wide, too far for our hallway, knocking into our hung-up coats. 'Sonny at your service!' and when Mum asked him if he needed a beaker, 'Nah-nah-nah!' To his own amusement and our horror, he raised a hand and made an opening and closing motion as if a puppet were talking: he intended to catch the spider with his bare hands.

Mum and I stayed at the foot of the stairs, supervising from a safe distance, and there were a couple of non-specific and muted sounds before he clomped back down. His limbs seemed to follow him haphazardly, making little effort to keep up.

Only then did I wonder, uneasily, if my door had been open and he'd seen Tutankhamun.

103

'Gone walkies out the winda,' he announced happily of the spider.

That would mean it was barely outside, I thought, twitching in the grass below our living room window, awaiting the first opportunity to clamber back indoors. This would just have to be a case, I knew, of hoping for the best and trying to forget, of getting on with life as if none of it had happened.

But Mum seemed satisfied, exhaling as if she had been holding her breath for several minutes. Then, 'Coffee?' and turning away briskly as if he had already accepted.

No, I thought, he should go: his bike was there outside and he had been on his way somewhere, or nowhere maybe, but anyway he'd been on his way and he should be back on his way. There was no need, surely, for him to stay for coffee.

But he was pleased: 'Grassy-arse!'

'Bird's do you?' she sang out behind her. Mellow Bird's: the jar with the little blue birds on it.

He laughed, 'Never say no to Bird's, me,' which had her turn in the kitchen doorway, lit from behind by a rare ray of sunshine, to tut at him but with a smile. He blundered past me and they were talking over my head as, I realised, people usually didn't: most people treated me and Mum as a pair and talked equally to us both.

'Three, ta,' he told her. Sugars, he meant, even though Mum hadn't yet asked. Mum didn't take sugar, said she was sweet enough. Opening the fridge, she announced, 'Oh, and top of the milk, too – aren't you the lucky one,' to which he jokingly said he'd be coming here again.

9

By the end of that awful weekend, I knew I was going to have to make some kind of a stand against Sarah-Jayne Todd, even if I didn't know how. My first opportunity came Monday mid morning, when Susan and I were in the porch, changing into our shoes, on our way out into the playground and Mandy was briefly with Miss Drake having an eyelash fished from her eye. With a hand to Susan's arm and my heart in my mouth, I took the plunge: 'Let's ...'

Let's what, though? As soon as I'd said the word, I didn't know what to specify because what did we ever do at playtime? Usually we'd hover and alight on something or somewhere – a skipping rope, the hopscotch squares – and then there we were, playing. Never before had we had to have a plan: off we'd go to play and then just end up playing. (And anyway wasn't that what playing *was*?)

So ... let's what?

But as luck would have it, at that moment the climbing frame, across the playground, snatched a passing ray of sunshine and seemed to tip me the wink. And it was a reliably good choice. We didn't use it for climbing so much as for hanging from, only ever hauling ourselves high enough to find a perch from which to swing upside down, which was so easy that even I could manage it: sitting balanced on the bar, folding forward but sinking my weight into my bottom, and then, at tipping point, dropping back into thin air with a thrilling whoosh of my hair ahead of me. We'd hang by the crook of our knees, swinging, luxuriating in the pull of our own weight for as long as we could stand the pooling of blood in our brains.

Ducked free from the sky and hanging upside down, I'd find my eye drawn to the woods that ran from the end of our playing field to the horizon. Royal hunting ground once upon a time, we'd been told, but now densely, darkly wooded, and bordered by barbed wire bearing threats of prosecution for trespassers. With a fire-gutted manor house somewhere in its blue-black depths and an ancient curse (its nightingales silenced), it was more fairy-tale forest than woodland; but to us, playing every day in its shadow, no more disconcerting than the tufts of wire-torn sheep wool and unearthly blue of the eggs on our classroom nature table.

Climbing up onto the frame on that Monday morning, though, my attention was snagged closer to home: Sarah-Jayne, Beverly and Caroline were sprawled with their anoraks as ground sheets on the playing field; Caroline reclined with her arms behind her head, Beverly cross-legged with her skirt stretched between her knees as a surface for daisy-chain-making, and Sarah-Jayne with her legs tucked to her side and her eyes flashing any sunshine that spilled from between the rolling clouds. I didn't realise they were singing until I caught a sustained low note, which Mandy – cured of the eyelash – also picked up and claimed to be from the previous day's chart show. A new entry, she said, called 'Puppy Love', by Donny Osmond, and this sparked the revelation from Susan that her nan was getting a puppy now that Alan had died; but before I could ask who Alan had been, Mandy cut across with 'Deborah's scared of dogs.' Mandy acted big about dogs because her dad was the local hunt's kennel master, but more fool her, I thought, because – I could just see it – a pack of wolves might be racing her way but she'd stand there gormlessly sucking on her plait stub.

I knew not to rise to the bait but on this occasion there was no need because Susan came sweetly to my defence: no way, she said, would I be scared of a lovely little puppy. And this particular lovely little puppy of her nan's was to be a spaniel, she said, which distracted Mandy into talk of the glories of spaniels. I hung there grateful to Susan for having come to my rescue, but the truth was that I was terrified of puppies; they didn't have fewer teeth and claws just because they were small. In fact, if you thought about it, they were proportionally more teeth and claws, and, worse, didn't yet know not to use them.

Too fresh in my memory was a long-ago visit with Mum to some people, somewhere, who had had a puppy that, for the whole afternoon, had never left me alone. Spurred on by my shrinking away, it had raked my bare shins while Mum tried her best to laugh along with its owners, who made no move to stop it, to scoop it up or restrain it, not even when they had clearly tired of the whole performance. At the end of that long day, when Mum yanked me along the street to the bus stop, she hissed, 'Why do I ever take you anywhere if you're just going to show me up?' Only later on the bus, as we sat side by side in silence, staring from the window, did she complain to her reflection, 'Why didn't they shut that bloody awfy wee thing away?'

Susan and Mandy were discussing the Donny Osmond song, Susan admitting she'd missed most of the chart show because her brother had nicked the radio to leave it between stations in the hope of picking up messages from aliens. I'd missed the show because of the spider escapade, but kept that to myself. Mandy had heard it in its entirety and been impressed by another new entry, which she said was about someone ringing up someone's mum. Susan was mystified as to how that could possibly be a song and Mandy completed a rotation – dropping her feet to the ground, releasing her grip on the bar, flexing her hands to bring blood back into them – before elaborating: 'The phone operator keeps coming on and saying' – she lowered her tone, to sound officious – '"forty cents more".'

'Oh, that's American,' said Susan, 'cents is American,' which was somehow enough to summon Wendy seemingly from nowhere, hurling herself at the frame, hoisting herself up onto a bar and yelling, mid somersault, her own take on American: 'Yew dirdy ray-at!' Wellied feet thudding to the ground (wellies for Wendy whatever the weather), she told us her mum booked with the operator every New Year's Day to talk on their neighbours' phone for a couple of minutes with an uncle in Canada, and

Canadians too had cents, she said, but he was old and boring and, in fact, aliens would be better. Her parting shot, before she went haring off, was that her brother's friend rang people in the phone book and asked them if their fridge was running and when they said yes he told them to run after it.

This tickled Mandy, like at Brownies when a mention of cheesy feet had led to the idea of cheesy knees and she'd laughed until she choked and nice Mrs Peters had had to turn vicious and bash her between the shoulder blades. Now she was asking me in a fake voice, 'Is your fridge running?' and in a pretend-puzzled voice I fed her the line – 'Yes, of course' – but despite several goes she was laughing too much to manage the punchline, and Susan tutted indulgently ('Oh, you two'), and before we knew it the bell was ringing and we had managed the playtime without even thinking again of Sarah-Jayne.

Even better, the weather held, that day, and later, after tea, it was fine enough for us to meet up in the park, the three of us standing on a swing each and wrenching ourselves ever higher amid the sashaying bats. From on high, we spied over the hedge into the Dixons' living room window to see what they were watching on telly, and heckled their disdainful cat. Slowly, the incoming tide of dusk saturated us, dissolving us until my friends were no more than points of light bobbing here and there in the opalescent gloom.

The next morning, though, I was back to earth with a bump. During our first lesson, Susan had glimpsed a copy of *Jackie* in Sarah-Jayne's bag and at break time was keen that we tag along for a look at it. I remembered once taking a copy down off the shelf in Smith's and Mum saying, 'That's for the lassie with more money than sense,' although I'd only been after a receipt to be able to enter the Win a Pony. Now Susan wanted us to crowd around as Sarah-Jayne turned the pages, to crane over her shoulder and come up with the required oohs and aahs in response to make-up tips and boyfriend advice. Bobbing at the knees, she implored me, 'Don't be like this.'

Like what? I hadn't said a word. Not yet I hadn't. But now, I thought, I might as well, so I took a breath, and took a running jump at it: 'I don't like her.' There: it crash-landed between us, sounding shamefully babyish. But I heard it for the truth that it was.

Startled, Susan lowered her voice: 'Sarah-Jayne?'

My heart squeezed. Beverly and Caroline were taken in by Sarah-Jayne and good luck to them, good riddance. But Susan? True, she wasn't clever at schoolwork – her attention hopping, skipping, jumping – but surely anyone could see that this new girl was ... well, what? I wanted to say she was a liar, although I couldn't think of any actual lies she'd told. It was more that she was somehow all lies, I thought: made of lies; one big lie.

Susan whispered, 'You don't like her?' and she sounded sad – perhaps for Sarah-Jayne, perhaps for me, perhaps for herself for being disappointed in me as, I realised, I was in her.

Mandy had gone to Miss Drake for a plaster for a paper cut but now came stomping back, and, having overheard something of what was being said, gave her own verdict, 'Sarah-Jayne's all right,' but in a tone to make clear that she considered Sarah-Jayne a lot more than merely all right. But Mandy would say anything to contradict me. I ignored her and for Susan's sake I tried again: 'She's bossy,' even as I knew that wasn't quite right. I tried again: 'She's a show-off, she thinks she knows everything,' which did feel a better fit – it was true, surely, of all the talk of boyfriends, parties and grown-up drinks – but Mandy said, 'It's *you* who thinks you know everything,' and before I could come back at her with *Oh change the record* – an expression of Mum's – Susan stepped diplomatically between us and decided for us that we'd stick to the climbing frame.

That morning, our respective perches gave us an odd view: the two boys in our year, Neil and Ali, as usual belting a ball around what stood in our playground for a football pitch, but with Sarah-Jayne, Caroline and Beverly grouped at the touchline. Sarah-Jayne was flanked by the other two, their arms slung across one another's shoulders turning them into something of a three-headed beast, and they were crooning what we now knew to be the puppy love song: how a young heart 'really fee-ee-ee-eels'.

Susan wondered aloud, 'What are they *doing*?' and good question because the boys made an unlikely audience, or no audience at all, playing on regardless of what was evidently a well-rehearsed performance being enacted for them. The three girls were swaying in unison, all harmonies and gestures and postures: hands on hips, hands pressed to hearts. But why would the boys be interested in a song about love? The little 'uns would be a better bet, I thought, and indeed several were drawing close, agog, entranced. I had an odd feeling that the two boys were being picked on, although surely no one could be picked on by being sung to, and softly, and admittedly quite well, about love and hearts. And if the girls were making fun of anyone, I felt, it was, somehow, of themselves: they were shrieking at one another, at their exaggerated flutters and coyness, the batting of eyelashes.

A closer look at the boys, though, showed the efforts they were going to in order to look nonchalant: they were round-shouldered, besieged and burdened by the unwanted attention. Neil was flushed, although that was nothing unusual for him. I could never look at him without thinking of Snow White – the coal-black hair, chalk-white face and rosy cheeks – which for me wasn't in his favour. Mum had taken me to see the film years back and the best bit of the treat had been the little tub of ice cream from the lady with the lit-up tray, although I probably shouldn't have believed Mum that rum and raisin was the best choice. As for the film, I hadn't managed to make much of the story (dwarves in a forest, a glass coffin) although it did beat *Fantasia* – the Brownies' Christmas outing – which hadn't had one at all.

I couldn't find it in myself to feel too sorry for flustered-looking Neil, because in all the years we had been at school together he had barely spared me a glance and never more than a scowl. Thankfully he was going private for secondary because otherwise – being brainy – he'd have been coming with me to the grammar, the pair of us stuck with each other every day at the bus stop. According to Mum, the cold shoulder ran in the family: his mum was a doctor at our health centre and Mum said she was no better than the men, only ever interested in lecturing ladies to lose weight, which took some gall because frankly she was no sylph.

But if no one's heart warmed for Neil, everyone – even Mum – had a soft spot for his sidekick, little Ali, despite him being one of the rough-and-ready Rudges, as Mum called them, living in one of the farm cottages. Mum said Ali was like a wee auld man, which, from her, wouldn't usually be complimentary but in this case was said fondly.

As we perched there on the climbing frame, Miss Drake passed at a clip to scoop up little Dawn Fletcher, with word of some medicine to be administered. Pausing to witness the display, she laughed – 'Oh goodness, those poor boys!' – as she turned on what in a Scholl stood for a heel. 'Really, girls!' she called jollily to the trio, in her wake. 'Leave those poor boys alone!' and we three on our perches, relieved at having been shown how to react, chuckled along with her. But as soon as she had clopped past with her charge, Mandy observed, 'Just look at that hippy skirt.' Miss Drake's knee-length skirt was cream-coloured and printed with big pale pink roses; it might have been made of bedroom curtains. I let Susan be the one to take issue with Mandy.

'Miss Drake isn't a hippy!'

Sometimes Mum said our neighbours the Porters were hippy, other times she said beatnik.

Mandy huffed. 'I was talking about the skirt.'

'But hippy is all floppy and snazzy and clashing.' Susan looked to me for backup. 'Isn't it?'

'Sort of "way out",' was the best I could offer.

Mandy dipped backwards, with a whip of her plait, and upside down her face was especially belligerent. 'Well, Sarah-Jayne says it's hippy.'

Ah.

'When?' Susan and I, in unison.

'Loos. Break.'

So, when she'd gone to spend a penny, as our teachers would say, she'd overheard something. I was annoyed with myself for asking, but, 'Did she say it like it was good, or bad?' Because I knew by now that no observation of Sarah-Jayne's on anyone's appearance was likely to be neutral. But all we got from Mandy was what counted, upside down, for a shrug.

That afternoon, we had art and crafts so that Mr Hadleigh could go off into the staff room to do his headmasterly form-filling and phone calls. For art and crafts our tables were pushed into pairs: we six girls sitting together. This particular session, Mr Hadleigh had set us cutting up fabrics from which we would be making bunting for the upcoming summer fete. Holding up one scrap, Susan despaired, 'I honestly think these were pyjamas.'

'Mr Hadleigh's pyjamas,' said Mandy.

Susan pointed out that the pattern was of daisies.

'*Mrs* Hadleigh's, then,' said Mandy.

Mrs Hadleigh always wore trousers, which she called 'slacks'. Mum said she was a bluestocking because she taught history evening classes in town.

Susan was thrilled. 'Bringing his wife's old pyjamas to work! He should get the sack!'

'His wife's old *bloomers*,' said Mandy, and then Beverly made a show of sniffing a handful of the fabric, confirming, 'Yeah, pongs of old ladies.'

Like Mrs Cobb's house, Susan said. Mrs Cobb ran the village shop and her house was joined on at the back.

'That's cats,' said Mandy, to which Sarah-Jayne offered that she preferred dogs because you know where you are with a dog.

'On the end of a lead,' said Beverly, then, to a quizzical glance from Sarah-Jayne, clarified, 'The other end.'

'*Master's* end,' chirped Susan.

'Or mistress,' said Mandy, which had Susan nod emphatically: *Quite right, well said.*

Mandy told Sarah-Jayne that we'd had a narrow escape this term from having to visit old people: only Brown Owl's bunions had saved us from having to do volunteer badge at Brownies. Susan corrected her: we could have volunteered for something other than visits to the old people's home, such as cleaning the village hall. And that was when Sarah-Jayne told us she was thinking of having her birthday party there, in September.

The hall, I thought: disco music and flashing coloured lights and that vast, vibrant car park.

'Oh, you must!' Susan urged. 'That'd be brilliant!' and around the table came a hum of accord: *you must, you must.* My blood was already up and dancing to the thump of the bass line. I could soon be going to a party at the hall – all those Saturday nights of being kept awake by the beat, the slamming of car doors, the shouts, and now, soon, that could be me, too, raising that racket.

Caroline cocked her head in a parody of contemplation: 'Hmm, and what shall I wear?' *Mirror, mirror, on the wall . . .*

We each had a party dress and Caroline's was the best: dark purple velvet, with buttons that my mum called mother-of-pearl. Very cheek, Mum said of it. Mine had a pattern of sunflowers, which she approvingly called the peasant look but which I now worried might make it a hippy dress.

Sarah-Jayne said as an aside to Caroline, 'Best bit about parties: the excuse for new clothes.'

My sunflower dress was getting small but Mum said we wouldn't replace it because I'd soon be beyond all that. Parties, she meant. I wouldn't need anything special, she said, for going to a film and the Wimpy.

Susan enthused, 'You could invite loads of people! You can fit everyone in there – like when there's a wedding. You could have hundreds.' But Sarah-Jayne winced, and Susan backtracked: 'Not hundreds, then. But – you know – everyone.' She beamed around us, because that was the point: *everyone*.

Sarah-Jayne laid her scissors aside. 'Not everyone,' she said quietly, and there followed a silence in which we all floundered before Mandy blustered, 'Yeah, because not the little ones, all running around.'

'Yes, and if it was me,' Susan piped up, 'I wouldn't have my cousin Terry,' although she didn't elaborate and that was the first I'd ever heard of any cousin Terry.

Sarah-Jayne merely said that not everyone was any good at parties.

I froze. Would I be any good at a party – the type that happened at night at the village hall?

'Like Virginia,' Mandy blurted, which had Sarah-Jayne turn to her, matter-of-fact: 'Virginia shouldn't be left out.' She added that Virginia had such beautiful big eyes. Chastened, we all rushed to agree, *Oh she does, she does*, although Beverly said her lenses were what made them big. None of us would ever consider excluding

116

Virginia: that wasn't what Mandy had meant; it was what she'd thought Sarah-Jayne had meant.

Susan explained that Virginia didn't like a lot of noise and would have to go outside sometimes even at Brownies. She glanced around us and we confirmed it: often Virginia would be sitting on the steps outside with Tawny Owl (a teenager from town), taking deep breaths.

There was a flutter of uncertainty around the table – would this do?

'Still,' decreed Sarah-Jayne, 'she should be included.'

But *of course, of course*. And then Beverly said that if she had a party at the hall, her sister could only come if she brought her friends. 'She's a right moo,' she said, snapping a thread with her teeth, 'but she's got some really hilarious friends.'

With a lift of her eyebrows, Sarah-Jayne asked: 'Any of them boys?'

They tittered.

'You don't want to make Neil jealous,' Beverly said.

Neil?

'Or maybe I do,' said Sarah-Jayne with a sideways glance.

Neil, again? What was going on?

Mandy had recovered sufficiently to be able to ask, 'You gonna have vo-ka at this party?'

'VoDka,' corrected Susan, helpfully.

'VoDTka,' Mandy repeated, reddening.

Sarah-Jayne gave her a fond, forgiving look. 'I'm sure Max'll sneak some in for us, if we ask nicely,' and we all knew to act appreciative, but I was wondering if I would have to drink it. Would I want to be floaty?

'But I tell you now' – and she rolled her eyes,

117

amused – 'I'm not going to have his old records – we want a disco!'

And yes, we did! A disco! But, then, would I know what to do at a disco? Would I dance like Mum did, to the radio, in the living room?

Sarah-Jayne laid aside a triangle of green gingham and said, 'And guess what my birthday present is going to be, from dear ol' Max,' before announcing into the expectant pause, 'Pierced ears.'

Gasps.

Beverly said, 'Lucky beggar.'

Not even Susan had pierced ears; she had that gorgeous little baby bangle, but not pierced ears, and duly she wailed, 'I'm not allowed until I'm eighteen!'

'Sixteen, me,' said Mandy, which had Susan turn indignantly on her: '*Six*teen?!'

Caroline said, 'My mum says it's not my body till I'm eighteen,' and Sarah-Jayne sympathised, saying that was just mad, to which Caroline spread her arms in wordless assertion: yes, because what's this if it's not *my own body*?

Susan checked. 'But can you really have your ears done when you're eleven?'

Sarah-Jayne said there was no law against it.

My mum had some old clip-ons in a drawer but they pinched so she never wore them. She said pierced ears on children were for gypsies and Catholics.

Mandy wondered, 'Will it hurt?'

Sarah-Jayne raised her eyebrows – who knows? – and Beverly said no pain, no gain. Then Sarah-Jayne explained that the proper present was to be an actual pair of earrings but obviously she had to be pierced first.

She'd already seen, at the jeweller's, the earrings she wanted: gold hoops.

'Gold hoops!' Susan swooned.

Mandy said that the holes could get infected: her mum had said so, and we all knew that as receptionist at the health centre, she'd know.

Sarah-Jayne agreed that they had to be kept clean, dabbed with something that you were given by the piercer, and the sleepers turned regularly through the flesh. 'You have to do it last thing,' she said, 'before you go to bed, for two weeks, but as long as you do that, you're fine.'

'And anyway,' said Bev, 'Neil could kiss them better.'

There she went again: picking on Neil.

Susan wanted to know what her mum and dad thought of it all, which amused Sarah-Jayne: she wouldn't be telling them, she said, until it was done. Act first, she said, then face the music. And, anyway, Max would talk them round, she said, as he always did: 'That man's my guardian angel.'

Guardian angel. I liked the sound of that. Could my dad be that, for me? Being actually dead, he should be better at it than that Max man, although the downside of his being dead was that he wasn't around to stand up for me against Mum.

Susan asked if Sarah-Jayne's sister would be going along to the piercing and Sarah-Jayne said no but she'd then be taking her bra shopping.

Not even Caroline, who had definite bosoms, had a bra. *Braz-i-air* was what we always said amongst ourselves whenever the subject of bras came up, often adding for good measure an impression of the lady on the Playtex advert: *Ooh, my girdle is killing me!*

No one spoke a word of that now, though, and Sarah-Jayne continued, 'We're going to a department store, where they fit you with them.'

Department stores, up in town: Mum always said she was going to take me one year to see their Christmas windows. With a sigh, Sarah-Jayne told us, 'My sister said I should wait until I'm twelve, but Max said do you want your little sister growing up to be a women's libber, with it all flopping about all over the place?' She put an index finger to her temple and made a screwing motion to an outburst of laughter.

Mum said those libbers have the right idea: *What's good for the goose is good for the gander.* Sometimes she said with a roll of her eyes, *H-where would we be, in life, h-without the menfolk, eh?*

At that point, Mr Hadleigh came back into the classroom in a haze of cigarette smoke, and we bowed our heads over the bunting pieces.

I wondered how it might be to have someone to take you on missions that were secret from your mum. Jeannie was my best bet. She might track Mum down and come into our lives and then I too could have someone who would take me on shopping expeditions to department stores. She was the sort to do it – I could tell from those photos – and she would know as soon as she saw me to step in, to help me. Your ma, she'd laugh: don't you go tellin' your auld ma.

10

The business of the bra bothered me for the rest of that afternoon: the 'flopping about', the screwy finger. Mum herself complained at people flopping about but for her this was goodnight kisses when we saw them on telly: mums and dads and kids giving goodnight kisses, *all soppy and flopping about like that and doesn't it make you sick.*

Mum didn't wear bras; was she floppy? I imagined some ladies might be – Mrs Peters, with her dappled, crêped cleavage – but my mum was nothing like Mrs Peters. Mum was bony, not bosomy. When I got home from school, I had a quick look and didn't detect any flopping, but possibly floppiness was brought on by specific activities of which hoovering wasn't one. Mum was busy hoovering Mr Watt's cut-off, with which she was usually so pleased – *that man has been good to us* – but today she looked cross, shoving the roaring vacuum around. The radio was on in the background: Alan Freeman. Wendy had once asked Mr Hadleigh why no ladies were on the radio and he'd said their voices were too high to be heard properly, and she'd said, 'Like bats?'

Spotting me, Mum switched off for a momentary breather and asked me how school had been. I mentioned a few things, including the bunting-making in the afternoon, and then when she started the hoover up again I hooted over the commotion that the new girl had said she was getting a bra for her birthday. Unzipping my anorak, I exclaimed, 'Her *sister*'s taking her!'

Despite having to yell, I'd done a pretty good job, I judged, of sounding casual. Switching off the hoover again, Mum said briskly, 'Oh aye, I can believe that.' She struck her hands against each other as if to knock them free of dust although the hoover should have been picking that up, and blew her hair out of her eyes, then told me that she had seen the sister. 'Glamour puss,' she said, sourly, as she hauled the hoover away for stowing beneath the stairs. 'Dolled up and sunning herself on the doorstep, puffing.' After the slam of the cupboard door, she was back in the doorway, inclined against the jamb as if to catch her breath. 'Been trouble, that one, I've heard.' *Hair-d*. 'Gave her parents the runaround, got in with the wrong crowd.' Turning into the hallway towards the kitchen she called to me, 'And don't you ever try that, because I won't come chasing after you.' And from the kitchen, 'I've had enough trouble in my life, as it is,' sung out as if not specifically for me but in general, to the universe. 'You make your bed and you lie in it.' But then as if I had answered her back she was there again, like a jack-in-the-box, in the living room doorway. 'It's hard enough being a parent without having it all thrown back in your face, so don't even think about it.'

Which, seeing as I had no idea what she was on about, would have been difficult.

The next day, Susan, Mandy and I kept to the climbing frame – literally hanging around – while the other three were back at their boy-bothering but now taking it up a significant notch. The striking of various poses had developed into more of a dance. They kept to the edge of the pitch, toeing that line, bright heads bobbing as they stepped to one side or the other in formation, with Sarah-Jayne pride of place in the middle, wiggle-hipped in jeans, her flares flapping. The dance was quite complicated, a specific number of steps one way and then the other, and from time to time a neat little twirl. ('Oh, that's good.' Susan was shiny-eyed. 'Isn't that good?') As before, there were precise, expressive coordinated gestures as if to implore, to beseech: sweeping arms, uplifted palms. ('They're as good as Pan's People!')

The polished routine had appeared in the playground as if by magic. As they belted out this song about heartache and being misunderstood, they made a good job of bringing anguish into their voices, although it didn't extend to their faces, and the way Beverly kept her eyes trained on the boys managed to make it, from her, more of a dressing-down.

We couldn't help but watch, suspended there on the frame. It was impressive but at the same time, I thought, the trio did look stilted, like puppets. Their dancing was quite unlike how Mum danced in the living room when something she loved came on the radio: like a flame, flickering bright but at the same time dissolving away, humming, head tipped back and eyes half closed, giving herself over to it, lost in it, and breathless but not, I somehow knew, just from the exertion. She would call to me over the music, *Isn't this one great? Don't you just love this one?*

Now, some of the infants – Michaela, Glenis, Graeme – wandered close to the performing girls but not too close, staring slack-jawed, and then, in no time, apparently satisfied, having seen and heard enough, they snapped away and skipped off. Neil and Ali played on, and if not admitting defeat they did give signs that they were finding the game hard going, their kicks at the ball accompanied by grimaces and groans. But apart from occasional furtive glances, they didn't acknowledge the inexplicable visitation at the edge of the pitch. Why, I wondered, were they suffering it? Surely they could see those girls off with a sharp word or two. Had it been any of the little ones making such a spectacle of themselves there, they would have been swiftly dispatched. But perhaps it was hard to know how to phrase the objection, to demand an end to the singing – because what could possibly be wrong about singing?

Susan swung down from her bar and, eyes shining, put it to Mandy and me: 'You know what? We should do that. We should go and learn some words and do a song like that.' It occurred to her: 'The phone operator one.'

Mandy was horrified. 'In front of the boys?'

'No, just for ourselves! Well, for *any*one.'

The phone operator song? I was unsure how that would work, but then I realised it was ideal, because we could act it out. It had parts: the one who calls up, then Sylvia's mother, and the operator. Perfect. But Mandy was already objecting that the one who was calling up was a man; one of us would have to play that man, she said, which made clear that she wouldn't.

I couldn't be bothered to argue with her. 'You can be the operator.'

That too, though, it seemed, was a problem: why, she objected, should she be the operator?

Presumably she was angling to be Sylvia's mother, but now I was irked and as a point of principle I wasn't quite ready to give in. 'You did say you liked the operator bit.'

'I *do* like the operator bit, but that doesn't mean I have to *be* it.' She glared. 'I'm nothing like an operator.'

As if any of us were.

Susan spoke soothingly, did her best: 'Operators are great! They get to hear *every*thing.'

We had a further problem, though, it was occurring to me, because there were the in-between bits. 'There's someone else,' I said, and in an effort to explain, I sang a couple of snatches: *Sylvia's mother says* and *the operator says.*

Susan was floored. 'Oh Gawd, yes, who'll say the sayses?'

But as luck would have it, that was when Wendy stepped up. We promptly enlisted her, and in no time we had it more or less worked out even if in places it was a challenge to coordinate.

(*No, that's not the operator, that's the person calling up!*
No, LISTEN! It IS!
Don't boss me around!
Yes, don't boss her around!)

The one remaining stumbling block was that none of us had caught the name of Sylvia's mother. Missus A-something.

125

'Abey?'

'Aylia?'

'How is that a name? That's not a name!'

Perhaps it was, though, because we knew from telly that Americans had all kind of names, like Randy. Wendy's suggestion that until we knew better, Sylvia's mother remain 'Missus A-something' gave us a way forward if at first controversial.

(*We can't do that! Everyone will laugh!*

Well, LET them laugh. We can laugh first! We can make that the funny bit!

And we can't know EVERYthing, how can we know everything?)

With the song itself progressing well, we started work on the presentation, retreating behind the toilet block at dinner break for privacy. Wary of copying the others, we nevertheless agreed on a few gestures because to stand stock still there in front of our audience might feel awkward. We didn't intend ours as a dance, though, but more of a show. We had an actual story to our song, unlike their puppy love, which, when you thought about it, wasn't much more than a whine.

On the way back into class, Mandy wondered, 'But *why* won't the mum let that man speak to Sylvia?'

Susan said it was because Sylvia was going off to marry someone else.

'So?' Mandy wasn't having it. 'She could just tell him that herself, couldn't she? Why does her mum have to do it for her?'

She did have a point, although I doubted any of us had escaped being on either side of a door at which a mum claimed a friend couldn't come out to play because

126

of bath time. I reminded Mandy that the song claimed Sylvia was busy packing: that was probably why. But Wendy, chewing pungently on a lime-flavoured Opal Fruit, said, 'Missus A thinks he might be a bad influence, and mums don't like that.'

We knocked for Wendy that evening and worked on our act in the park, and the following day, just as it was coming together, the other girls' show began falling apart, its unravelling a performance of its own: the carefully prescribed moves replaced by a riot of squeals, by shrieks of laughter and gleeful shoves of one another over the line onto the pitch. The only response from the boys was that they modified their range, to give the mayhem a wider berth.

Those girls had no staying power, I thought, and it made for nice timing because our own act was pretty much ready to go. And when they had exhausted themselves with all the shoving and squealing and had sloped off to the loos to fix their hair, we four took the stage, as it were, if a different one and of course not a stage at all, just a bit of the playground, and nowhere near the football pitch.

From the outset of our performance, the little ones were entranced, which in turn drew an appreciative Miss Drake ('Oh this IS good, isn't it, it's a whole proper little sad story'). Mid song, the original trio reappeared and assembled at a distance behind Miss Drake, to watch. Sarah-Jayne smiled her smile and cocked her head; Caroline observed from beneath luxuriant lashes; Beverly latched her hair businesslike behind both ears. We had their attention and I sensed it was benign but, still, I didn't feel as – I only then realised – I had imagined I would. We got to the end but it felt as if it had missed its mark. What, really, I wondered, as we took our mock-bows to applause, had we been hoping for?

Beverly's sole comment was 'You need more dancing,' and Susan started to explain to her, 'It's not really dance-y,' but Sarah-Jayne cut in to say, 'It's good.' She nodded, decisive. But I had to grit my teeth, because *Who asked you?*

11

From then on there was no more of their singing at the boys but something of the spectacle found its way indoors in Beverly's behaviour towards them. Over the next few days in class, she was often whipping around in her chair, literally turning on them, excitedly subjecting them to demands and protests, upbraiding them at any opportunity, indeed inventing such opportunities.

'Don't!'

'Give—'

'Where's—'

'Why've *you* got the—'

The boys were baffled, dumbstruck, which was merely more grist to Beverly's mill because had no one ever told them it was rude to stare? Beverly never stinted when it came to putting people down and keeping them in their place, but even by her own standards she was, in those few days, ferocious. In high dudgeon she slammed and snatched – books, pens, rulers – and whatever it was that she was up to, it had the appearance of a game if without the jubilance or artfulness; and one which, from the looks of them, the boys evidently weren't in on.

Sarah-Jayne and Caroline played no part, nor appeared bothered, nor attempted to counter all this, nor even acknowledged it. Sarah-Jayne worked away as usual, head down. Perhaps she did feel sorry for the boys, though, because whenever she took her book up to Mr Hadleigh's desk, I noticed, she chose the route past their table even though this was such a squeeze so as to have her turn sideways and rise on the balls of her feet to edge past, balancing herself by a light, friendly touch to Neil's shoulder.

It was Wendy who opened our eyes to what was going on. During the drive to swimming the following week, as the coach began the stretch of journey between the village and town, Wendy went rogue, scampering up and down the aisle on various baffling missions, and on one of these sorties she lunged in on me and Susan and challenged, 'You know what? Sarah-Jayne loves Neil!'

At first we wouldn't hear of it, because anyone could see those three girls were, for whatever reason, at war with the boys. And anyway, Susan reminded her, Sarah-Jayne loved David Cassidy.

Wendy said, 'Yeah, but she can't marry David Cassidy, can she.'

She couldn't marry Neil, either, I pointed out.

'In six years she can,' and, bolstered by the thought, Wendy yelled down to the back seat in taunting sing-song, 'Sarah-Jayne loves Neil!'

Saaaar-ah-Jayne loves Neee-il.

This provoked outrage from Beverly – 'Shut your face! Don't be such a baby!' – and doe-eyed indignation from Caroline, but from Sarah-Jayne herself came an

130

emphatic folding of arms, a theatrical roll of her eyes, and a smirk: a pretty show of being caught out and hauled into the spotlight.

I sat back, confounded. Neil, though? Snow White Neil? From where I was sitting, I could see one of his ears, and its reddening suggested that what we'd all just heard was news to him, too. I was baffled: Neil was different from David Cassidy in more ways than I could count.

Susan, similarly puzzled, turned to me: 'Would you love Neil,' she asked, solicitously, 'if it was you?'

It *is* me, I thought, I *am* me, and no, I wouldn't, I didn't; but before I could say so she was pondering aloud as to how no one could help who they fell in love with, and Mandy gave the most ridiculous example she could think of, which was Mr Hadleigh: what if you fell in love with Mr Hadleigh? This provided some welcome relief, the three of us having a laugh at Mrs Hadleigh's misfortune to have done just that, but then Susan was serious, saying, 'If I had a boyfriend – when I do – I think he'll be blond.' She sounded worried.

I thought of Tutankhamun. I couldn't see his hair because of his death mask but there was no question that he would be what my mum called a brunette.

And Spanish, Susan was saying, which, it seemed, was the problem because could a Spaniard be blond? Then for no apparent reason she was adding that she wouldn't want a boyfriend with a name like Bill or Harold or Ted. And – another worry – 'I wonder what you *do*?'

'*Do*?' Mandy leaned in.

'With a boyfriend. I mean: do you' – she cast around – 'go swimming?'

'Pictures,' said Mandy. 'You go to the pictures.'

And yes of course the pictures, Susan agreed, and Mandy was saying her mum and dad had gone not long ago to see the *Dad's Army* film and for a moment we were all lost to envy. I tried to recall if Mum had ever said she had been to the pictures with my dad. I did remember that she'd been to see *West Side Story* with her auld pal Jeannie and *H-What a fillum!* and she was going to take me to see it if it ever came back around.

You must never, ever let any man near you, but obviously Mum had, because she'd married my dad. So, how had she known? When and how had my dad stopped being some man and turned into her boyfriend? She had once said to me that she'd told him that he had a way with him; she had said it jokily although I couldn't tell who the joke was with or on. I could imagine her saying it to him with that sidelong look of hers, *Och, you've a way with you*. At least I thought that was what she had said; but, gazing through the coach window at the fields, it occurred to me that it could've been a simple 'away with you'.

Susan was wondering if Sarah-Jayne and Neil would get married; Mandy pointed out that he'd have to love her, too, in return. But he definitely would, argued Susan, because how could he not? She was so pretty. I knew it would be madness for me to try to deny that, but still I was unconvinced: it felt to me as if Sarah-Jayne might have got everything of herself from a dressing-up basket – if a dressing-up basket could offer up eyes and noses and lips – and it could all just as easily fall away. (*I'll huff and I'll puff and I'll . . .*)

Susan was saying that when they did marry they could

live up on the Ridgeway, in one of those big houses. Actually, Neil already did, although with his mum and dad rather than with Sarah-Jayne. Susan said that was what you want when you're married: a nice house, a nice big house. And sitting there on the coach, I recalled, dimly, how Mum and I used to go on visits several bus journeys away to people I couldn't now quite remember. Then some names came back to me: Pam and Mick, Brian and Sue. It was at one of those houses that there had been that puppy. And, possibly, children: the name Joanne came to mind, and Nicola, yes, there had definitely been a Nicola because Mum had had a way of saying the name for me, making a joke of it between the two of us, her nose in the air and pronouncing it from on high like someone singing in a choir or reading the BBC news, Nee-co-laaah. Now that I thought about it, I hadn't known what was supposed to be funny about it beyond the way she'd said it.

Those people – yes, and there'd been a Doug and Sheila, I remembered – had been two or perhaps even three buses each way: one bus into town and then at least one other onward elsewhere. Mum would pack barley sugars for me; she said they helped, although with what she didn't say. Travel sickness, boredom. But she always said travel sickness was all in the mind – everything was in the mind except presumably what my dad had died of – and certainly boredom was all in the mind because where else could it be?

While Susan and Mandy were talking over me about the future wedding of Sarah-Jayne and Neil, I recalled the brightness of a kitchen, not the details of the kitchen itself but the brightness of it, which came perhaps from an expanse of light floor tiles whereas our kitchen at home had a dark speckly lino on the floor. And – it was coming back to me – there were beakers up on a counter. At home we had no counters as such, just a draining board and what my mum referred to as *the surface* ('Just leave it there on the surface'). And, wonderfully, in those beakers there had been ice cubes, diamond-bright and sweetly tuneful. And at one of the houses – it came rushing back to me as the coach pulled into the car park at the pool – there had been sticks of celery in a jug and next to it a saucer of salt and you were expected to help yourself, to serve yourself a sprinkle of salt then take a stick of celery and dip it into your salt. But even better than any of that, the bright jug had had a word on it: *Salou*. When I had asked Mum about it, she had said it was a souvenir from a holiday. There was – fabulously – a place called Salou. The letters had been painted in bright colours (blue, red, yellow) and maybe the celery itself hadn't been so great – come to think of it, the celery had tasted of nothing, really, except perhaps wee – but what had made serving myself so special was that jug. I remembered it catching the sunlight on a table in a garden, around which the grown-ups were sitting. Gardens down our road weren't for sitting in – they were for clothes lines and rabbit hutches and there was the Porters' vegetables and old Mrs Goodchild grew tall flowers in rows like the Porters' potatoes – although Mum did sometimes balance a chair on the paving slabs by the drain.

Back at school that afternoon, class had barely begun (exercises on adverbs, *The girl walked . . . [slow], The boy ran . . . [quick]*) when Beverly slapped a folded piece of

134

paper onto the boys' table, as if throwing down a gaunt-let. The response on her own table was a pantomime of panic: Sarah-Jayne and Caroline both lunging in pursuit of the note, their chair legs squealing across the floorboards, eliciting from Mr Hadleigh the obligatory rebuke, '*Girls* ... '

Little Ali had moved like lightning and held the slip of paper aloft, beyond the reach of the interested parties.

Beverly commanded, 'Open it for him.'

Whatever it was, it was intended for Neil.

Sarah-Jayne made a show of mortification, pressing both hands over her mouth then clapping them to her cheeks, and Caroline made something of tending to her, laying a comforting hand to her arm. The boys exchanged glances, then Ali unfolded the note, grinned as he read it and displayed it to his friend, which pro-voked more squealing from Sarah-Jayne and Caroline and distantly from Mr Hadleigh another '*Girls.*'

The three of us, at our table, gawped.

'Well?' Beverly demanded of a startled-looking Neil and to a mere frown from a resigned Mr Hadleigh (*Girls will be girls*).

Neil shrugged, but fairly happily, which seemed to do the trick, because jubilation erupted from Sarah-Jayne and Caroline (nothing more from a thoroughly defeated Mr Hadleigh); but Beverly thumped the boys' tabletop and demanded of Ali, 'What about *her*?' indicating Caroline, who unlike Sarah-Jayne didn't squirm but rose to it, tipping her chin, eyes gleaming, giving us a glimpse of the future Caroline who in not so many years' time would be smoking in the bus shelter and sunbathing on the war memorial.

Ali, too, shrugged – as ever, Ali-amenable – and at this Beverly turned to the room to let us all in on it: 'They're going out.'

Going out? I suspected there was more to it, but still I half expected the four of them to get up, open the door and leave. Whatever it really was, this 'going out', it was cause for celebration, Beverly's pronouncement bringing room-wide murmurs of admiration and approval so that the air itself was transformed, shimmering over and above each individual appreciative utterance.

Possibly Mum would shed some light, although as ever I would have to choose a time when her focus was elsewhere so that I wouldn't come in for any flak. The perfect opportunity presented itself that evening when she was down the side passage, emptying the pedal bin into the dustbin. Rocking on the lip of the doorstep, the metal strip biting pleasingly into the soles of my slippers, and smashing softly into and out of the fly curtain, I called after her down the passageway.

'Guess what?' I offered it light-heartedly.

'What?' came echoing back. *H-What?*

'That new girl says she's going out with Neil Hammond.' On the spur of the moment I decided to hold back on Caroline and Ali. For now one pair was enough. A test case.

'Going out?' she called back, sounding suspicious, which had me shrink back, retreating into the kitchen onto the sure ground of the lino, the fly curtain shrugging me off.

From down the passage came the distinctive clang of the dustbin lid and then the fly curtain exploded into

136

sparkles around her emerging form. She said, disapproving, 'That's a bit forward, isn't it?'

Was it? *Forward*. It sounded as if forward wasn't good. Neither, though – I knew – was backward. Virginia at school was lucky, Mum always said, that the operation on her brain hadn't left her backward.

I told her that I didn't know *where* they were going and she huffed a half-laugh; she seemed to think I'd been making a joke. Perhaps, then, I concluded, you didn't actually have to go anywhere, or perhaps nowhere much, perhaps just to the park. I hoped I wouldn't bump into them there.

'It's a nonsense,' she disparaged, but then washing her hands she said over the running water, 'Don't you get into any of that before you have to.'

That.

Before you have to.

Which implied that at some stage I would.

Drying her hands on the tea towel she gave me the warning look and I turned to get out from under it, back onto the step, which left me looking at Bert and Lil's fence.

'Kids these days,' she rued, and I had the sense that – annoyingly – she was including me in that.

Later that evening, around nine, when I'd gone to change into my nightie and then was heading back downstairs for my supper, I heard to my horror that the Sonny boy was in our kitchen. But why? And how? I hadn't heard the doorbell.

I froze on the bottom stair, unable to retreat because I was already in Mum's line of sight, not that she was actually looking. She was focused on the hob, on the milk pan, although conversationally she was in full flow: '... and missy here' – a jerk of her head in my direction – 'coming home from school with talk of courting!'

Courting. But even as I squirmed to hear it, this did confirm that 'going out' meant going to the pictures, even if the cinema couldn't actually be got to.

'Wee kids!' She was making sure to sound amused. 'And I said to her, believe you me, you've plenty of time for all that!' She was making out that we too had had fun with this, when in truth she'd told me off in advance for something I wasn't doing and had no intention of starting.

Still without as much as glancing in my direction, she addressed me: 'Stop skulking there.'

All right, all right: tugging my dressing gown around me (*Age 6–8*), I readied myself for sickly Ovaltine fumes, but what I walked into was cigarette smoke. Mum, who hated anyone smoking, was letting him light up in our kitchen. He was on the back step, the fly curtain hitched aside in a handful of its own strands to make space for him, and had just lit a cigarette. Now he extinguished the match with a shake and chucked it over Bert and Lil's fence, which Mum, intent on the milk, didn't spot. He glanced my way but seemed not quite to see me. I sensed myself gliding across the surface of his eyes.

'Yeah, well,' he announced into a plume of exhaled smoke, 'way of the world, now. Start young, don't they – screaming and chucking their damp little knickers at some pop star.'

He was stupid, because we all loved that song – '*Leap up and down and wave your knickers in the air*' – but no one ever actually did it: it was just a song. And anyway my knickers were never damp, because Mum was adamant about airing. She gave me a sidelong glance but, like him, didn't quite seem to see me. I felt invisible there in the kitchen doorway at the same time as spotlit.

He shouldn't be here, I thought, hanging around like this, even at this time of the evening when usually we did nothing. This was our time, even if we did nothing with it. I felt as if he'd walked in on me falling asleep. Even my feet felt bare; well, they *were* bare – and no reason they shouldn't be – but they actually *felt* bare. Bared. Mum was acting as if everything was normal, as if people were forever popping round and standing chatting while she heated my bedtime milk. But *open house* was a frequent complaint of hers about the Porters: *It's open house over there.* She was avoiding my gaze, or more than avoiding it, actually batting it away with her brisk, bouncy manner, and I knew why: if she saw herself in my eyes she would see how false she was being, like when she stood in front of the mirror and held her tummy in. This was unfair: I couldn't help having eyes. I couldn't help being in the kitchen, either, because it was she who made me turn up for supper. I didn't even like Ovaltine (*Don't be silly, you have to have something, last thing*). And now I was going to have to go to bed with smoke in my hair.

But now, turning the knob and lifting the pan clear of the red-hot ring, she directed my attention to something on the surface on the other side of her – 'See that?' – and she sounded natural again, and pleased, even excited. 'See what Sonny's brought us.'

It was something shoebox-sized.

And she told me: 'A tape player!'

A tape machine! For us? Forgetting myself, I darted around her and stood over it, gazing down at its chunky, deliciously pushable buttons, *Play, Stop, FFW, Rewind.*

We didn't have any tapes, though. But Mum was saying that he'd be recording us some, 'All the stuff I love!' to which he chipped in, 'Yeah, yeah: no Slade. I get it, I get it.'

Dramatically, she sang, '*The Witch Queen ovvvvvv*' – her face close to mine, conspiratorial – '*Uh-New Orleans.*'

We did both love that one, and 'A Horse With No Name', and 'Gypsys, Tramps & Thieves': anything that sounded mysteriously faraway. And usually I loved it when she sang, although I wasn't quite sure about it with him here, even if he didn't seem to be paying attention, staring smart-eyed into his own smoke.

Reaching over my head into the cupboard for my mug, she said, 'Isn't that great?' and she sounded so happy that I too was happy but at the same time sad, too, at how normally she never got a present from anyone except the box of Maltesers that I bought for her from the village shop for every birthday with the money she'd given me to do exactly that.

With a teaspoon handle she levered the lid from the Ovaltine tin, releasing the sickly stink, and spooned what I thought of as the ash into my mug. For once I hardly minded because I was busy thinking of the tapes I could have. This could really be something. Suddenly, anything and everything was possible: we'd be dancing around the house and we could even have it playing when I was in the bath or going to sleep. Anywhere!

I couldn't wait to tell my friends; I'd be the envy of them. Susan did have a record player at home, but Mum said the problem with a record player was that you had to buy the records and there were only so many times you could listen to them before you'd had enough and were on to the next thing, which meant money down the drain. We did have the radiogram in the living room, but the record-playing part hadn't worked for as long as I could remember. We had a record – just one – propped up against it, Simon & Garfunkel's *Sounds of Silence*, which Mum said had been my dad's, but with a wrinkle of her nose and a roll of her eyes she said she couldn't dance to that. The cover featured two serious-looking men and I wondered if my dad, too, had been serious. One of the men resembled a training teacher we'd had for a time at school, who'd told us to write poems about the Victorians: spirit yourself back, he'd said, to one of those dark satanic mills and really try to bring it to life for us, make it real, imagine perhaps you catch your fingers in one of those gigantic looms. I'd loved doing that poem and had thought I'd done really well with the splintering bone but when I'd told Mum she had gone to complain to Mr Hadleigh.

'Sonny does discos,' Mum was saying now, impressed, stirring a little of the warmed milk into the powder, but he cut in, 'It's my mate who does 'em. I'm just the magician's assistant.' Then he said they would be up at the hall this Saturday. So, it might well be him, I thought, who would lower the needle at midnight onto 'Hi Ho Silver Lining' or 'Spirit in the Sky'. Mum poured in the rest of the milk, stirring vigorously (*No one wants lumps*), the teaspoon ringing on the china, while Sonny was saying that his earnings from the discos were going towards some travel.

'Oh aye and where you off to?' She sounded disbelieving.

Salou, I thought, was where I'd go – first stop, Salou – but his reply was disappointingly unspecific. 'Anywhere that ain't here.'

Mum handed me the mug and I tried to dodge the Ovaltine stink.

'Sweet eff-ay for me here,' he added, which had Mum warn him in a low voice, 'Earwigging,' which presumably meant me and was unfair because I just happened to be here and whose fault was that and how could I possibly help but hear what was said right in front of me? I didn't want to listen to him anyway. And in any case he hadn't said anything bad. I could go now, I supposed, take my mug into the living room, but actually I wanted to hear about the travels.

'Big wide world out there,' he said, but Mum said it was probably all pretty much the same when you got there. That wasn't true of the toilets, though, if she was to be believed. Then she said to him, 'Just don't go on any plane.'

He shot her a grin. 'Don't fancy a bit of Concorde?'

He was being ridiculous: Concorde was for the Queen and businessmen.

Sloshing tap water into the milk pan she said chances were he'd be stuck on the runway for two weeks with a gun at his head. True: there was always some hijack or other on the six o'clock news. Every week we saw another, some snub-nosed plane brought low and seeming to stare blankly ahead, the humiliated hulk of it on the runway.

Mum reminded me to take a biscuit. Sonny was saying

he'd like to make a go of running discos, which surprised Mum: 'Building trade not for you, then?'

When the cigarette was clear of his mouth he said, 'Not my idea of fun.'

She snorted. 'Not meant to be fun. It's work.'

'Easier ways to make a living. You try being on a site, even in this.' The weather, he meant.

He wouldn't know that sometimes she had to do leaflet deliveries in the rain.

'Och, no fear,' she said, scrubbing the pan. 'I've never known a June like it. There's a word for it where I come from,' and she said it: 'Dreek.'

'*Two* words where I come from,' he said: 'Pissing down.'

Mum said to me, 'Come on, now, get drinking that up.'

'But yeah,' he was saying, 'dreek'll do. Pretty bloody dreek.'

'Och, well,' Mum rinsed the pan, 'I'll leave the building sites to you men.'

'Women's lib only go so far, yeah?' He seemed to find that funny. He blew a torrent of smoke into the evening air. 'Suit yourselves, you ladies.'

'Too right,' she said, turning off the tap.

He seemed to be thinking, for a moment. 'Old man got me the job.' He shrugged. 'It's okay for now.' Then, 'Kids next year gotta stay at school till sixteen. Geezers crammed in at those desks, birds parking their prams in the playground.'

Mum was drying, now. 'You're lucky you've no national service.'

He squashed the cigarette butt into a jam-jar lid, which – I marvelled – she must have given him for that very purpose.

'Like *Dad's Army*,' he said.

'My sister's husband copped for the last year of it,' Mum said, 'And in his case, a bit of friendly fire wouldn't have gone amiss,' but Sonny was already saying that the site opposite the school was giving him the creeps. Mum was incredulous but he insisted: 'Blokes all say they can sense someone. Used to be some creepy old cottage. Some old bird.'

'Miss Kirkwood?' Mum hooted.

'They say it's like she's still there, watching, breathing down your neck.'

'Och, they're having you on, sunshine. Miss Kirkwood has better things to do in the afterlife than hang around here breathing down your scrawny necks.' And to me: 'Had geese, eh? Miss Kirkwood, you remember?'

I did. Daphne and Doris. Terrifying.

To him she laughed, 'Those are your old birds. And you did have to keep on the right side of them. It's probably them who've got it in for you. Geese ghosts.'

'Vicious,' he agreed. 'Nip your arse.'

No one ever said arse in our house.

I kept my nose in my mug and Mum busied herself wiping the surface with the dish rag. 'Right enough that cottage was an eyesore because she had no one to help her, poor auld geril. But she was nae bother.'

He enjoyed repeating, 'Nay bother,' then turned serious: 'Yeah, well, but you don't know, do you – people might be different when they're dead.'

She wiped her hands on the tea towel and said, 'What people are, when they're dead, is dead.'

12

At school the next day Neil and Ali were somehow persuaded to sit with Sarah-Jayne and Caroline on the playing field during all three break times ('Look at those lovebirds!' said Susan, thrilled), but even the girls themselves looked as though they'd got more than they'd bargained for, holding themselves as self-consciously as if balancing books on their heads. Beverly was overseeing the foursome, pacing the vicinity to police the boys, barracking them for imagined misdemeanours (*Oi! Watch it!*) and administering shoves to shoulders. She'd have made a good goose. But apart from that, nothing much was going on. From what I could see, Sarah-Jayne directed what little conversation there was as if conducting an interview, tilting her head this way and that, but now and again she reached for Caroline to prettify her, to fuss with her hair or rearrange her collar, Caroline's grateful moon face illuminating her in return. In class, that afternoon, I overheard her bolstering Caroline with talk of how much Ali adored her, and with a secretive smile Caroline raised her eyes to the heavens in thanks for her incredible luck.

That weekend, at the park, there was a fair amount of talk about it between Susan and Mandy – would Sarah-Jayne still love Neil if he grew a beard? Would Caroline have to go to tea at the Rudges'? – but come Monday, everything changed again when, after an air at dinner break of offence taken and resolve made, Beverly informed us in passing, 'She's chucked him.' *Chucked?* Even by Beverly's standards this was stark. Susan – wide-eyed – asked the reason, and Beverly, scooping up some pens, said with an air of cheerful resignation, 'No spark.' A shame, she implied, but there you have it. You can only do your best. Win some, lose some.

'No spark,' Susan repeated respectfully but I was puzzled that anyone could have considered Neil a candidate for spark.

But, then, what *was* spark? And was there – would there have been – any spark between Tutankhamun and me? In my imagination he and I would sit together beside a pond of waterlilies, which, now that I thought of it, probably wouldn't be considered sparky.

Nothing had been said about Caroline and Ali but we all understood that their going out, as the supporting act to Sarah-Jayne and Neil's, would now also have to end. In a way, then, Caroline's loss was worse, visited arbitrarily upon her, and indeed all that afternoon her big eyes were particularly soulful. Sarah-Jayne, by contrast, seemed stung rather than wounded: grim but practical, picking herself up, martyred. Life lesson learned was what her bearing conveyed.

By Tuesday, though, this was old news, when along

came one of our most eagerly anticipated annual events: the arrival on Mr Hadleigh's desk of a boxful of fundraising 'Sunny Smiles' booklets. Each page of the floppy, pocket-sized booklets from the Children's Homes Association featured a black-and-white photograph of a smiling orphan to be liberated into our possession for a donated coin or two. Every year, these pictures were collectibles and, craning over one another's shoulders, we would have to be quick about our choices. Trade was brisk, and bartering rife.

There were always the predictable favourites – the blond and blue-eyed and beaming – but even in our backwater, and at our tender age, we could be discerning as well as charitable, choosing to shell out our precious pennies not always or only for the obvious candidates but for those who were differently, distinctively appealing. Someone endearingly buck-toothed, perhaps, or humorously bespectacled. And each year a different trait or characteristic would, unaccountably, find favour: braces, perhaps, or hearing aids, to say nothing of variations in skin tone. Inevitably, though, there were the stragglers – the ferret-faced, the boss-eyed, or those with an unflattering mole or downy upper lip or too severe a haircut – and in those cases we had to trust to a grown-up to make the best of it ('Oh, that's a characterful face! Reminds me of my Auntie Renee!') and to cough up. Not my mum, though, who said charity begins at home and sent me each year to try the Porters because they were a soft touch.

It was from the grown-ups that we learned words for those in the booklet who were blighted through no fault of their own, 'handicapped' and 'half-caste', and now, fifty years on, it occurs to me that I might have thought of myself as a kind of half, back then, because, after all, I was one parent away from being orphaned. But – incredibly – I don't remember thinking about it at the time. Perhaps I'd assumed that, if necessary, Jeannie would be found and come to my rescue, striding into my life like a character in a storybook, tossing her raven-black hair. Not until I had a baby of my own did I wonder whether Mum had made any plans for all eventualities, but even from the safe distance of decades I couldn't bring myself to ask her. Or perhaps especially then: not the most comfortable time in my life for me to acknowledge the knife edge we'd been on.

That Tuesday, the Sunny Smiles were distributed among our tables to a rising hum of excitement over which Mr Hadleigh hectored us about the timely collection of funds. We were raring to get ahead, to scramble through what was always at first sight a blur of coaxed and cultivated smiles. We were preparing to air our preferences and defend them ('Well, *I* think that's a *sweet* smile'), or perhaps to admit to mistakes or even confess to a whim, throwing our hands up ('I just don't know what it is about this one but . . . '). That was how it had always been. But now, after the initial buzz, a hush descended on our side of the classroom, broken only by Beverly advising Sarah-Jayne how to proceed ('So, you choose who you want . . . '). Sarah-Jayne leafed blankly through the booklet, and on either side of her, Beverly and Caroline did the same, studiously neutral, resisting any leap to judgement, waiting for her word. Sarah-Jayne alone was to be judge and jury.

The suspense extended to our table but after a long,

tense moment, Mandy cracked, exclaiming to nobody in particular, 'It's a no to this one. Because just look at him!'

From where I was sitting, I couldn't, quite; but Sarah-Jayne was able to turn right around in her seat for a good view over Mandy's shoulder. Then she raised her eyes to Mandy's with a look like Mr Hadleigh's whenever he said *If you've something to say then speak up because we'd all like to hear it*. I flicked through to the corresponding page of my own booklet and saw that there wasn't much wrong with the boy in question; not much right, perhaps, but really not that much wrong. Sarah-Jayne was correct, then, that Mandy had been too quick to judge, and harsh. But I knew that Mandy's outburst had been because she had lost her nerve, like that time when she had seemed to suggest Virginia shouldn't be invited to parties. Now she was digging herself deeper with some mumbling about the boy's eyes being too close together. Sarah-Jayne returned regally to her own booklet and made a show of considering this, raising the photo and holding it to the light, giving every appearance of struggling to understand what Mandy was claiming to see. Shamed, Mandy could meet no one's eye, so Susan rushed in with an attempt at distraction.

'This one, here' – she scrabbled through her own booklet – 'has such a sweet smile.'

Sarah-Jayne slid her eyes politely to Susan's. 'She does look a bit pleased with herself, though, don't you think?'

'True,' Susan said, too quickly, and turned the page.

That night I had earache, and Mum said to fight it but in the end I had to have a Junior Disprin, which did the trick; but the next morning she was muttering worryingly and mystifyingly about mastoids, which, whatever they were, would be worsened by swimming. Despite my protests she sent me to school with a sick note in place of my swim bag.

I spent the session miserably confined to the spectators' gallery, the only compensation being that invalids were first back on the coach while the others were still wrestling with their damp clothes in the changing room. I bagsied the seats just in front of the precarious back seat, and then, when Susan and Mandy joined me, we saw that we were in for a peaceful journey because Virginia had had one of her spells and needed to sit with Miss Drake, which in turn would keep Tracy down at the front. When I remarked on our luck, though, Susan and Mandy exchanged a knowing look.

'What?'

They were evasive, but some probing on my part revealed that they were worried for Virginia.

'Why?'

A notable pause. Then, from Mandy, 'Because of Miss Drake.'

'*Miss Drake*?'

'Miss Drake,' confirmed Susan; and with a jut of her chin Mandy delivered it up: 'She's a lezbeen.'

A what? I wasn't sure that I had heard properly over the roar of the coach; the word hadn't sounded like anything except perhaps a has-been.

'A lez-bee-anne,' Susan corrected, and Mandy flushed, which suggested that whatever this was, it was as new to them as it was to me. They, too, were on uncertain ground. This had arisen, I suspected, from chat in the changing rooms. What was it, though?

150

What – now – was wrong with Miss Drake? This had to be about more than her legs and her skirt. Images of her came spinning through my mind: perpetually sunlit, joyfully rushing around. But instead of asking *what*, I found myself asking *who*: 'Says who?' And their instant caginess confirmed that I was bang on, that I'd hit a sore point. They hadn't expected to have to account for its origin. The accusation was supposed to be fact; not just something that someone had said. My question was a bright light swung into their eyes. 'Who says this?' I was impressed by how indignant I sounded, as if I alone were to be the arbiter of all matters lezbeeanne. I had no doubt who'd said it, and sure enough the pair of them hefted their hangdog gazes to the back seat.

Then Susan started back-pedalling: 'But she does say it's very sad' – *she*, Sarah-Jayne – 'because it's unnatural, like when something goes wrong with you before you're born ...'

'... and if it's a puppy,' growled Mandy, 'you drown them in a bucket, because it's kindest.'

What?

And 'unnatural' – Miss Drake? The soap-and-water lass. Clopping around in those Scholls of hers, she had to be just about the most natural person I'd ever come across. '*Unnatural?*'

Susan confided, 'Because she likes other ladies.'

What other ladies?

She tried to clarify, '*Likes*-likes,' and raised her eyebrows but in a way that managed to be solemn.

Mandy added, 'Thinks they're sexy.'

I was baffled. 'Like on Miss World?' But we all loved Miss World, and precisely because the contestants were sexy. We all watched, every year, and then all talk the following day was of who we'd have voted for. We never actually said sexy – we said pretty and sweet – but it was what we meant.

Susan tried again: 'Wants to marry.'

That made no sense: 'You can't marry a lady if you're a lady.'

At that point, we had to pause our discussion because the coach was parking up in front of the school, pitching us into the scrum of disembarkation. We scrambled to our feet, hauling down our bags and collecting up coats, to join the protracted shuffle down the aisle to the door. We were almost last to leave the coach, with only the Sarah-Jayne trio behind us and they were still on the stairwell steps when Miss Drake came dashing back across the playground, calling up that because she'd been helping Virginia into school she had left her own bag on her seat – could someone please just reach around and grab it for her? Sarah-Jayne glittered and obliged, but then when Miss Drake had trilled her thanks and turned on her wooden heel, Sarah-Jayne glanced around us, gathering up our gazes, and, accompanied by something in the air like laughter if not an actual sound and from none of us in particular, emphatically wiped her hand on her trousers.

13

I wish I could claim that what I did later that day was in solidarity with Miss Drake, a gesture of resistance and defiance, but in truth I was just scared; I just wanted to get away from my friends.

That dinner time, Miss Drake clip-clopped over to our side of the room, all smiles, to request some help with the bunting for the fete. She addressed us as a group but somehow Sarah-Jayne was at the centre of the exchange. And how, I marvelled, did she do that – magic herself up at the centre, without moving a muscle, so that it was as if she personally was being asked and she alone would make the decision as to whether help would be forthcoming? She received the request respectfully, gave it a lot of attention, eyes bright, allowing Miss Drake to enthuse about the bunting and how grateful she would be for any assistance, but she remained non-committal and I saw how she was giving Miss Drake rope in order to keep her dangling. In the end, Miss Drake got a chilly smile and had to slope off, hoping for the best.

I had been too slow and cowardly to offer myself at the time, but Miss Drake's use of the word 'volunteer' had given me a chance, and when we'd cleared our plates away, I made my move. Susan, surprised, asked where I was off to and I said I was going to volunteer.

'Volunteer?'

'Do the bunting.'

She was concerned. 'With Miss Drake?'

Mandy hovered.

I trotted out the justification that I had privately been rehearsing: I needed to do this for my Brownie volunteer badge.

But we'd just about finished with Brownies, Susan said; depending on Mrs Peters' bunion, we might never be going back.

As if I hadn't heard her, I pointed out that if I got one more badge then I would have more than anyone else.

'Do semaphore instead,' said Mandy, and demonstrated, waving her arms robotically. It was a badge that, so far, none of us had done; none of us knew any semaphore and Susan was intrigued by the display, asking Mandy, 'What did that just say?'

Nothing, Mandy said: she'd just been waving her arms around.

Ridiculously, I said I hated semaphore.

Susan's suggestion was that I volunteer at church with the flower-arranging but this struck me as like when Mum said charity begins at home and I could volunteer to do the washing-up (not that she would ever let me do it, because *If you want something doing, do it yourself*).

I was getting tetchy, now; I said, 'Yes, or I can just go next door, now, this minute, and *do some bunting*.'

She was grudging in her defeat – 'Well, just be *careful*' – which I answered with a lofty tut and, mimicking her sulky tone, came back at her with, 'It's just *bunting*.'

So, off I stomped to Miss Drake's bright glass box of a classroom, feeling conspicuous and indignant, none of which was improved by Miss Drake's obvious surprise to see me: she didn't seem to know why I was turning up. 'Deborah?' Solicitous, with a careful smile: *How may I help?*

I nearly asked, *Do you want to marry a lady?* Instead, I pulled myself together and said about the bunting and the volunteer badge, before regretting that perhaps this had me sounding mercenary. She didn't seem to take it that way, though, or didn't care, because she cheerfully made room for me at the bench.

Thinking back now to the smile she rustled up for me, I wonder, not for the first time, if in the eyes of adults there was something disconcerting about me. It seems to me that I was an easy enough kid, no trouble, diligent and trustworthy. I wonder if people saw me as hobbled by my home life, my history, dragging along with me my dead dad and my fish-out-of-water mum. It's possible, though, that none of this went through Miss Drake's mind, then or at any other time; perhaps her sole concern, that dinner time, was the bunting that needed doing and here, happily, was a volunteer. Her welcome might well have been genuine. She was saying how good of me it was to turn up and I was saying I loved bunting, which wasn't so; in truth I wasn't even indifferent to it but actively disliked it, those pyjama bits and their poor pretence at jauntiness.

'Great! And you've come on your own?'

I said that I, alone, was doing the badge. 'Mandy's doing semaphore,' I heard myself embellish.

'Semaphore!' She laughed. 'How interesting,' and did something with her arms that might or might not have been an actual message. And then as she shuffled piles of fabric she asked if I helped Mum at home, and I said how Mum said if you want something doing it's best to do it yourself and Miss Drake smiled and said, 'Ah.' Then she asked me what I wanted to be when I grew up and that too, I knew, was small talk, but it was a question I liked. An Olympic swimmer, maybe, I said, to which she murmured gratifyingly about my swimming abilities. 'Or a vet,' I said. 'Or an archaeologist.'

'Treasures!' she enthused, and then she said it was good to have options but that she had always wanted to be a teacher because she loved little children. I told her that my mum said kids should never have been invented, at which she laughed as I had known she would. 'Your mum's so funny,' she said, as people so often did, and I liked it that they said it even if I myself couldn't quite see it. 'Or I might run a disco,' I said, remembering Sonny's weekend work, his saving to go travelling. *Spirit in the skyyyyy*. 'If,' I added, 'girls can do that.'

She said, 'Why not? And I wish you could do ours for us! I've still to book one for the wedding.'

Wedding?

'So much to organise,' she said.

'Whose wedding?' My heart was thumping.

She was sweetly puzzled: 'Well, mine.'

My blood sang inside my ears. 'You're getting married to a . . . ?' Husband?

'Mr Hoggatt.' She laughed. 'I'll be back next term as

156

Mrs Hoggatt,' and she gave me a look to show me that I too could laugh, which dutifully I did but the feeling inside me was so much better than laughing; it was as if I were breaking the surface, kicking up from the murk and bursting into the air and light. Because I was right! I had been right! Everything was as I had thought, Miss Drake was as I had thought she was, and there was no unnaturalness nor any need for buckets.

After our productive bunting-making session, I skipped off to find Susan, encountered her in the porch and dished up my news with a *Guess what?*

She was thrilled: 'Miss Drake? How do you know?' As if my knowing, itself, was the achievement. How did she *think* I knew?

'She *told* me,' and I added that they were going to have a disco.

She drew a deep breath: 'A *disco*!'

The wedding was to be in the holidays, I told her, and imparting this filled me with such pride and excitement that it might have been my own.

She was scarcely able to contain herself. 'We should tell the others!'

But I wasn't sure I was quite ready for that. This was mine – my discovery, my revelation – or, now, mine and Susan's, and I wanted us to savour it together for a little longer. But then Mandy came back from the stationery cupboard and sensed at once that there was something going on. She gave Susan a look that slid beneath her defences, and duly Susan spilled the beans.

'Married?' Mandy was sceptical. She'd fallen hook, line and sinker for whatever it was that she'd heard in the changing rooms and I felt oddly triumphant, vindicated because I was right about her, too. *You're plain stupid*, I thought, giddily, *and if they told you to jump off a bridge . . .*

But Susan gleefully affirmed it for her – 'I *know*!' – and then to me: 'Who to?'

'He's a Mr Hoggatt.' Admittedly, this was the drawback: the man's name.

Mandy glowered. 'What do you mean, "a Mr Hoggatt"?'

What did she mean what did I mean? 'I *mean* she's going to be *Missus* Hoggatt.'

'Mrs Hoggatt!' Susan was awed, as if it were a title like HRH. And again, 'Let's tell the others!'

But must we? I wanted them to stay wrong for a while longer. This – the truth – was mine; I'd done the work of finding it, while they'd sat around amusing themselves with nasty rumours. Let them stew, I thought. Let them rot. Why should we go to them with our news for their dissection and approval? That sly, calculated, theatrical wiping of Sarah-Jayne's hand had had nothing to do with the truth, and she'd known it. To her, the truth was neither here nor there.

I grabbed Susan's arm, to try to shake some sense into her. 'Sarah-Jayne makes things up about people.'

Susan attempted to laugh this off. 'Oh, I think she just didn't *know*, that's all. She was just *thinking* that. But' – brightly – 'now we *do* know!'

And then suddenly there they were, the three of them, coming into the porch as a deadening of the light.

'Guess what!' heralded Susan. 'Miss Drake is getting married!'

Sarah-Jayne tilted her head and came up with the quizzical smile that, habitual as it was, amounted to no reaction. But Beverly could be relied upon to step into the breach and provide that. 'What?' she derided. 'To a *lady*?'

Susan tutted fondly. 'No!' *Dumbo*. 'To a man, a mister, a Mr Hoggatt. She's going to be Mrs Hoggatt, next term. She told Deborah.'

Sarah-Jayne's gaze switched to me and if I wasn't mistaken there was a small nod of her inclined head in affirmation, perhaps even admiration. 'Well,' she said, 'congratulations are in order,' and for a second I thought she meant for me, for having discovered the truth, but she was already turning on her heel and heading for Miss Drake's room, with Susan in her wake wittering about the disco. I took off after them; all I knew was that I didn't want her in there.

Too late: she was already knocking, but didn't wait for permission before cracking open the door and treating Miss Drake to a peek. The rest of us, behind her, stopped short. We heard Miss Drake's greeting – 'Sarah-Jayne!' – which sounded open and inviting. Sarah-Jayne went in, and we all crowded into the now open doorway. Miss Drake was at her desk and Sarah-Jayne sauntered over the black-and-white tiles to rest the fingertips of one hand on the edge of the desktop, staking her claim, then softly, winningly said, 'Deborah says you're getting married.'

A jolly smile from Miss Drake. 'Yes, and not long now! Lots to do.'

Sarah-Jayne asked lightly, as if joking, lady-to-lady, 'No engagement ring?'

I hadn't thought to look for one. Perhaps because my mum didn't have one, just a wedding ring. Miss Drake laughed and briefly splayed her bare hand as if to check.

'Heavens no, not in here!' Not in the hurly-burly of the infants' room.'

Sarah-Jayne bestowed a sympathetic smile. 'Is it diamonds?' and Miss Drake said something about opals, asking if Sarah-Jayne knew what they were. Beside me in the doorway Caroline whispered, '*I* do,' and then everyone else was muttering, sharing various insights and opinions on gemstones. None of which Sarah-Jayne even acknowledged, pressing ahead, asking Miss Drake if she had a photo, 'Of your intended.'

Intended. That was a new one on me, and sounded impressively grown-up.

Miss Drake hesitated – 'Er, yes, I think so, yes' – and took her purse from a desk drawer and rifled through it. Sarah-Jayne shot us a glittering smile, as if none of it – legs, lezbeeanne – had ever happened. Miss Drake handed her something – 'Here, that's Dave' – and together they looked down at the photo.

'He has a lovely smile,' Sarah-Jayne said, which somehow gave us permission to herd into the room, and there we all were, crowding around the desk, craning for a glimpse. I was at the back; I couldn't see. Susan could, and came up with her own grown-up word, *handsome*, at which Miss Drake laughed, embarrassed. 'He's very kind,' she allowed, 'and he's very funny. He makes me laugh,' and again she laughed, as if even to think of him making her laugh was making her laugh.

Mandy croaked, 'Where did he propose?' which was a good question, and the answer didn't disappoint: 'In our local pub, would you believe! Not very glamorous or romantic, I'm afraid!' and on cue we all laughed and Sarah-Jayne gave a pretty roll of her eyes: *Men!*

'He was drunk,' Beverly said, but Miss Drake took no offence, just said he'd better sober up before the actual wedding. This was when Wendy burst in, demanding, 'What? What is it?'

'Miss Drake's intended,' called Susan.

Wendy came skipping over. 'Your what-id?'

'She's getting married,' Susan explained. 'To Dave here.' But Wendy wasn't interested in the photo, bellowing, 'Oo-oo-oo, can I be bridesmaid?'

Miss Drake said that was a kind offer but she had a lot of nieces queueing up.

Half-joking, Wendy pleaded, 'But just one more!' and Mandy said, 'You should have all of us,' which was a bewitching image and suddenly we were as one, *You should, you should!*

And then Sarah-Jayne said, 'My sister's getting married.'

'Oh, is she?' Miss Drake leapt at the distraction.

'You gonna be bridesmaid?' Wendy was wide-eyed.

'Of course,' said Sarah-Jayne to sighs, and Miss Drake said that sounded lovely and when was it to be? In the spring, Sarah-Jayne said. 'She's marrying Max. He's great.'

'Well, isn't that nice.' Miss Drake was returning the photo to the safety of her purse.

'Max is *really* funny.' Sarah-Jayne glimmered with private reflection. 'My sister doesn't deserve him.'

Miss Drake's attention was with Wendy, who was asking if she was going to have a baby. 'Gosh,' Miss Drake blushed, 'all in good time,' but it was too late because now there was a chorus of pleas, *Oh, go on, go on, Miss Drake! Have a baby!*

161

Ah, but, 'When I have a baby I'll have to leave here.'

We fell silent, because we hadn't thought of that, and because Mr Hadleigh had appeared in the doorway. 'Miss Drake' – which was for our benefit, because whenever he thought we weren't listening he called her Gillian – 'a quick word, if I may.'

She thanked us as if we had all been in there for the bunting and we trooped past Mr Hadleigh, leaving the room to the pair of them.

Outside, Sarah-Jayne mused, 'No baby on the way. Not shotgun, then.'

When I told my mum the news, that evening, she said, 'Oh aye? And who's the lucky fella?' and then, 'Mr Hoggatt? Who's he when he's at home?' She wondered if he was the man whom Peggy Peters had mentioned a while back: apparently Miss Drake had met someone at a friend's wedding. I said I didn't know, but then, instead of leaving it there, added, 'There's no shotgun.'

She stared at me. 'Who's been talking to you about shotgun weddings?'

No one, I said, shrinking, stung, realising I'd made a mistake even if I didn't know what the mistake was.

'Right enough,' she said, hard-faced, 'and mind you keep it that way.'

14

From that day onwards, in the blink of an eye our sturdily shod, downy-calved, soap-and-water Miss Drake was a fairy-tale bride-to-be and all the talk was of the dress and flowers and what kind of car would take her to the church and whether she should have a pageboy, and what might be her Something Blue. I should have been happy for her – I *was* – but the turn-about had left me doubting the ground beneath my own feet, because if she, clopping sweetly around in her Scholls, had unwittingly come so close to downfall, what lay in wait for the rest of us?

It was possible, I supposed, that I had misunderstood and was making too much of Sarah-Jayne's snide wiping away of Miss Drake's touch and Susan and Mandy's whispers of unnaturalness: me, scaredy-cat, prim-faced, perhaps failing to get what everyone else knew for a joke. Or if not an actual joke then something we should all expect in time to go through: each of us under suspicion until – respective intendeds in tow – we proved ourselves to be normal.

Still, no one else came forward to volunteer for Miss Drake, because they had a new distraction: a mini transistor, Susan told me, being smuggled into school in Sarah-Jayne's bag and around which everyone was gathering in the house at dinner break to catch the end of Dave Lee Travis. After which, I witnessed, they blew back into the classroom like dandelion clocks, giddied and radiant. This radio, Susan reported breathlessly, was Sarah-Jayne's very own; she was able to listen in secret in her bedroom at night.

But to what? There was nothing on at night, I said. Except perhaps the news.

Mandy put me straight. 'There's *advice*.'

Advice, surely, was what was in those leftover magazines at the doctors' waiting room: *How to clean a burnt pan*, and at the top of the page, drawings of pans and scrubbing brushes and aprons twinkling like stars.

But no: Mandy gloated, 'Last night, Sarah-Jayne says, this man was ringing up' – 'Don't!' Susan, scandalised, flapping at Mandy's words – 'because he's married but he can't stop going off with his wife's sister.'

From the nature table, Wendy bellowed, 'Canoodling,' and, her lips puckered and eyes popping, turned her back to us and sinuously ran her hands all over her own shoulder blades.

Susan was keen for me to come along and listen to DLT but I stayed alone in Miss Drake's classroom the next day, inventing for myself a succession of fete preparation tasks. Alone there, sifting tombola from raffle and ticketing the donations – the unwanted gifts of abrasively scented toiletries, the bottles with incomprehensible labels that had been souvenirs but then back home had lost their shine – I couldn't help but dwell on what Mum said about friends: more trouble than they're worth, looking out for number one, only ever waiting for a better offer. I'd always listened, but before now, I realised, I hadn't let it worry me. I had come to know it for the kind of thing she said, her very own theme tune; and perhaps, also, I had been hoping, deep down, that what might have been true for her in her life might not be so for me in mine. Anyway, most of us at school weren't really friends, thrown together as we were and getting along as best we could. So, it wasn't as if I had been expecting much. But Susan? Although she and I might not be best friends – Mandy in the middle of us – I'd hoped for better from her. She'd never told stories about people nor much listened to them, before Sarah-Jayne turned up.

I had two dinner breaks on my own in Miss Drake's room before, at the end of the second one, Susan came to find me, insisting on her pleasant surprise – '*There* you are!' – when we both knew I'd been there all along. She was determinedly breezy, all hop-skip-and-jump, but her gaze was deferential. She had some ground to make up with me and she knew it. No point, though, I warned myself, in being less than gracious. And there was no denying that my heart had lifted to see her. So, truce, I decided, or at least for now, for a start.

'What we've been doing' – over in the house, she meant – 'is trying the levitation again.' She was shy and solicitous. 'It's really interesting; I think you'd be interested,' although in the next breath she was playing it down: 'But we're just trying.'

More rubbish, I thought, if of a different kind from

Donny Osmond, but I kept up the smiling. She leaned back against the door, slotting her hands behind her tailbone, bouncing softly on the knuckles, and said that levitation needed concentration for it to work, 'And you're good at that.'

Well, compared to you, I thought, which wasn't saying that much.

'It's to do with the power of the mind, and you' – her eyes shone – 'you're a brainbox.'

And that was all it took. To my own surprise as much, no doubt, as hers, I went with her across the playground to the house the following day, telling myself that it was just for once, just for a change, and I'd merely hang around while they did whatever they did.

Going into the front room, I avoided anyone's eye to make clear there should be no counting me in, and that I was there only as a favour to Susan and for a well-earned break from my work in Miss Drake's room. But as it happened, no one spared me a second glance – they were all too busy, Mandy vigorously drawing the curtains and Susan darting across the room to help Beverly lift the topmost table from the stack, its tubular hollow legs clanking against the others and ringing in the bones of my skull. And when the three of them began clearing the centre of the room of chairs, hauling them bumping and shuddering over the hairy carpet, I felt I could no longer stand aside but should muck in. Sarah-Jayne, though, kept to a corner in consultation with Caroline in a manner suggesting Caroline was the one to be levitated. Caroline, though – heaviest of us all? But perhaps that was why, I thought: a proper test of their so-called powers.

166

When the table was in place, Caroline perched on it and swivelled to raise her socked feet to the wipe-clean surface, then adjusted her skirt more comfortably and decorously over her hips before reclining.

Sarah-Jayne checked, 'All right, Caz?' as she took the head end like a high priestess.

Caz?

Caroline's response was to meet and hold Sarah-Jayne's gaze, her eyes slotting back in their sockets like a doll's.

Then the others stepped up, closing in around her, and I managed to position myself beside Susan, aware too late that this wasn't the best move in that it brought me face to face – nose to nose, even – across Caroline's body with Mandy and Beverly. Susan whispered to me, 'And now we just ...' as she slid her hands, palms upwards, beneath Caroline, but she had Caroline's shoulders, whereas I had her bottom. I considered going in at an angle, aiming more for the small of her back, but Beverly, opposite, was shovelling up a buttock and in the interest of balance I would have to do the same. I tried hard not to think of the bulkiness in Caroline's knickers that we'd all glimpsed, recently, when she'd been doing handstands.

Caroline stared stoically upwards as if into a dentist's lamp, and on that tabletop she seemed able to hold herself more lightly than usual, as if poised for lift-off. How long, I wondered, before it was accepted that nothing was going to happen and we could give up on it? How long were my hands to be wedged beneath what Mr Hadleigh would call Caroline's derry-air?

Sarah-Jayne closed her eyes and Mandy and Beverly

copied, although in their case the effect wasn't cere-monial, Mandy looking crestfallen and Beverly vacant. I cheated, merely lowering my gaze. For a couple of minutes my hands were surprisingly snug but then my wrists began to ache; they were at the wrong angle but I couldn't flex them, couldn't risk wriggling or fidgeting, nearing any possible pad. I should have driven a little deeper in, I realised – it was my own reticence that had done for me and my hands half in and half out and slightly cocked probably made for at least as much dis-comfort for Caroline as for me. I wished in a way that she was even heavier, because then she'd have just nicely flattened everything and that would have been that.

In other respects, though, the session was passing easily enough. Silence buzzed in my ears but not unpleasantly and definitely preferable to DLT. If this was all it was, I thought, and if this was all that was required of me, I wouldn't mind spending my dinner breaks lulled by the tick-tick-tick of my blood cooling in my calves and, outside, the infants' whoops and shrieks strewn through the air like streamers. My thoughts turned leisurely to the afternoon ahead. It was too wet for rounders, so we'd probably do some reading and I thought I might treat myself to a return to *Tom's Midnight Garden*.

But then, just when I was settling into the session, it was over: all around me was a snapping-to within an air of resignation. Somehow it had been collectively decided over my head that this attempt had failed. They were surprisingly buoyant, though, as they busily righted the room, and then on the way back across the playground, with Susan musing aloud as to what else might be pos-sible with the powers of the mind and Mandy saying a settee would be nice. Sarah-Jayne said nothing actual could be magicked up because the power of the mind was instead about making things happen, but Susan had a neat way around that, suggesting we make someone donate us a settee, which led to talk of donations in general and how none of us ever won the boxes of chocolates at the fete. Always just the bubble bath, complained Caroline, to which Sarah-Jayne said that bubble bath was brilliant but Caroline said chocolate tastes better, and Susan told Sarah-Jayne about the big box of chocolates that Mrs Peters donated every year, which she must buy specially because no one would have a big box of chocolates spare in their cupboard.

Unless she's a Weight Watcher, said Sarah-Jayne, but Susan said she was slim, and Mandy said apart from her bunions.

As we settled down at our tables, ready for the afternoon lesson on local history, Susan began burbling about how it wouldn't be long before we'd be levitating Caroline now that there were two brainboxes on the case. 'You two grammar school girls,' she said admiringly of Sarah-Jayne and me. Trust Susan, I thought, to confuse grammar with private.

Sarah-Jayne leaned across to ask me if I'd had an interview for the grammar and I said no, explaining that the headmaster had dropped by – touring all the local primaries, Mr Hadleigh had said – and I'd been sent into the staff room to meet him. In truth, the staff room had been a disappointment: simply a desk – with telephone – against a wall, and in the middle of the room two hard-backed and scratchy-fabric armchairs arranged at an angle to each other, between them a small table

holding an ashtray. In that ashtray had been a smoulder-
ing, reeking pipe, and folded into one of the armchairs
like a broken umbrella had been a tall, bony man in some
kind of black cloak, his legs crossed and the uppermost
dangling in my direction, trouser-hem hoicked to expose
a pallid, sparsely furred shin. His huge teeth, bared in a
false smile, were like knuckles. Gesturing to the vacant
chair, he had asked me what I had been playing in the
playground. Horses, I told him, and reaching for the pipe
he said, 'Horsewoman in the making, are you?'

Horsewoman: was that, I'd wondered, a kind of centaur?

He asked me, 'What makes a good horsewoman, do
you think?'

I had no idea and the best I could come up with was
the right kind of oats.

Sarah-Jayne was saying that because she was new
to the area her application had been late, so she'd had
to go up to the school, to the headmaster's own office,
which, she said, stank of pipe smoke, and it struck me as
odd that her future headmaster too was a pipe smoker.
Perhaps, I thought, teachers progressed from cigarettes
to pipes as they rose in rank.

Susan chipped in with 'You'll have to wear that jacket
they all have, with the badge on it.'

'Blazer,' Sarah-Jayne said. 'Crest.'

Beverly said the only uniform rule at the comprehen-
sive was to wear black and Caroline said with a regretful
moue that purple would be a so much better match for
her eyes, and fluttered her eyelashes for a laugh.

'And you have to have a briefcase,' gushed Susan.

'Max has bought me one,' Sarah-Jayne said. 'So, I'm
all hunky-dory.'

I didn't yet have any of my uniform; Mum was waiting for the second-hand sale and hoping they would offer briefcases, too, because we had no idea where they came from and she suspected they cost a bomb. She said she might ask Mr Watt if he had an old one spare. And then there were the extras, the optionals, such as the school scarf: if there wasn't one in the sale but I was willing to wait, she said, I could have one for a Christmas present, if I liked.

Susan whispered that we were going to look so smart, the pair of us, together on the coach every day, and I looked to Sarah-Jayne to put her right but she merely tilted her head and smiled and my heart plummeted to my plimsolls. Because no, surely not, this couldn't be true: she couldn't be coming to the grammar. She was going private! Mum had said! Mum had promised, or kind of, as good as: *That sort always do.* And anyway the grammar was for serious types – that too she had always told me – and I had pictured girls and boys writing stories about how it would have been to be a centurion, but now Sarah-Jayne would be strutting in there looking like an air hostess, with her *Jackie*s and that transistor in her briefcase, and everyone would look up from their centurions and think her fabulous. Because misguidedly, maddeningly, everyone always did; even, it seemed, that horrible headmaster. Mum had said grammar school places were like gold dust but Sarah-Jayne had stalked into the headmaster's office and he had showered her with it like confetti.

All that afternoon, I sat stiffly on a swelling sense of injustice. Sarah-Jayne just happened to be clever. She didn't have to try, she didn't work for it, nor even seem to want it. Cleverness just settled over her as she sat around smirking and biroing *DC 4 Me* on her hands. Whereas me: Mr Hadleigh always said I went all around the houses before coming up with something interesting, which to my mind had had me sounding gratifyingly like an archaeologist. But now I wondered if whenever he said I was imaginative he was secretly making fun of me, imagination being merely the best I could do, a kind of consolation prize.

Forget settees, I thought hotly; forget chocolate boxes, perhaps even as an emergency forget the WH Smith pony, because if I had a power, if I could harness the power of my mind for anything, it would be to have Sarah-Jayne gone. It took my breath away to think how close we had come to never having known her, how mere chance had had her and her family turn up here in our village. Then again, I supposed, I could hope that the reverse could be true in that fate might not have quite finished with her and would somehow see her back on her way. Yes, and if and when it did, I vowed to myself, I'd be there to see it. I would keep on its case, on its tail, I'd dog it and, if and when the time ever came, I'd be there to see it done.

Perhaps that was why I fell in with them yet again the following day as they surged across the playground towards the house. We were barely halfway across, though, when all hell broke loose, Sarah-Jayne seizing Caroline, frantic and elated amid shrieks from the others of *he's back, he's there, he's back* and Beverly wolf-whistling and Susan and Mandy waving wildly in the direction of the building site over the road. And there, I saw, hitching his long limbs around on a platform on the scaffolding, was Sonny. He hollered back a greeting – 'Hiya, girls!' – and then, turning to join his two smirking fellow builders, called casually over his shoulder, 'Wotcha, Deb,' thereby well and truly dropping me in it.

As one, the girls rounded on me in a whirl of jubilation and incredulity: 'He knows you! He knows your name!'

That is *not* my name, I thought, and spluttered something about how he'd saved us from a spider, which fleetingly worked because then the spider copped for the hysteria – *Spider! Spider!* – in the midst of which I remembered that there had in fact first been the tortoise. I should have offered up that tortoise because now the cries were of 'Your house! Your house!' because to rid us of a spider, he'd have had to come to my house, to have been *inside* my house. But no, I thought, it wasn't like that – like what? – and I was gabbling about the roadside, about how I'd gone there to get help, and I even mimed flagging him down ('Semaphore,' announced Mandy) to try to make the point that only chance had it that he was the one I'd ended up escorting home.

But Sarah-Jayne was calling me brave ('You just . . . ?'), pressing her hands to her heart, acting awed and astounded, and even as I did my best to look unbothered by all the fuss, I was frantically trying to make sense of it. What was he to them? He was nothing like David Cassidy or Donny Osmond or even our own Snow White Neil Hammond. He was rude and cigarette-smelling and too big for his boots. What was I missing?

'She doesn't have a dad,' Susan told Sarah-Jayne, presumably in explanation for the need for spider rescue, as Beverly was demanding of me, 'Where was it?'

Just up on the main road, I told her, by the bus stop.

'No, the *spider*!' and uproar, hilarity, and *ha ha very funny*. 'The *bath*,' I said, but already Mandy was asking why we hadn't gone next door for Bert and yes, why hadn't I insisted to Mum that I fetch a neighbour? No way should they know that Mum had specifically told me to go and waylay Sonny. Why *had* she? Why *hadn't* she asked me to call for Bert, or for Mr Porter? Or Mrs Porter – Mrs Porter wouldn't have been scared of a spider, she practically farmed them in that house of hers, although she wouldn't have been able to lean over the bath with her bump and then that spider would have given her a grisly runaround. But Mum would never have the neighbours in. *Knowing our business*, she said, although what *was* our business? And did everyone have business? Or did we have more than others? Or was there something about our business, whatever it was, that made it crucial to keep it to ourselves?

Sarah-Jayne was asking me his name, and my reply had her reel in delight: 'As in "Smiles"!' Then, 'What's he like?' but immediately to the others: 'He is *so kind*, isn't he, helping them like that.'

Them. Me and Mum.

'And brave.' Returning to me, 'Did your mum not mind?'

Mind?

'When you came back with him. Because' – a knowing glance around the others – 'he is such a *lad*, isn't he,' said admiringly and to appreciative laughter. '*My* mum,' she said with satisfaction, 'would've had a *fit*.'

This, too, was popular and enthusiastically taken up: *Mine, too! And mine, and mine!* And my heart thumped

174

because why *didn't* Mum mind? Why *did* she let him in our house all the time, saying words like arse?

Next, Sarah-Jayne wanted to know where he lived, and that too I could answer: 'Tracy's.'

Beverly blurted, 'He's her *brother*?' to widespread derision because everyone knew Tracy's brother was Trevor and he was seven. 'But what, then?' she hammered back. 'Is he an orphan?' and I might have tried to explain had Sarah-Jayne not put out a call for Tracy, who arrived in no time, Virginia in tow, to confirm that Sonny was indeed living in her house, adding a sacrilegious 'Worse luck!'

'He'd be very welcome to live in mine,' purred Sarah-Jayne, and I kept to myself that I was with Tracy on this, who was busy further disgracing herself with 'He *stinks* of aftershave, and our whole house whiffs of it.' She fanned herself vigorously for the benefit of Virginia, who obliged with a twinkling inside her bulbous lenses.

'Aftershave!' Sarah-Jayne swooned.

I didn't recall any aftershave but perhaps it had worn off with the cycling. Then again, I wasn't sure I'd have known it in any case. Was it like soap? I knew from the telly adverts that men had their own special soaps, on ropes. Tracy was proclaiming that Sonny's ponged like toilet cleaner, which Sarah-Jayne chose to ignore, asking instead why he was living in her house. Tracy said he was working for her dad, learning the trade, which caused a flutter, presumably because learning a trade sounded noble or manly.

Sarah-Jayne pressed: 'Yes, but why does he live in your house? I mean, Miss Drake works for Mr Hadleigh but she isn't living in his house, is she.'

'Imagine if she did!' and Mandy adopted a ridiculous, fluting voice: 'Toast, dear?'

Tracy said, 'No, but Miss Drake lives with her mum and dad. But *he* can't live with *his* mum and dad because they're *miles* away.' Then she said, 'Southend or somewhere.'

Where had she got that from? I stopped myself from saying Rainham, but she'd already thought better of it. 'Somewhere,' she revised, 'not near here.'

Susan said with deep concern, 'Southend is right over by the sea,' which had Tracy whip around and turn on her: 'I *know*!'

Sarah-Jayne exclaimed, 'Southend?' the palm of one hand steadying her heart at the thought of the near miss, of being so nearly thwarted by geography.

'Not Southend,' Tracy was saying, 'just somewhere, and he hasn't got a car, so he can't come from home. He's only got his bike. And good job, too, because he can buzz off on that all the time.'

Sarah-Jayne glanced at me – it confirmed my story – then was back to Tracy: 'Off where?'

Tracy shrugged. 'Just . . . around.' Where was there to go, she meant, around here?

Sarah-Jayne looked up at the now-vacated scaffolding, and Beverly said to her, 'He might bump into you.'

'With any luck.'

Tracy blared, 'Or he just hangs around playing his records.'

Sarah-Jayne: 'Records?'

Tracy corrected herself: 'Tapes.'

For Sarah-Jayne the distinction was neither here nor there; what mattered was 'Who of?'

Another shrug. 'Slade and stuff. Wizzard.'

A frisson all around, because for a boy this was acceptable, respectable; this was boy music.

But Tracy backtracked: '*Did*.' *Did* play tapes. 'Now he's dumped the tape recorder because he's doing discos.'

Sarah-Jayne's gaze sharpened. 'Discos?'

The whole group echoed, 'Discos?' and for a disconcerting moment it was as if they had all been there in my kitchen to overhear that conversation.

Tracy went on, 'His friend does them, and he helps. Saturdays. Goes off in the van.'

Beverly interrogated: 'Where?'

'Weddings, twenty-firsts—'

Susan burst out, 'He could do Miss Drake's wedding!'

Sarah-Jayne said quietly, 'He can do my party.'

And now it was as if they had all stepped up around me, although in fact no one had moved.

Beverly said to Tracy, 'You should've got that tape player off him.'

'I tried.' She upended a mauve Spangle on her tongue. 'He was shoving it in his bag and I said where are you going with that? And he said he didn't need it and I said I'll have it but he said, "It's spoken for."'

And Sarah-Jayne repeated, thoughtfully, 'Spoken for.'

15

The levitation session did go ahead, after the kerfuffle, although it took a while for everyone to settle, and when eventually there was silence except for the occasional rumble of Beverly's tummy, my thoughts could turn properly to what had just happened outside. Had it been some kind of a joke? Sonny, chewing and slouching and picking his nose, not that I had ever actually seen him picking his nose but I was pretty sure it was only a matter of time. Calling to him and waving and whistling like that: had they been teasing him? Or perhaps, somehow, teasing themselves – like when they'd danced and sung to Neil and Ali on the touchline. Or me? It couldn't be – could it – that someone had seen his bike outside my house and all the fuss was something to do with that?

Susan was still skittish when we were packing up, and pushed us: 'Don't you think she was a teensy bit lighter, this time? Do you think we might be getting somewhere?'

She: the cat's mother, as, inexplicably, Mum would

say. Caroline was sitting up on the tabletop, hugging her knees, attentive, awaiting the verdict like a gymnast at the Olympics about to receive her score.

Mandy wasn't having it. 'But isn't she supposed to fly up in the air?'

Susan was perplexed – 'I haven't the foggiest' – and looked to Sarah-Jayne, but got no help; Sarah-Jayne shrugged, as if all this nonsense hadn't come from her in the first place. But then she decided, 'I suppose it could kind of happen bit by bit; it probably does have to start somewhere.'

Caroline was looking pleasantly expectantly around us, and Susan asked her, 'Could you tell, Caz?' (*Caz!*) She was wide-eyed: 'Could you feel anything?'

Beverly answered for her, 'She can't tell,' meaning it wasn't her place to be able to tell, and agreed with Mandy, 'A bit of shifting isn't levitation,' but this gave Susan all she needed:

'Aha! So, you *did* feel it!' She glowed with intrigue and delight. 'That "bit of shifting".'

Beverly said, flatly, 'That was just shifting,' and Mandy shored her up with, 'They have to go right up, they have to hover.'

They. Like *they* have to go in a bucket, I thought.

Susan muttered a mildly rebellious 'Well, I think they do have to start somewhere. She's not a rocket,' which provided some light relief, and Caroline made a vrooming gesture. Cheered, Susan said to me, 'I just feel there was a difference, this time. Because before, she was like a sack of potatoes.'

'Charming!' Caroline said good-naturedly to more laughter, with Susan rushing to say she hadn't meant it that way, although it was hard to imagine how else it might have been meant. She tried again with Sarah-Jayne, 'But you felt maybe just a little tiny change?' to which Sarah-Jayne raised her hands, non-committal, and said it was impossible to tell from where she stood.

Which was convenient, I thought.

But then as we filed into the hallway Sarah-Jayne remarked, 'If it *is* starting to work, you know who we have to thank.'

Susan, owl-like: 'Who, who, who?'

With a nod in my direction, Sarah-Jayne smiled the smile that was no smile and said, 'Well, *she* was what was different, this time.'

Not only was that a transparent attempt to butter me up because of what she imagined, ridiculously, as my connection to Sonny, but it was just plain wrong: I'd been there the previous day, or had she forgotten? She kept it up, though. In the porch, changing back into my plimsolls, slotting my outdoor shoes onto the rack beneath the bench, I glanced up to see not Susan standing there waiting for me, as I'd expected, but Sarah-Jayne. Everyone else had gone; there were just the two of us. She must have been quick off the mark, across the tiles in the instant that Susan was up and away through the doorway back into class. Even more impressive was that she'd given Mutt and Jeff the slip, presumably by a deft doubling-back.

She tilted her head in that way she assumed to be winning, and dropped her weight onto one hip in a manner she probably considered appealing but that gave her the look of having been plonked there, unbudgeable. '*So*' – the smile – 'you *know* him.'

No, I thought, I don't. I really don't. Nor do I want to. And I took exception to the unspoken accusation: *Why didn't you say? You could have said.*

'You've *talked* to him, you've' – an ecstatic flick of her eyes skyward – '*walked along the road with him*!' and a self-mocking little laugh before she was back to searching my gaze for what else I might be keeping from her. 'And all this time,' she lamented, 'we've been seeing him up there on that scaffold and wondering about him.'

Two days at most.

'He *likes* you.'

So?

Except he didn't. Well, no, he didn't *not*; that wasn't it.

Beverly reappeared – there was never any keeping her at bay for long – and hovered over Sarah-Jayne's shoulder for the next question: 'Do you think he'll come round your house again?'

'Why would he?' But this was, upon reflection, too strenuous a denial.

She made a show of humouring me: 'Well, *I* don't know. To say hello. To see if you're all right. He might be cycling by and just ... drop in. I mean,' she rocked on the balls of her feet so that she loomed over me, 'he's not *banned* or anything, *is* he.'

Beverly said, 'You can't cycle by Deborah's, it's at the bottom.'

I answered her back with 'He does ride across the fields.'

Sarah-Jayne said, 'Oh, he does, does he? He gets everywhere, doesn't he.' And turning on her heel, heading into class, 'How am I ever going to keep track of him?'

★

Later that afternoon, when we were all up from our tables at the sink, filling our water pots for our paintbrushes, she asked me where had he been going when I had flagged him down, and I said he was just riding about.

She asked me, 'Is he saving up for a car? Do you know?' and when I said no, she said, 'He isn't, or you don't know?' but she was already wondering what type he might want and when Susan excitedly suggested red she had to explain that wasn't a type. 'A type is like a Mazda, which is what Max has,' and then she said to everyone, 'We need to know who the friend is.'

Beverly frowned. 'What friend?'

'The friend who got his tape recorder.'

In my mind's eye I saw it sitting there on the kitchen surface in my house.

She asked me, 'Did he mention a friend?'

'Girlfriend,' leered Beverly, to a playful thump from Sarah-Jayne and jeers from the others.

'Can you remember?'

Mandy blared, 'Oh she never forgets anything, she's like an elephant,' and enacted a swaying trunk, which had me thinking, even as I knew I shouldn't, that she should avoid doing impressions of elephants.

Susan asked, 'Did he say he was taking it to a friend?' and Sarah-Jayne said, 'Well, he wasn't taking it to an enemy, was he.'

At the end of the afternoon, we had ten minutes to spare before home time to talk amongst ourselves while Mr Hadleigh went to see a man about a dog, but I volunteered to tidy up the library corner so that I could have some peace. There, straightening the spines, I thought how this was all too much and how they had it all wrong.

Friend. Girlfriend. It was almost funny how wrong they had it. And should I just own up to our having the tape recorder? Because if only I could think, there had to be a way to do it. 'Oh, *that*!' I could say: I could come in tomorrow, and say I'd found it at home, that I'd asked Mum – 'What's this?' – and she'd said, Oh, *that*! And she would have told me that it was Sonny's old tape recorder and he had been going to chuck it away.

And there would be some truth in that, I thought, because his friends wouldn't have wanted it; his friends had discos; they would have no need for some old tape recorder. It was nothing, really, that tape recorder; for me and Mum it was great, but to someone who had all that sort of stuff it would be nothing and he'd have been glad to get it off his hands. He would never have given it to Tracy, because she thought he stank. Well, so did I, if he only knew, but the point was that he didn't know, whereas Tracy wouldn't have spared his feelings. He'd have needed to get shot of that tape recorder: no use to him, lying around taking up space in his lodgings, his Gibb-digs. Mum had done him a favour in taking it. She was good like that with him. Look at how she'd given him coffee. And that lid as an ashtray. I suspected she felt sorry for him, stuck here in the village. Maybe the tape recorder had been in exchange, kind of, for the coffee. Mum might have mentioned the offcut from Mr Watt and Sonny would have realised that we needed second-hand things. But anyway, the point was that my mum wasn't Sonny's friend. Of course she wasn't – she didn't have friends, she didn't like them, didn't believe in them. They were only ever looking out for number one. She wouldn't have a person as a friend even if they tried. He wasn't her friend.

When we got out of school, Susan gazed admiringly into the clear sky and said her Auntie Mary and cousin Diane were coming over for tea but if they were gone before too late, should we go to the park? Should she come and knock for me and Mandy, if she ended up free after tea? I was about to say yes when into my mind's eye came a flash of that bike against our hedge and I said no, unfortunately no, because Mum had told me that I had to help her with some leaflet delivery. And then I fumed all the way home, with a lump in my throat.

Back home, I opened the front door to the scent of newly mown grass, sweet as a clean sheet, and from beyond the kitchen the rhythmic rasp of the mower that she'd have borrowed from Bert, topped by our radio blaring from the windowsill. A song was starting up as I stepped into the hallway and I knew it – deep down and from way back – by the first few notes on the guitar, which were more or less the same, like a hum or the tapping of a fingernail. Then came the voice singing – '*It was the third of June*' – but more like talking, or telling, and behind it the guitar persisting with those same notes, like fast breathing. Something had happened, I remembered: this was a song about something having happened, something bad, something sad, which was why the singer sounded as she did, as if she wanted to tell us but also she didn't, and I remembered just as she said it: Billie Joe McAllister jumped off the Tallahatchie Bridge.

The singer was singing of heat so heavy that even to hear of it in the shade of the hallway I could barely summon the energy to breathe. We used to have summers like that, I thought; we had always had summers like that, before this one. Endless days when the most that Susan and Mandy and I could do was lie around on itchy grass, sucking dry the caustic lollies made from cordial by Mandy's mum in their ice box, the fluorescent orange and deadly dark blackcurrant juice bleeding from the grainy ice onto our lips and tongues.

I went to make my presence known from the back step before escaping up to my room, leaving Mum to her sullen progression back and forth across our dandelion-soured patch of grass and then to the heaving of the mower clattering and bumping, bashing and scraping down the side passage on its return to Bert. I lay on my bed but couldn't rest, my blood leaping time and time again at what I imagined to be the drop of a bike against the hedge or the yapping of Susan's flip-flops as she came up our path on the off chance. Above me on the wall, Tutankhamun looked kind and wise but I was hearing nothing from him, not that I was asking. He was no use: safely dead, what could he know of any of the problems I had?

That night, when I was changing into my nightie, I spotted the first star and contemplated making a wish. Could I wish that the invisible hand of fate give Sarah-Jayne and her family a little push and send them on their way? I knew, really, that my sheer desperation for her to be gone was nothing so pretty as a wish. We didn't go in for wishing, much, at home, only on Christmas Day when we had a chicken and Mum gave me the wish even when she'd won the wishbone because, she said, there was nothing she wanted. Which wasn't true because she was forever saying *What I wouldn't give for* (an automatic washing machine, someone to cook my tea for me).

Privately, I doubted the wishbone was transferable, and anyway I felt obliged to wish as she would have done had she kept it for herself, and despite there being many things for which she declared she would give everything (a proper pair of boots, an electric blanket), I'd heard her say there was only ever one wish worth making and that was for a long and happy life. Which was two, surely, and, as such, pushing your luck.

16

The next day, the building site was deserted but that solved nothing because Sarah-Jayne acted tragic and abandoned all the way across the playground, the others fussing and clucking in her wake. And then at the house when everything was arranged and we were stepping up around the table, she broke away in a performance of frustration and dejection, muttering that she couldn't concentrate, just couldn't do it, wasn't up to it. The others stood awkwardly by, at a loss: Mandy gnawing her lip, Beverly blank-eyed and like a Dalek run down on power, and Susan flustered in her sweetly old-fashioned manner: *Dear-dear, dear-dear.* Caroline remained Sphinx-like, as did I in my own way because I refused to give Sarah-Jayne the attention, to pay court. I was disappointed, too, because I had come to love these sessions, how we were suspended in the soft rain of dust motes, our heads bowed and eyes closed, held by one another in our deep hush.

Sarah-Jayne was pacing tight circles as if digging deep

to retrieve her composure, while I considered speaking up to cut myself loose – *I think I might . . . I just have to –* but then she halted, looked up and around, directly at me, as if I had already spoken. It must have seemed to the others that we exchanged a glance, although actually she had taken me by surprise and I was merely gawping gormlessly back at her. And then as if at what she saw of herself reflected in my eyes, she gathered herself, drew herself up, even gave herself a shake before advancing on the table in a show of resolve: *to work,* said her demeanour; *we're back in business.*

The impression she gave was that she and I were in league, and I couldn't think – not then and there, on my feet – how best to deny it. No need, though, because, it seemed, Mandy could be trusted to do that, weighing in a mere minute later with 'This isn't working,' and I could almost hear the obstinance swelling in her lower lip. The snapping open of Beverly's eyes, too, sensing prey. Distinctly audible, beside me, was Susan's little gasp at the disloyalty. But Sarah-Jayne was unfazed and gave Mandy short shrift: 'We'll just have to try harder, then, won't we.' And that was that: Mandy told.

Susan was left unsettled, though, and took it upon herself at the end of the session, as we tidied up after ourselves, to try to rally us with a lot of excitable chatter about how close we were to success, how impressed she was by the power in the room. And in a way she succeeded, because on our way back to the school building the mood was notably lighter, if not actually about the levitation. As we strode across the hopscotch squares, Sarah-Jayne wanted to know from me if Sonny had had a cup of tea when he was at my house, and although my instinct was to deny it – to deny everything – I told myself to relax because what, really, was a cup of coffee? Especially when it had been in return for tussling with a spider with his bare hands. So I spoke up. 'Coffee.'

'*Coffee*?' Susan would be thinking it a step up from tea, not knowing that we still had a caddy – because for Mum there was no bigger waste of money in the world than tea bags – and opening a jar of Bird's had simply been less bother than making a pot. Then Sarah-Jayne wanted to know how many sugars and I could tell her he'd had three, which was uncontroversial compared to Susan's dad's five and Mandy's grandad's six. 'White or brown?' she asked but before I could reply she pronounced brown the choice for coffee (we didn't have brown) and preferably crunchy brown.

'Like in cafés,' Susan enthused, and mimed licking her fingertip and running it around inside a bowl, and Caroline claimed to have it sometimes sprinkled on porridge.

On those French holidays of hers, probably, I thought. Sometimes Mum and I shared a Russian slice in the café area of the bakery in town and the sugar in there was in lumps: luxurious lumps, for crunching and for stealing in case my luck turned with the Smith's competition.

Then discussion turned to the matter of biscuits, yes or no, but I didn't know, hadn't seen, because I'd left them to it, which I didn't want to say so I went for a simple no, which was probably the truth because Mum always said a little of what you fancy does you good but that biscuits weren't for willy-nilly. In our house they were kept for elevenses and supper. Then Susan made the mistake of saying that men didn't really bother with biscuits, and we all put her right on that because think of Mr Hadleigh, although personally I wasn't sure he quite counted, spending his days in a ladies' world and doing as ladies did. Mandy said there were biscuits that were especially for men, like Rich Tea, and we all contemplated the slap in the face that was the offer of a Rich Tea.

At home our biscuits were fig rolls and Garibaldis because of the fruit, although at Christmas we had brandy snaps, which despite looking weirdly nude as they lay in their plastic tray under the cellophane were delicious and did a good job, too, of sticking to our teeth, of staying around, which, in a way, if you thought about it, made them good value.

As we took our places at our tables, back in class, Sarah-Jayne leaned across and said pleasantly to me, as if we were in the middle of a completely different conversation, 'You *might* have special powers, you know. Sometimes people themselves don't know they have.' And again, 'You *might*,' with an encouraging smile as if she were speaking of a voucher that were I to root around in the bottom of my bag, I might be lucky enough to find.

I did have a special power, sometimes, which was to make Mum let me have my way but think it her own idea. That was how, occasionally, I got to stay up to watch *Steptoe*. Or perhaps it wasn't a special power, because there was a trick to it, to do with hanging around while at the same time lying low: a fine line and a matter of holding my nerve until – hey presto – Mum stepped into the breach to say *Tell you what* . . .

That evening, at about half past eight, I was

considering trying to work a little of that particular magic; it was late to be calling on Susan but a half-hour in the park would be better than nothing and her mum never seemed to mind about bedtimes. My mum, though: if I came out with it and asked, she'd almost certainly say it was too late for a school night. I could aim, though, for *Tell you what, why don't you nip out for half an hour, it's a lovely evening.* I'd need to gaze out at the stubbornly light sky in a way that was appreciative – it's so light! – at the same time as weary (it's so light . . .), and then she might get the idea.

For the time being, though, she was upstairs, doing some hand-washing. If I was lucky enough to get *Tell you what,* she'd want to know that I had everything ready for tomorrow, and it occurred to me that I hadn't handed over a letter from Mr Hadleigh, a reminder of the fete on the Saturday after next and a request to those parents who hadn't yet signed up to help on the various stalls to make their mark in a tick box. Mum had already committed to the tea tent, on an earlier letter, but she still had to sign the slip to say she'd read this one (*Yes, sir, no, sir, three bags full, sir,* she so often grumbled when signing his slips). She couldn't do it now, in her rubber gloves, so instead of taking it up to her I left it where it wouldn't be missed, beside the kettle, but then went upstairs anyway.

I had to talk to her back as she hunched over the washbasin. 'That ber-loody fete,' she said, pausing in her drubbing and leaning heavily onto the rim. 'Fete worse than death.' After a big sigh, she said, 'Thank God Sonny'll be coming along.'

My stomach clenched. '*Now?*'

She blew a strand of hair from her face. '*No,* to the *fete.*'

To the ...?

I couldn't think what she meant.

'Sonny?'

'Yes, you know' – she was giving something a good wringing – 'spider man. Disco king.'

Conscious of my silence, I made myself speak although what I said was so obvious that I felt silly to be saying it. 'But what would he do at the *fete*?'

'Liven it up a bit?' She glanced over her shoulder: 'Pass me that bucket, eh?'

The fete wasn't meant to be lively. It was ... well, it was a fete. 'But the fete's all ... ' In my bewilderment I came up with nothing more than 'Crochet.'

Crocheted coasters. Crocheted tea cosies.

What was wobbling inside me felt like laughter, but wasn't.

'*Bucket*, Deborah.'

I lunged with it as if into a lions' den and she lobbed the wrung item into it, where it landed with a wet smack. 'There's always booze in the tombola. He'll have his eye on that.'

Was she joking? She didn't sound as if she was. I had to press on:

'He can't come to the *fete*.'

She half turned towards me so that she could rear back, mockingly. 'Last I heard, this was a free country.'

'But it's the fete.' I sounded pathetic, she was making me sound pathetic. 'It's for people at school.' And their families. She knew that. She knew it! 'Other people don't come.' We went to the fete to support the school – that was the drill – and not because any of us actually wanted syrupy pink hand lotion made by Teresa Dunkley's mum.

She spun around, holding something aloft, droplets spattering the lino. 'Och, for goodness' sake, Deborah, have a heart, the poor kid's got nowhere to go at weekends.'

Not true, I thought, not true, because he goes to discos.

She was back at the basin and squelching the life out of whatever it was with the heels of her hands, like we did with the Resusci Annie at swimming. 'Are you going to begrudge him a flutter on the raffle and a fairy cake in the tea tent?'

More wringing, a deluge into the dingy suds.

'Probably the biggest excitement he's had in months.' The exertion was making her nose drip; she dabbed with the back of her rubber-gloved wrist. 'And anyway he can make himself useful . . . he can help put that tent up.'

'But the dads do that!' Susan's and Mandy's dads, all jokes and jumpers.

She snatched up the bucket, on her way to the clothes horse. 'Well, he can *help* the dads!' Pushing past me in the doorway she gave me a bug-eyed, accusatory look – *What's your problem?* – then stopped at the top of the stairs to tell me, 'It's not easy being eighteen on your own away from home for the first time. Be charitable.'

She could talk! She was the one who never stopped saying charity begins at home.

'He'll tag along with me.' The words bounced around her in the stairwell. 'He'll be nae bother, he won't be laughing at you gerils if that's what you're worried about.'

And my breath caught in my throat because did she really not realise? She was the one who would be laughed at.

'If I've to stand there with the twinset brigade doling out cornflake cakes,' she said as she thumped down the stairs, 'I could do with a sidekick.'

And fury shot through me, right up from the soles of my feet and fiercer than any I'd known, because why couldn't she be a *proper* mum? Like other people's mums, in cardies, who said *sweetheart* and *you tried your best* and *as long as you're happy*, and who put plasters on grazed knees. Why was I stuck with this mum? No dad, and this mum! Stomping to my room, what came roaring into my mind was *He'd be ashamed of you*. My dad. Yes, he would. Because what he would have wanted when he died, I seethed, more than anything, was that you look after me, properly. But now look.

That night I barely slept. I couldn't have Mum and Sonny turning up together at the fete. She sporting her defiance like some elaborate headdress, and he like a jester scampering around her pleased as Punch and making his stupid remarks. Perhaps I could say, on the day, that I was ill; but then she'd probably go regardless. Other mums talked temperatures – *A hundred and two!* – but we didn't have a thermometer because that was pandering; we didn't even have plasters, because nature should take its course and best left well alone. If I told her I felt sick, she'd probably tell me to fight it and leave me with the bucket. Once she'd committed herself, as she put it, she didn't like to let people down: she was quite prim about that. The problem was that anyone seeing them together would know that he had been to our house more than just the once. And then wonder why I had kept that to myself. It would be pretty clear to everyone where that tape recorder had ended up.

After worrying all weekend, I struggled at school on Monday to concentrate in the fug of disinfectant and Banda fumes, with sunlight knifing through the slats of the blinds and the floorboards lurching and creaking all around me with each and every footfall. Mid morning, when we were up at the drawers to retrieve our maths books, to be left to our own devices while Mr Hadleigh went around the back to whack the boiler with the broom, Sarah-Jayne started on again about Sonny – Sonny-Sonny-Sonny, how he probably thought this and would probably like that – on and on, and then, turning with her book towards her table, dispensing a fond pat to my shoulder.

Slumping back down at my own table, I just said it: 'I think he might be coming to the fete.' My blood flashed through my heart and panic scorched the roots of my hair, but at the same time I didn't care, because it was off my chest and let them have it, let them make of it whatever they would because much better now than on Saturday hence when Mum came swinging through the school gate with that awful Sonny in tow.

Sarah-Jayne's smile dimmed fractionally, and I slapped open my book at the dreaded long division.

'To the fete?' she queried, and I knew without looking back up that she was glancing around the others, her question echoing off their stony faces. 'How come?'

Oh, my thoughts entirely. You tell me!

'With Tracy?' Susan, doing her best to be helpful.

Beverly was blunt: 'He wouldn't come with Tracy.'

'Who else does he know?' Sarah-Jayne was genuinely puzzled.

Beverly lost no time in reminding us: 'Deborah.'

There was a pause before Sarah-Jayne leaned across to my table, to coax it from me: 'Is he coming with *you*?'

I didn't know what to say. After a moment, she gave up on me, sitting back in her chair like a doctor finished peering down my sore throat. But then she said, 'Clever you,' and laid her hand over mine. 'Spooky you,' her voice as warm as the hand, and to the others she announced, 'She's using her powers to make this happen.'

I didn't dare draw breath. I couldn't make head nor tail of this. Was she making fun of me?

'Like she's hypnotising him?' Susan was hopeful; and Mandy with arms outstretched swayed from side to side in her chair to mimic a lumbering stride, intoning, 'I'm going to the fete . . . '

'No,' Susan told her, 'more like in *Bewitched*,' and she whirled to Sarah-Jayne to ask if she'd seen the episode when Queen Victoria had been accidentally magicked up, but in the next breath asked me, 'Does it run in your family? Powers, like with Samantha and her mum.'

Mum and I loved *Bewitched* and Mum's favourite was the mother – 'Loves to throw a spanner in the works, that one' – but whenever Endora was up to her tricks my tummy flipped and stayed flipped until poor Samantha realised and managed to reverse the spell and make everything all right again. Luckily Samantha was quick to catch on and that gleam in her eyes was what made her so pretty, I thought, rather than her cute little nose, as everyone else thought. And everyone else thought her nose did the wiggling, to cast the spells, but if you looked closely it was actually her mouth.

'Your mum *is* funny,' said Mandy, brightly; then to Sarah-Jayne, 'She's Scotch.'

'Yes,' said Susan, 'but only like Ronnie Corbett.'

'What, short?'

'No, a *bit*: just a bit Scotch. You have to listen carefully to hear it; it's kind of underneath.'

Mandy enthused, 'She says "wee",' but then leapt to, 'And she doesn't believe in God.'

I must have said so, I supposed, at some point.

'*My* mum doesn't believe in God,' said Caroline.

'Or the Queen,' Mandy continued.

Beverly objected, 'But we can *see* the Queen, on telly.'

'No,' Susan explained. 'Doesn't believe there should *be* a queen, that anyone *should be* the queen.'

'No one's better than anyone else,' said Mandy, not speaking of her own belief but of my mum's.

'Deborah's mum isn't like a mum,' Susan continued, pleasantly, turning to me to explain herself. 'She lets you eat your tea in front of the telly,' before back to Sarah-Jayne: 'She's not all polite like mums are, if you know what I mean.' She seemed to mean it as a compliment.

We had to eat tea with our plates on our laps because the table was covered with Mr Watt's books. I did know how to set a table: I'd had to learn for my hostess badge.

'She's young.' Caroline spoke up, approvingly.

Sarah-Jayne enthused, 'Oh, I'd love to have a young mum; we could go shopping together. My mum's such an old fogey.'

Peals of laughter: *Fogey*!

'But you've got your sister,' Susan soothed. 'You can go shopping with her.'

Sarah-Jayne removed the lid from her biro with her teeth. 'She's *boring*. Max is the one who's fun. He says we're better off by ourselves, so we escape,' she said, 'and he takes me to lunch and we have wine.'

Wine! Wine!

You have to get used to it, Sarah-Jayne was saying, like with coffee, but Susan was back on track, asking me, 'If it's like a spell – Sonny coming to the fete – what about when he wakes up from it?' She looked around the others. 'Because people do, don't they. They don't stay under a spell for ever. What if he wakes up and he's at the fete? He's going to wonder what he's doing there,' to which Mandy voiced the confusion of a disoriented sleepwalker: 'All these doilies!'

But Sarah-Jayne had an answer to that: 'He'll just think he's there to help her mum,' and she turned to me with a question in her eyes.

Tea tent, I told her.

To the others, she said, 'He'll think he's there to do that. Because he's helpful, remember; remember that spider.' She sighed. 'Anyway, it doesn't matter, because what matters is that we *get him there*. That's all we need, because then' – the tilt of her head and an opening of her arms to present herself in all her glory – 'there's me.'

17

On the news that teatime was a plane crash. Everyone had died. The wreckage was scattered over a scrubby field that could have been anywhere but was in fact a stone's throw from Heathrow. If the air traffic controllers had looked through their window they might have seen what they had missed on their radar screens: the plane stalling and dropping to the ground. It had been left to a couple of boys of my age, out on their bikes, to witness it and to go and find help, knocking at the door of a retired nurse.

On our telly, that wreckage seemed still to be steaming, although that might have been rain. Some bits looked like a plane but most was rubble, as if a giant in a rage had set about it with a hammer. Smithereens was the word. 'Jesus,' breathed Mum, in disbelief. The newsreader was saying there had been a traffic jam of sightseers and Mum whispered to herself, 'What's *wrong* with people?' then got up, switched it off and left the room, stranding me there in the dead air of the living room with only the company of my blood trudging through my veins.

After what I judged to be a respectable interval – as if giving her a head start – I tiptoed in search of her, and from the hallway spied her on the back doorstep, on the far side of the fly curtain, her arms wrapped around herself as if she were cold. It *was* cold – evening chill seeping down the hallway – and I wished she'd shut the door even if that put her on the other side of it. She was the one always going on about keeping the heat in. How long, I wondered, could I stay there in the hallway before she became aware of me? How much closer might I get, if I tried, before she would snap around and see me off with a searing tut? But really I knew not to approach. Standing there, I thought of how she had only ever held me at roadsides, her demand of 'Hand!' like a reprimand, as if I were scheming to give her the slip.

I retreated to my room and found something to occupy me, attempting to draw Tutankhamun using a sketchpad and set of coloured pencils that had been birthday presents, although the yellow pencil was a poor substitute for gold. All in all the portrait attempt was an uncomfortable experience, not just because I was useless at drawing but because the sighing of the pencil nib across paper was unnervingly noisy when there was nothing to hear of Mum. Normally by that point in the evening she would be clattering around in the kitchen, washing up, drying and putting away, without any help from me because *If you want something doing* and then at seven we'd be settling down together to watch *Z Cars*. Was the *Z Cars*-watching still going to happen? If it didn't, I thought, the evening would be like a Sunday but without even the distraction of baths and hairwashes.

I kept an eye on my clock and a few minutes before seven put aside my drawing and went downstairs with a bit of bustle to give due warning. The hallway wasn't cold, so the kitchen door must be shut, and as far as I could tell she wasn't in there. The living room was empty, drowsing in its hues of brown and orange, and I hadn't heard her go upstairs. She might, I thought, be drawn from wherever she was by the theme tune, so I switched on in time for the set to warm up, and my plan worked, because when the music started she did appear (she *had* been upstairs), if reluctantly, refusing to catch my eye and perching on the far end of the settee. But then it didn't go as I had hoped, because I couldn't settle into the story and anyway after mere minutes she rose, saying she was going for a soak. It wasn't a Sunday, so unless she had thought ahead to switch on the tank, there wasn't going to be enough hot water.

I stuck it out with *Z Cars* while above me the presumably tepid water thundered into the tub, but not long after the racket had stopped came the shriek of the doorbell. I held my breath, awaiting instruction from upstairs, but there was nothing, as if she hadn't heard it – unlikely, because, as she often said, that was a ring to wake the dead. Who could it be at this time of the evening? It wasn't pools night: Wednesdays, when Mr French called for the coupon and coins. Fighting shy of the letter-box flap, I trod softly into the hallway and three quarters of the way up the stairs to stage-whisper a plea: 'Mum?'

The response came like a slap, if muffled by the atmospherics of the bathroom: 'I'm not in.' Wilful was how she sounded, I thought, wilfulness being something to which in others – specifically me – she took exception (*Don't be wilful*).

Occasionally we had religious people on the doorstep, dressed as if for a funeral, and Mum had a way of dealing with them: *No thank you*, said with a distinct lack of gratitude and her nose in the air as if she were Rose from *Upstairs, Downstairs*, if Rose were Scottish instead of cockney. She'd come out with it right in the middle of whatever it was they were saying, and shut the door on them. It worked a treat, but I knew there was no way I could do that.

A second scream of the bell was too much and had me dash back down and lunge for the latch; and there on the step was Sonny, all insolence and insinuation. He uttered a reflex *Hi* but had clearly forgotten I existed. Just as clear was his expectation that I would step aside so he could shoulder past. But Mum wasn't in – well, no, she *was* but she'd said she wasn't, which made it doubly important that I didn't yield. With my heart shooting blood into my face, I offered up the lie – she wasn't in – sounding as wobbly as one of the school recorders, and braced for a telltale slosh above us or the grunt of a limb on the surface of the tub.

'Yeah?' He grinned mid chew, and held back on *Where's she gone, then?* saying instead a simple 'Oh well,' and tonguing the gum forward onto his sharp front teeth, playing casual, which we both knew for a lie. *I know your little game*, his look said. He may or may not have known that the cause of the trouble was wallowing directly over our heads. Turning away, he thrust an offering. 'Give her this, then, yeah?' A cassette tape.

As soon as I'd closed the door and was safely alone, I skim-read his scrawl on the label, deciphering 'Hey Girl Don't Bother Me' and 'Meet Me on the Corner' and 'Close to You' and 'Lady Eleanor' and 'Hold Your Head Up'. Mum liked most of those, she'd be pleased with them with the exception of the Carpenters – he'd mis-judged there, I thought, with some satisfaction. I put it down and went upstairs, dithering outside the bathroom door until she detected my presence and called crossly for me to come in. Prim, she'd accuse me: *Good God, it's nothing you haven't already seen.* She said there were no secrets in our house. Such secrets did, though, exist in other people's houses: remarks here and there had me pretty sure that my friends didn't see their mums naked. I was careful to keep from them that in my house it was different. Yet another way in which we were different, added to no dad nor grandparents nor aunts, uncles, cousins, no dinner table, no bedtime stories, no family photos, no Sunday roasts.

She was lying there in the bath with her eyes shut tight and chin tipped to the ceiling, steadfast in submission like when she sunbathed. Above the shallow waterline halfway down her body squatted a mass of hair like a whole other being. She was waiting, pointedly, for what I could tell her, so I came out with it: it was Sonny at the door and he'd brought a tape, which I'd left for her on the room divider. She gave a nod and then, still without opening her eyes, said I should think about getting ready for bed. She didn't really mean it – it was far too early for bed – but she was telling me to keep out of her way. So I crept away again, back to my room. Less like sun-bathing, I decided, and more as if she were wounded. I knew from experience that there was nothing I could do to help, and that it would pass. Give it a couple of days, I reminded myself, and she would be more or less back to normal. I couldn't quite help wondering, though, if she wouldn't be up to the fete.

The next day at school we had visiting musicians, two ladies and two men with mandolins and bongos, and break times were drastically shortened – no more than loo breaks – to give more rehearsal time before the performance of our improvised collective piece to the infants at the end of the day. So, there was little time for any Sonny talk.

Back home, that evening, Mum was quiet and I tried for her sake to be the same but found it hard to stop myself filling the silence, and at teatime when she was dishing up I rattled off some details of the day, to which she half listened and gave half-hearted responses (*That right?*). Then as we were taking our plates to the living room, she raised her voice as if to argue with me: 'You don't get a second chance,' and for an instant I took her to be referring cryptically to the contents of my plate, the 'crispy cheese pancakes' or so claimed the packet although they never were crispy and anyway I wasn't sure I'd want them to be. Then I remembered this was her lament for people killed in accidents. And indeed: 'You're just going about your business, then ...' Furious, desolate, she clicked the fingers of her plate-free hand. 'Pff!'

I didn't know what to say: I did wish people could have a second chance, like Mr Hadleigh's son bouncing off that car; I felt awful that they didn't, and I would have apologised to them if I could.

'Could've been me on that flight,' she said, bitterly, plonking down beside me on the settee and squaring the plate on her knees. 'Could've been you.'

Well, not to nitpick, but we'd never been on a plane nor were we likely to – for this, for once, I was grateful – and anyway if we did we'd go to Spain whereas this one that had crashed had been heading for Brussels.

'Whole families on that flight.' She speared her pancake; it oozed yellow. 'Wee gerils like you,' she accused. 'Three wee sisters. A babby.' She sawed off a forkful, then chewed. 'And no one remembers you. Och, folk *say* they will – they *think* they will – but they don't, because life just' – with her knife she gave a vicious swipe – 'goes on.'

I didn't know what to do or what to say, and wondered distantly if while she was distracted I should take the opportunity to practise squishing peas onto the back of my fork as we were taught in school but which, if she saw, infuriated her (*H-will you just shovel them in!*).

'Some teenage kiddie, taken along with his dad on a business trip for a treat.' She put down her knife and fork. 'All that work,' she said, and I presumed she meant the cooking. 'All that work you put into a kiddie,' said as a matter of fact, as if speaking to someone else, anyone else. 'All that work, just for it to be wasted.' She put the plate aside on the arm of the settee and said not entirely truthfully of the pancakes, 'These are cold in the middle.' She didn't say if I too could discard mine, so I ate dutifully onwards.

After prunes and custard – my least favourite pudding, not counting Lil's gooseberries – I said I was going to the park, and despite the drizzle she raised no objection so

I zipped myself into my anorak and set off. I wasn't in fact heading to the park; I wouldn't risk coming across anyone I knew, although that was unlikely on such a damp, dreary evening. I wasn't heading anywhere in particular. Just away from the house. As I tramped the circuit of church, village green, shop, bus stop, school, and trudged past all the crazy-paved driveways and bay windows, I tried telling myself it was nothing new for her to complain about the work of raising me. In any case, it was something that everyone said, just a joke that all grown-ups made about their children even if it was true too and much more so for my mum because she was alone with me. But whenever my friends' mums and dads said it, there was a punchline, one which my own mum would never say aloud although I imagined Auntie Jeannie, should she ever turn up, might say it for her with a playful chuck of my chin: *Och, but she loves you really!* Mum might never actually say it but it had always been there, or so I'd assumed: like two halves of a heartbeat, any complaint about laundering my smalls followed by an unspoken but-I-love-you-really. That was what I'd always heard, or had thought I'd heard. This time, though, when she'd said over the pancakes about all the work she'd put into me, there had been nothing to follow it but silence.

Adrift, I kicked my way along the choked gutters. Mr Hadleigh always said we were lucky to live somewhere leafy, but Mum said those leaves spend half the year dead in the gutter. My problem was that I had nowhere else to go. Wendy sometimes went to her dad (*A breather for poor old Dilys*), Susan spent some of her holidays with her nan and grandad, and Mandy sometimes stayed with

Susan if her mum and dad had to go somewhere like a wedding or a funeral. For me, there was never anyone but my mum.

The anorak hood amplified my breathing and I could no longer distinguish the drizzle on my face from snot, and then to cap it all, as I turned into the lane behind the church, on the far side of the water that was bubbling from beneath a manhole cover to pulse and shimmer on the asphalt like snakeskin, was the last person I wanted to see. Sarah-Jayne too was in anorak and wellies, yet somehow she was what Mum would call cheek, even if the doughty little black-and-white dog at her side could have come from the Famous Five.

I called across the floodwater that I was out for a walk, as if it was nothing, as if this were normal, although then I made the mistake of adding, 'To see who's around,' when obviously no one was going to be around on an evening as bad as this. And indeed, 'There's no one,' she called back with the habitual cock of her head and glint in her eyes, 'except me,' and she made a little joke of it: that gesture again, an opening of her arms to present herself: *Give us a twirl.*

Holding the dog lead, she was the picture of proficiency. Zipped up and booted, even if in a plain old anorak and wellies, she looked as if she might be on her way to do some showjumping rather than simply walking a dog. I had never come across her outside school; this was new territory. 'Well, and ...' I indicated the dog. Because I was intrigued by that dog. Sarah-Jayne was always so full of everything she had in her life but although she had once said she preferred dogs to cats, she hadn't ever said she *had* one. Together we regarded the animal, who stared politely into the middle distance.

I asked, 'Is he . . . ?' *Yours*.

'She.'

Sorry, 'She.'

'Lucky,' she told me, which I took as a declaration before realising it was the dog's name. And now that the dog had been dignified with a name, an acknowledgement was called for – 'Hello, Lucky!' – although I knew I sounded unconvincing and it got me scant canine regard in return.

'She doesn't bite,' Sarah-Jayne prompted, perhaps a little sarcastically but not unkindly, and thus bidden I made the move, splashed through the flood to venture a stroke of the dog's silky head, which was stoically borne.

'She's actually quite old.' Sarah-Jayne's voice was lowered as if to spare her companion. 'She was my grandma's, but my grandma died, so . . . '

Before I could think better of it I'd said, '*Not* so lucky.' I did mean it, though. No Sunny Smiles for dogs. No Sunny Muzzles.

Sarah-Jayne agreed, fussing the dog's ears: 'Bit of an Orphan Annie, aren't you, huh?' Then with an indulgent roll of her eyes, 'Max is such a meanie, he says she's not a proper dog.'

What was a proper dog? A red setter? Dalmatian? Corgi?

'A gun dog,' she said.

A *gun* . . .

'A Labrador, a retriever – fetches the bird you've shot.'

The bird you've . . . ?

With a playful widening of those too-blue eyes, she said, 'Max loves all that. Shooting. Hunting.'

I thought of the local hunt gathering every Boxing Day on the green and Mum saying they should know better, grown people racing around after some poor wee tod. Something of this must have shown on my face because she sympathised, 'Oh I know,' but added with a smile, 'It's natural for men, though, isn't it. It's an instinct.'

Just as I began to wonder how much longer this chit-chat would have to go on, the drizzle seemed to draw itself up, gather itself to hurl itself down, giving me the perfect excuse. I raised my palms into the downpour to demonstrate defeat – time for me to give up and dash home (in fact I'd be heading to shelter in the lychgate) – but Sarah-Jayne yelled over the roar that I should come to her house and before I knew it she and the dog had made a run for it and I couldn't just turn tail and go, so found myself sprinting to catch up with them.

The three of us went belting up the lane to the vicarage. We clattered to the top of the steps, where Sarah-Jayne opened the vast sleek door with a shove and kick just as I did our tatty, tricky, sticky one at home, and then we were inside, gasping in a cavernous porch with an inner door, the glass in its panes so dense and luminous as to seem molten. She reached around me to pull the main door closed behind us, and a hush clapped over our ears as if we had jumped under water. So, I was inside and there was no going back, not for now.

Following her, I extricated myself from my wellies, conscious of my threadbare socks on the smart black-and-white tiles. From somewhere she had taken a towel and was tussling with Lucky, drying the dog's paws, before she opened the glass door, which with a whumpf released us into the house and enabled the dog to skitter away.

The hallway made a rapt audience for Sarah-Jayne, showering her with glints and gleams as she slinked her way ahead of me over the shiny chequered tiling and beneath a sequence of small chandeliers. From somewhere, a stream of cigarette smoke rode a wave of breathtakingly tangy cooking smells. I hesitated on the doormat before surrendering to the seductive slide of my socks over the tiles, and then momentum carried me past someone who was sitting in a cubbyhole beneath the stairs. Someone with tangerine-lacquered toenails and a phone cord coiled around her fingers and wrist, smoke jetting from her nostrils. She was speaking into the receiver tucked awkwardly between chin and shoulder, her tone faintly disputatious ('Yup, yeah, I know'), and as I passed she glanced up, but blankly. Her eyes, narrowed against her own smoke, were replicas of Sarah-Jayne's, as if I were inside a hall of mirrors.

Sarah-Jayne inhaled ostentatiously and, as she backed into a door, nudging it open with her bottom, she stage-whispered something about being in training for Sonny.

Sonny, I thought, disappointed, and anxious: *Here we go again.*

'But maybe I can get him to give up,' and she wrinkled her nose, before saying of whoever we had just passed, '*She*'s not supposed to smoke *indoors*.' She spun ahead of me into a kitchen, in which was a drizzle of radio voice and that dizzying fragrance everywhere like steam. At home, our kitchen strip lighting came on like a cold shower but here somehow even the lighting was warm. Sarah-Jayne crossed to the fridge, saying something about Max saying a smoker is like an ashtray next to you on the pillow. Taking from the fridge a tin of dog food and holding it aloft, she said with a hitch of her eyebrows, 'Still, I'll just have to get used to it, won't I,' and, 'The things we do for love.'

On the far side of the kitchen were French doors – not the sliding patio doors of Caroline's house but a pair of proper old-fashioned doors – and somewhere beyond them, in what looked from the warmly lit kitchen like darkness, would be that pool. A pool, I thought, in a garden, just outside a house, a home: how magical.

And then from another doorway, one I hadn't even yet registered, emerged a silvery lady. Tinker Bell was my first thought, if admittedly bigger and older and with none of Tinker Bell's malevolence. But definitely something of Tinker Bell in how she came swooping in from thin air and by some light of her own.

'Ah!' she said to Sarah-Jayne.

'Deborah,' said Sarah-Jayne, gesturing at me with the fork with which she was doling muck from the tin of dog food. 'From school.'

As if we were friends.

The lady – her mum, presumably – tilted her head and smiled, a look I knew so well, but in her case, for all its sparkle, there was a softness to it.

'Going to the grammar,' continued Sarah-Jayne.

'Ah!' Up a note, now: this, for her mum, seemed to ring a bell. 'Well, hello, Deborah!'

I heard myself simper in reply.

Sarah-Jayne was telling on the dog: Lucky hadn't been persuaded as far as the park, she complained, even before the rain.

'Oh Lucky,' the mum remonstrated, 'you old fraud, you,' and then she was back to me: 'You'll have to forgive us, Deborah – we're still all over the place after the move.'

It didn't look like that to me.

'And will you be joining us for supper?' The mum glided towards a cooker that was built like a steam engine.

Supper? How late did she think I was staying?

'What are we having?' Sarah-Jayne slammed the fridge door, almost obliterating her mum's answer, 'Spagbol,' which sounded strange and foreign, like Battenberg, and then there was talk of some kind of mousse, Sarah-Jayne asking why they couldn't have that and her mum citing a missing ingredient – another name I didn't recognise – and Sarah-Jayne saying Max should get it when he was next in London. Then she told her mum we were going up to her room – we were? – and her mum said they would be eating at half-seven. Too late for tea, but far too early for supper.

18

Even climbing the stairs in that house was pleasurable, each of my steps sinking slightly to be bounced back to me, as if I were being given a series of leg-ups. In my house we thumped up and down our stairs and they met our tread just as abruptly, ringing hollow, audibly the planks of wood they indeed were beneath the thin brown carpet. These stairs in Sarah-Jayne's house sang softly of our ascent as they aided it, and unbelievably the carpet was a rosy peach. At home we had a single flight, but here was a halfway landing with its own window and more than a simple turn in the staircase, spacious enough to accommodate a table with a potted plant and a whole room, a bathroom. Passing, I glimpsed behind the half-open door a bath which, free-standing and raised on a platform, was more like a statue of a bath. Making my way on upwards, I had the sense that I could wander up and down and around corners, in this house, and through doorways like in a fairy tale. It was, in its own way, something of a palace.

Even her bedroom door was made of elegantly pro-
portioned and cream-painted panels, unlike the scuffed
watery-white board that was my door at home. And
behind the door, a deep hush unfolded to embrace us.
My room at home smelled of emptiness, the air flat and
thick in my throat like cardboard.

True, the posters on Sarah-Jayne's walls struck an
odd note: the faces of Donny Osmond and that man
from Sweet stuck here, there and everywhere over an
old-fashioned wallpaper of cream and pale blue stripes.
I said I liked them, because something had to be said – I
couldn't not mention them, huge and everywhere as they
were – but then actually as I spoke the words I wondered
if there wasn't some truth to them. Because those posters
were certainly something; they had a certain something,
stuck all over those neat polite stripes.

'Do you?' She glanced around at them, doubtful,
then asked me about the posters in my own room, and
although I had no intention of confessing to a poster
of a boy thousands of years dead, I found myself doing
exactly that. She and I were clearly so very different from
each other that there was no point pretending otherwise
and trying to meet halfway. Better just to be who I was,
I thought, and leave her to deal with that.

I'd still ventured no further than the threshold; she
was across the room, framed by the huge window and
somehow lit by it despite the gloom outside. She turned
from the view, surprised at what I was telling her, her
eyes bright and gaze sharp, to ask about my poster:

'The mummy?'

'Well, the mask,' I said.

And with a little laugh she said that yes of course she

had meant the mask, 'not the *actual* . . . ' and a wrinkle of her nose, which in turn made me laugh because, no, not the dried-up old bandaged, brain-drained body.

'That mask,' she enthused, 'is beautiful.'

Yes, I thought, as pleased to hear her say so as if the mask were my very own. On that, then, it seemed, we could agree.

'That mask with the . . . handle?' she faltered 'It isn't a handle, is it, under his chin?' and she put her fist under her own chin. 'But what is it?'

A relief to be able to admit that I myself didn't know.

She shrugged. 'Well, maybe it *is* a handle!' And I agreed maybe it was, probably it was, and then somehow that was funny to the pair of us. If you had a great big heavy gold death mask you probably would need a handle.

She sat down on the bed, patting for me to join her on a shimmery rose-pink satin quilted bedspread that was both delicate and substantial. Mine at home, made of what Mum called candlewick, was mustard-coloured and smelled of dust however much it was aired. Sarah-Jayne had a bedside table – my dream – which was white-painted, its little drawer with a golden handle, and – beyond my wildest dreams – against the far wall was a matching dressing table, with a single mirror rather than the weirdly askance three-winged one of my mum's. She spoke warmly of Tutankhamun, saying that he was very dishy, and I made sure to smile in return although no way would I forget her snide comment about his sandals. She was trying her best to be polite, though, which counted for something. And to my surprise the effort seemed genuine. She was different, here, from in school.

'Very dishy and very suntanned,' she said.

Well, that was gold, I thought, although yes, probably beneath all the gold he was, when he was alive, also very suntanned.

And then: 'Have you seen how tanned Sonny is?' and before I despaired to hear him mentioned again, she said, 'Suntanned Sonny,' and laughed, inadvertently flashing a filling. 'Sonnytanned,' which did strike me as quite funny.

Looking for a distraction from talk of Sonny, I glanced around for the radio to which she was rumoured to listen at night, from which she heard advice to married people who were running off, but there was no sign of it. For something to say, I said she had a lovely room.

She said, 'It's a bit scary at night.'

That was hard to believe. Those soft wallpaper stripes? The bright gold of the dressing table handles, and the steady gaze of its uncomplicated single mirror?

'Shadowy,' she said.

Well, yes, it was big, I thought. That could be scary.

'And those cupboards ...' She indicated a row of white doors in the wall.

Yes, I did understand, because no one wants more doors than necessary in a bedroom; one is enough to worry about.

'But I've got my troll.' She said it so lightly as to make a joke of it, taking from the drawer of the bedside table a squat, bruise-coloured, heavy-featured and tangle-haired creature and waving it at me, dancing it in front of me, showing it up for the grotesque it was. 'Stupid thing,' she allowed, 'but I wouldn't be without him.'

I made sure to look appreciative but my treacherous

thought was *Wait until I tell Susan*. The infants liked trolls. Tracy liked trolls. I knew better than to breathe a word to a living soul about how I played with old make-up bottles.

Sarah-Jayne was saying how she couldn't wait to get married because then she wouldn't be alone at night, even if she had to have someone bristly next to her on the pillow.

'Sideboards,' I said, only then thinking to translate, 'sideburns,' and admitting, 'Me and Mum call them sideboards.'

She glittered, appreciative. 'You're so funny,' she said. 'You two, you and your mum.'

I made sure to smile but again I was uneasy because what did she know – what did she *think* she knew – of my mum? What had she heard? It was impossible to see what was in her eyes.

I should go home, I thought. Or go, anyway.

'And when I'm married, I'm going to have four children.' She presented the wish itself as an achievement and unsure quite how to respond I said, 'Four's loads.' It was three more than me, for starters. And if one was hard work, what was four?

More seriously, she said, 'You know, you and me are the same, really.'

What?

'Being onlies.'

But what of her sister?

She guessed what I was thinking. 'My sister doesn't count. You've seen her.'

What did that mean?

'She's old.' From the bedside drawer she took a hairbrush and began tearing through the troll's lurid mane.

'We never played together. She was already grown up when I was born.' And then she was back to the subject of her own children, how it would be fun to have four, best to have two of each, and she was going to call them Kurt and John-Joe and Vanessa and Melissa.

I wasn't sure I'd ever heard any of those names and my mind was whirring: were they made up? 'Very up to the minute,' was all I could manage, and they did have a ring to them.

'It's best,' she said, 'to start young, having babies, because then you have more in common with them.' The glittery look again. 'Like your mum does with you.'

And again my stomach clenched. The faceted depths of her irises had me think of the fortune-tellers we made at school from folded paper, slotting them over our fingertips to work them open and closed, this way and that to a rising count before, at the chosen number, the contraption was splayed and the truth revealed.

Of her own parents, she said cheerfully, 'No one wants fuddy-duddies like mine.'

That lit-up lady in the kitchen? Sarah-Jayne didn't know how lucky she was. She was insisting, though, that I was the fortunate one. 'Your mum's more like a sister, except nicer than an actual sister,' she said with a roll of her eyes that I took to refer to the person of the tangerine toenails downstairs. I thought, doubtfully, of Mum, back at home, stiff-faced in her dressing gown.

'And if you have them young, you can get your life back when they've gone.' She rose, the bed bouncing in her wake.

Kids, she meant, and this was something that grown-ups said, but it brought back Mum's word, *work*; and at

218

my back, beyond the window, the sopping lanes of my route home opened like a chasm. Sarah-Jayne dipped gracefully onto the dressing table stool and, troll laid aside, her attention given over to the mirror, began brushing her own hair. Her layers made it easy for her; hers wasn't knotty like mine.

'My sister's left it late to start,' she remarked, conversationally. 'Twenty-six and only now getting married.'

This did now have me speak up; because to this, something needed saying:

'*He*'s thirty-five.' I remembered her having told us.

She shot me a look. 'But it doesn't matter for men, does it.'

Doesn't it? I said nothing. My dad could have been older, except he couldn't because by then he would have been dead. My mum had sounded disappointed when she'd once said to me, *We were just a coupla kids*, but all I could think was that if they had waited until they were older then they wouldn't have had me.

Sarah-Jayne turned to me, hairbrush rested in her lap, and her look was searching, and what she was after was a sign in my own eyes that I understood I was about to be given something in confidence and should treat it accordingly.

I sat up straight.

She confided, 'My sister's *had* boyfriends, but that's been the problem.' She was whispering but for once, I could tell, this wasn't for fun, for intrigue; her expression was – I was astounded to see – somewhere between embarrassed and scared. 'Bad boyfriends.'

Bad boyfriends?

Proper dogs, I thought, bad boyfriends.

'Boys,' she confided, 'who didn't want to get married, but just wanted to' – she glanced at the door, wary of being overheard – 'go around planting bombs.'

Bombs?

Bombs planted, birds shot.

'Well, one of them did. Or so we think.'

I sat there with my carefully straight face wondering what on earth this was. More rubbish like Miss Drake and levitation and Sonny?

Plant bombs *where*?

I hardly dared ask: 'IRA?'

'No, not them,' she said, turning back and regarding herself dolefully in the mirror. 'GPO.'

It took me a moment but the GPO tower in London, yes, there *had* been a bomb there: it had been on the news back in the winter and Mum had said you couldn't go anywhere these days although actually that was somewhere we would never have gone.

Sarah-Jayne's sister's boyfriend had planted that bomb?

I whispered back: 'Is he in prison?'

Her reply was barely audible. '*Going* there, we think. He's at court.'

I didn't know what to say to that. I didn't even know what to think. I had an odd sensation of wanting so much to hand this over to Mum while at the same time knowing to keep it from her.

Sarah-Jayne was back to her hair, methodical, bringing up a shine, and sounded bright again when she said, 'So, you can see she's really lucky to have Max,' and via the mirror came one of her smiles. 'He's such a gentleman.' But this business of babies, she said: leaving it too late would mean having to adopt and that just wasn't the same.

'Because they don't match,' she said, 'they don't look like you, those poor babies, and then everyone knows.'

Mr Hadleigh's boy, I thought, although it had been impossible to tell what he looked like under all the cuts and bruises. And those children in the booklets with their sunny smiles: not matching anyone, as if they were offcuts. And in Sarah-Jayne's family, with the startling eyes they shared: for them, there really would be no getting away with it.

'Not that I'd want to start too early, either,' she said. 'No one wants to be one of those teenage mums.'

My mum had been pregnant with me at nineteen. It was a lot for your dad, she'd once said.

'Twenty is good, I reckon,' Sarah-Jayne told herself in the mirror. 'Because that way, you can have a couple of years with your husband when it's just the two of you – marry at eighteen and have some time together, then start your family. Boy first, ideally, because everyone needs a big brother in their life.' She glimmered at me, via the mirror: 'I'll have to settle for a big brother-*in-law*,' and then, startled, cupping an ear, 'Speak of the devil!'

And indeed I could just about hear a man's voice downstairs, carping to someone – 'I've *said* . . .' – before a heavy tread on the stairs.

Sarah-Jayne was up, calling, 'Max!' and bounding onto the landing, leaving me to follow. Together we peered down over the banister onto the man who was trudging up. I saw a profusion of dark wiry hair – like Jason King, I thought, although this hair was depleted at the crown. 'Hiya, handsome,' she called down, striking a pose around the newel post that had me cringe, and anyway, I saw, he wasn't: he wasn't handsome. The problem wasn't so much the small, mean mouth amid the tangled hair of moustache and sideboards, but the eyes, trained on me, aimed at me, bullet-like.

I half expected Sarah-Jayne to exclaim apologetically that she was mistaken ('Oh, sorry, *not* Max') and that this man advancing up the stairs was in fact someone come to do something in the house. But blithely she continued, 'This is Deborah, from school,' to which he said nothing, not that I expected anything because dads never said anything and although he wasn't her dad, he was like a dad, or kind of, a flashy version. Or no, actually, no: he was nothing like a dad, merely as big and old as a dad. Nor – it was obvious – was he kind and funny, as she had so often claimed he was. He looked to be the opposite of everything she had said he was; it was like a trick had been played although on which of us I couldn't at that moment fathom. Whose mistake was this? Which of us was so mistaken? I had an actual physical urge to knock my head with the heel of my palm, as if water were trapped in my ears.

He was going into that halfway bathroom and she called after him, exaggeratedly plaintively, wheedling, 'Maaaax, when are we going to fill the pool? Because Deborah's such a good swimmer,' and grabbed me as if I were some kind of find, drew me into her ridiculous pose in a kind of bolstering. Adding to my mortification, she said, 'She'll show us all up,' which I scrambled to mitigate with a mumble about being unable to dive. But all he said – or growled – as he pulled the door closed behind him was 'Fill it *in*, more like.'

She smirked at me and pronounced him a 'grump' then confided gleefully, 'Just because he can't swim.'

In that, then, he was like my mum. The inability of so many grown-ups to swim was, as much as anything else, what made them seem to be from a different species, and a word of mum's came disloyally to mind: *throwbacks*.

As we returned to her bedroom she said, 'And he's in a bad mood because of you-know-who downstairs: Puff the Magic Dragon,' and that did make me smile, but in truth I was thoroughly unnerved. Even with him behind that bathroom door, and even though he'd shown no sign of wanting to be in the least bothered with us, I was trembling. So, with an appropriate show of reluctance, I told Sarah-Jayne that I should probably be going, making the excuse that Mum would be wondering where I was, although privately I doubted that. I hadn't yet seen the pool, though, she reminded me, and did I still want to? And, actually, despite or perhaps even because of everything, I decided that I did.

Haring downstairs to retrieve our wellies from the porch, we passed the Max-occupied bathroom without a glance, and the cubbyhole beneath the stairs no longer held the sister but along the hallway, shambling in the direction of the kitchen, came a quite old man with a folded newspaper under one arm. The dad, I presumed. He greeted us as if he had been looking for Sarah-Jayne – 'Ah!' – but then said no more and continued on his way. Dashing past, we heard him singing to himself, and Sarah-Jayne – onwards down the hallway – echoed the catchy refrain, '*Istanbul, not Constantinople*', hamming it up, embellishing it with a disco wiggle, then saying to me, 'I bet *that* was *straight* in at number one, a trillion years ago.'

Hilarity swept us down a side passage into the garden

before the shock of being back outside could make itself felt. As we went through the iron gate, the rain seemed somehow particularly wet, and the garden ahead of us was desolate. Sarah-Jayne crunched her way expertly across an expanse of gravel that seemed to swallow my every footfall but we made it onto the lawn, and as we picked up pace over the drenched grass she pointed to the outhouse that I had seen from the back when I'd crawled through the hedge. That, she said, was where you were supposed to change for swimming, and it had its own shower and toilet. To me, the pitched roof and curtained window, grimy though the panes were, made it look like a little house: a person could live in there, I thought. Or a troll. But it was full of junk from the move, she said. 'And Max's stuff: bits for his car; his gun.'

Gun?

'Rabbits.' For shooting them, she meant. '*Wild* ones,' she qualified, 'not *pet* ones,' and I did my best to look appreciative of the distinction although there had been nothing very wild about any rabbit I'd ever seen, and as we sprinted the final stretch to the paved edge of the pool I felt a prickle of horror at the thought of being in the sights of that man.

At the poolside I was taken aback. I'd been prepared for disappointment, but, actually looking right down into it, it was so much worse than I had imagined. It gaped, the opposite of a pool in every way, not just for the want of water but in laying bare how, for all the glitter, a pool was a mere hole in the ground. And this particular hole was deep and disturbingly shelving and had me think of a grave, but somehow even worse was the chrome ladder, ending blind above the drop.

19

As I'd left, she'd said to come back, and she had seemed to mean it; so, when there was no offer on Saturday from Mum of a trip into town, I did. I waited until a respectable hour, eleven-ish, and then, saying only to Mum that I was off out, I went back up to Sarah-Jayne's house, braved the door knocker, and then there she was, as if she had been expecting me.

As she ushered me down the hallway to the stairs I glimpsed through an open door a cream-carpeted room with walls of ice-cream pink, and in it was a thoroughbred of a piano. 'A grand!' I'd seen them on telly but never thought that anyone could have one in their house. Yet there it was, gleaming darkly in the pink room, and arranged across its lid were a lot of silver-framed photos.

'Baby grand,' said Sarah-Jayne. 'It's a baby grand,' with such confidence that I knew there must really be such a thing. I asked her if she could play and she said no but her mum did, a bit, sometimes: the song about a trout, she said as if I should know but I didn't, there being no trouts that I knew of in the charts (... *been through the desert on a trout with no name* ...).

She was impatient for us to be off upstairs but I couldn't tear myself away so she relented, indulged me, wading across the snowy carpet and lifting the lid; it folded back with a surprisingly unsophisticated but satisfying thunk to expose the keyboard. 'We're allowed,' she assured me as she pressed a key. The note seemed to claim all the air in the room to its purpose, ringing clean and strong and true. She did the same with another key and then once more was enough to have me join her, and how thrilling it was to press down with a mere fingertip and make the air around us ignite with sound.

We stood there pressing a random succession of keys and listening intently while staring back at us from the photographs were family members either sovereign or in couples in their silver frames. They looked as if they had permitted the camera's attention rather than submitted to it. The photos were in black-and-white rather than sunburst Kodak colour but the subjects in their suits, or wasp-waist dresses, mink stoles and kitten heels, didn't look old-fashioned so much as if they belonged equally to any era.

Seeing me looking, Sarah-Jayne asked what my dad was like, although she backtracked to check, 'Can I ask that?'

I was glad she had, because no one else ever did, although only then did I realise with a sensation like a misstep off a kerb that I had no answer for her. I had no memory of him, and Mum told me precious little. I fell back on 'kind'; it seemed to me what would be said of someone who had died, even if my mum had never actually said it.

Carefully, she ventured, 'He was very young, wasn't he.'

Who had told her? What had they said?

She spoke gently. 'What did he die of?' and dignified the question by looking long into my eyes. I was taken aback how those intricately whorled irises of hers were suited to solemnity.

This time I did have an answer for her, because Mum had told me. 'Leukaemia.' Would she know what that was? Some people didn't; Susan and Mandy hadn't, although Mandy had thought she did, telling Susan he'd taken too many tablets.

But Sarah-Jayne did know. 'Like in *Love Story*.' She sounded impressed.

Yes, I said, like in *Love Story* or so I'd heard.

'My all-time favourite film. It is *so* sad.' She gave my arm a comforting squeeze. 'Do you have a photo of him in your room?'

I didn't say no, and when she inclined her head to encourage me further I gestured at the photos in front of us to imply that it was a bit like them. He was wearing a suit, I said, and as I said so I burned at the injustice of him being buried away in our kitchen drawer. He should have a silver frame, I thought, and one day I would buy him one.

We left the pink room and were going up the stairs when she asked me how my mum and dad had met. She wanted the story, and I did have something that I could trot out. I told her what I'd been told: in London, I said, where they both working in offices near St Paul's. This she approved of, as I had guessed she would: she said it was romantic and I smiled although I didn't know that it was, actually, because Mum had said something about navvies in Dad's digs having consumption.

Sarah-Jayne said of her own parents, 'Mine are so old they probably met in the war or something.' She shouldn't do them down, I thought, she didn't know how lucky she was. Her mum, pearls skittering over her collarbone, silvery blonde strands slipping from tortoise-shell combs; her dad and *Istanbul, not Constantinople.*

I asked her about her sister. And Max, I meant, but I avoided saying his name, for fear of conjuring him.

She said it for me: 'And Max ?' She was eager to tell, and to take the credit: 'That was *me.*' She raised her eyebrows. 'He always used to talk to me at our club – in Germany – and one day I thought, "You are so nice, there's someone you need to meet!"'

As we went into her room she said how happy she thought they'd be together.

There was something I had been wondering, though: 'Don't they want a place of their own?'

She sat on the bed. 'Oh, but you know us – we're family, we stick together.' Then she was talking about how Max was going to make sure that the new house would be really modern; the kitchen would be completely fitted, which made it sound to me like a corset. 'No more dressers,' she added confoundingly. 'Just a breakfast bar.'

Caroline had one of those, I told her.

She looked pleased to hear it. 'And something else I'd love,' she said, 'is one of those baths that's kind of like a swimming pool.'

As big as?

'You go down into it; it's got some steps.'

I recalled the chrome ladder, and shuddered.

She said she wished Sonny would be building their new house for them, 'But Max would just say he was an oink.'

'An oink?' And this from Mr Piggy-eyes himself.

She laughed, '*Oik! You* know,' so I had to pretend that I did. 'But isn't that what's so loveable about him?' She tipped her head, so that her smile slid like mercury. 'Don't you think?' and before I could consider how best to answer, she said, 'I could be happy with him,' and her gaze drifted to the window. 'He wouldn't be going on at me all the time' – a glance back at me – 'or *any* of the time. I could be myself with him, just sitting up there with him on that scaffolding . . .'

In my mind's eye I saw him there, with everything too big for him but also somehow at the same time him too big for everything.

'So *alive* up there,' she enthused.

Well, he wouldn't be dead up there, would he, I thought. Although (only joking) I could wish.

With a tap to my arm, she said, 'You should levitate him in here for me. Float him from the scaffold through my window.'

Not knowing what to say, I mumbled that it might take some practice. And then we were laughing, and laughing at ourselves laughing, and it was clear that we both understood the levitation was a joke, and that it being a joke was in itself a joke, and it was as if a lid had been lifted, or a window opened, and I could, at last, breathe. Gesturing for me to sit with her, she said she was glad we were going together to the grammar.

'Max said I should go to private school but Dad said look at my sister. That was a convent, though, and Max always says to me they're all nymphos in convents.'

Yes, nymphs, I thought: will-o'-the-wisps, sylphs, little Charlotte in her boater.

'But for once Max didn't win and I'm glad because now I can go with you.' She glittered. 'He says he'll run me there and back every day but I want to get the coach. Imagine – you and me on the coach!' and then I did, I did imagine the pair of us with the village spinning away down the sequence of windows as we left it behind.

'With our books,' she enthused, 'different books for each subject.' I hadn't thought of that, and as she said the words 'French' and 'chemistry', breathy with wonder, I too was awed. 'In our uniforms,' and she leapt up, hands linked behind her head, jacking her hips to one side then the other: 'Sexy schoolgirl, Max says.'

Dropping her arms to her sides with a slap, she mock-despaired, 'Mum's taking me to that outfitter place, this weekend, you know the place,' although I didn't. 'So I'm going to have to stand around for hours in some dingy shop with some old bag saying, "Stand up strr-raight, dair," and calling Mum "modom" and me "mad moselle".' She bounced back onto the bed. 'Problem is, we're running late and there'll probably be nothing left and I'll end up having second-hand stuff with that awful jumble sale smell.' She grimaced, comically, and I obliged her with a laugh. And actually I didn't mind. Because she knew no better, I thought. There was so much she didn't know. And – really, truly, no word of a lie – I felt sorry for her.

20

That evening, I was at the park with Susan and Mandy, and kept to myself – I didn't know why – that I'd spent the day at Sarah-Jayne's. Arriving home late, I was horrified to see Sonny's bike slung against our hedge. What was he doing here? I glanced around to see who else might have spotted it; the road was comprised of closed doors, which lent it a tight-lipped look.

They were in the kitchen and, as had become usual, he was smoking on the back step. Mum called to me, '*There* you are!' annoyed, as if I had been evading her. I knew I would have to show my face. As I came into the kitchen, Sonny was saying to her, 'And you see them queues? Everyone after a gander.' She said nothing to that, so he said, 'Not every day you see wreckage like that.'

'You'd hope,' she muttered.

'Human nature,' he said.

'That's what I'm afraid of,' and then to me she complained, 'Chop chop, missy – time for your bed.' She looked tired. 'I'll get your supper started,' which was my cue to go and change into my nightie.

To my surprise, Sonny turned and addressed me: 'Seen you yesterday coming from the vicarage.'

Mum echoed, 'Vicarage?' and I managed to come up with something about having gone to see Sarah-Jayne, and left it at that. Because so what? Why shouldn't I? Luckily I was already back down the hallway and at the foot of the stairs, far enough away not to have to reply, when she called to me, 'Got pally, you two, eh?'

Pally. My gut tightened. *You know nothing.* I'd started on up the stairs when I heard him asking her, 'So, who's the dolly bird, up there?' to which she said, 'Och, that's the sister,' then, 'Well, I *say* "sister",' and, 'That's what Peggy Peters told me,' before going off about Lorna having been no end of trouble, 'Running around with types.'

She didn't know the half of it. I knew what types. Bombing types. I went a step or two further up the stairs but was listening hard; and a few more steps up, I stopped and perched on a stair four or five below the landing, keen to hear what she thought she knew.

'But now there's a big white wedding planned, so Peggy says.' *H-white h-wedding.* 'A decade late, though, eh? Bet the auld folk leapt at him. Get her off their hands. Loose ends tied up. You seen him, though? Flash Harry. Wouldn't trust him as far as I could throw him.'

The Max man: on him, then, we could agree.

Sonny said, 'Geezer with the Maz?'

The car.

Mum didn't respond to that – probably she didn't know what a Maz was – but instead said, 'I feel for them, the auld folks. Parading themselves as the parents when they'll know everyone sees the truth of it. And you wonder when the wee 'un herself is going to put two and two together.' There was some kitchen clatter. 'Pitiful, though, eh – playing happy families, splashing around in that pool up there when everyone can see right through you.'

That wasn't right, I thought, hotly, and she knew it. They weren't splashing about in their pool and she knew it, because I'd told her; I was the one who'd told her about that pool, and I'd said how it was drained, derelict, littered with leaves. But when did she ever listen? Really listen. To me, or to anyone. *Why don't you stop talking for once*, I fumed, *and listen*. She only ever heard what she wanted to hear, which was whatever she could fit into the story she wanted to tell, yet she was the one who always said people say all sorts. Well, it was *she* who said all sorts, and more often than not about me. *Och, missy here* ... But now here she was, dishing up this rubbish on Sarah-Jayne's family to sound big.

She yelled, 'Get a move on!' and from the volume it was obvious that she assumed I was up in my room.

Parading themselves, I seethed. Parading themselves as parents, pretending to be good parents when their daughter had in fact been running around with bombers (*Don't you show me up, don't you dare*). Was that what Mrs Peters had said about them? But Mrs Peters wore her hair in a bun, she was a cut above, and whatever it was that she had said to Mum, I didn't think she would have said they were parading. That, I suspected, was Mum's word. And it was so unfair. I'd been there, I'd seen how they were, *Hello, darling*, and *Istanbul, not Constantinople*.

They were happy. Well, with the exception of the Max man, but despite whatever Sarah-Jayne said he wasn't really family. They were a lot happier in that house, I thought with fury, than we were in ours.

Change the record. Because to Mum, a few people were all right – soap and water, a cut above, good to us – but so many, many more were do-gooders and chummy and rough-and-ready and hippies and tartars and common and boffins and gypsies and sheep. *Change the record.* And anyway, *You can talk*, I thought: you, with *that* down there on your kitchen doorstep.

I changed into my nightie, then went back down for my supper; she had already reached the stage of smearing the milk into the Ovaltine ash. With a glance at me she said, 'Oh, at last,' but she was still talking to him at the same time:

'And I'd like to have seen *me* do that. Talk about different worlds, eh? You run around with a bad crowd, you get yourself into trouble but then have your ma and pa pick up the pieces. Take you in, cover up for you. That type always land on their feet, though, don't they. Sail on through life. Don't care what they leave behind. Always someone else's problem. Someone else tidying up behind them.' She took the pan to the sink. 'Mind you,' she said, over the hiss of water into the pan, 'clever move. Get your folks to do all the work for you.'

It was probably the word *work* that did it. I took my Ovaltine through to the living room, along with what the packet optimistically termed a fruited shortcake, and as I went I felt their eyes bore into the back of my head even as I knew they didn't spare me a second glance. I sat down on the settee and let it sink in. I wouldn't say I was surprised, particularly. It made as much sense as anything else in my world at that time.

I did the maths. Sarah-Jayne's Lorna was twenty-six and even I could stretch to subtracting ten from twenty-six. *Pff! You never get your life back after that.* But Lorna had. From what I had seen, she was doing fine for a life, lolling around in the cubbyhole in that sparkling hallway, about to be fed with fabulously fragranced cooking but in the meantime threading the phone cord around tangerine-nailed fingers and, through a throatful of smoke, confiding in some friend. And she was going to marry that Max in a big white wedding and live in a house with a breakfast bar and ride around in a Maz. And all this she could do because her own parents had done the work of raising Sarah-Jayne. They had furnished that lovely bedroom and treated her to weekly copies of *Jackie* and let her talk to pool boys and taught her to walk a dog.

Before then, I hadn't known that a subterfuge of such magnitude could be done. If I was at all surprised, it was at how you might claim whatever you liked about your life, tell whatever story you liked, and no one would say a word.

At least on the face of it and for the time being you could get away with it.

I did then consider that it might not be true, or only partly true, distorted like hieroglyphics sometimes were, but I didn't think so. This wasn't thousands of years ago. Mum knew because Peggy Peters had told her. And Peggy Peters knew because somehow, gently, she always knew everything about everyone.

And anyway I just knew. Sitting there, blowing on the Ovaltine, fearful of it forming a skin, I had to admit to myself that I had already known. I hadn't realised that I'd known – but deep in my bones, I had. And now, I thought, it was like when Neil Hammond had brought into school a pair of 3D specs from a cereal packet and we had all had a go, and through those lenses everything was the same but different, and different but the same. Actually, no, I thought, there was one big surprise: that Peggy Peters had told my mum. I could picture how she'd done it, though: with a rueful grimace, a show of sympathy for an accident of birth like a birthmark so placed that the bearer wouldn't know unless told of it.

Mum had handed this news over to Sonny through the fly curtain and also, by accident, to me. *No secrets in this house.*

Come to think of it, there was an even bigger surprise: that everyone knew when Sarah-Jayne herself didn't. And she definitely didn't – of that, I had no doubt. *No one wants to be one of those teenage mums.* The thought of her swinging around that house, so pleased with herself, not a care in the world, brought tears muscling in on my throat. Which was in itself something of a surprise.

I sat there in the Ovaltine stench while on the other side of the door in the hallway Sonny took his leave, he and Mum stepping around each other, voices rising and falling, and I knew she'd be saying I'd better be getting missy away to her bed as if I wasn't nearly eleven and could do that for myself. I'd never had bedtime stories but for a time – years and years back – I'd been scared at night and she had sat on the edge of my bed as if waiting for something before giving up and saying, with

236

a squeeze of my blanketed knee, 'Right, I'm off, I'm bone tired.'

I sat looking down into my Ovaltine, at the skin forming and tightening. Across the village, Sarah-Jayne was where I'd left her, scampering up and down that staircase and along the hallway, and bouncing on her bed, and such thoughts of her brought to mind a spinning top: how, set spinning, it takes up the spin for its own and makes the most of it, makes magic from it, locking itself into a whirl so hard and fast that in no time it seems not to move at all, and looks as if it will go on for ever even as it's on the brink of a crash.

As soon as Mum had shut the door on Sonny, she was going to come marching across Mr Watt's offcut and poke her nose into my mug to see that I'd failed to make a start on it. *You turning your nose up at this now?* Well, yes, actually: I supposed I was. I couldn't drink it. I just couldn't. I'd had so many years of it and had hated every single mouthful. No more, I thought. Enough was enough.

21

Lying awake, that night, I resolved that it would make no difference who Sarah-Jayne's parents were or weren't. She was who she was. *Your secret is safe with me*, I beamed across the village on thought waves to her. Not that she knew it was a secret. But then that only made it even more important that it was safe.

The next morning, I told Mum I was off to the park. In fact, I was heading for the vicarage. Sarah-Jayne and I would be doing our usual, I thought – because that was how I thought of it, already, our hanging around in her lovely house, chit-chatting. That was what we did, now. I wouldn't have said that we were friends, exactly, because it wasn't that simple. Somehow, I felt, it was more than that.

Not until I was on my way there did I wonder whether the Max man was in on the secret. He might not be, I supposed: he'd met Lorna only in the last few years. He wouldn't necessarily know.

As chance would have it, he was the one to answer the

door, and as he towered over me, darkening the doorway, peering down as if I were some lower life form that had rolled up on their doorstep, I understood that nothing ever got past him. And possibly, deep down, I understood that was precisely why he was there.

It took everything in me to endure his hostile gaze. Merely to stand there needed a concerted effort, like in the pool when trying to swim underwater, to have the surface close over my head. He said, 'Diane, isn't it?' and I didn't correct him because I knew he'd made the mistake on purpose; and although there could be no other reason for me to be there he waited pointedly for me to ask, 'Is Sarah-Jayne in, please?'

To which he sighed softly but heavily – more of a groan, as if he were having a difficult time on the toilet – and then gave me a grudging, doubtful 'I *think* so.' But then, as if prodded in the back, he relinquished the space, because there she was, coming to the rescue, skidding to a stop in her socks. 'Step aside, big man,' she crowed to him, and greeted me with, 'Helloooo!'

As I shucked off my wellies and she went ahead of me down the hallway, I marvelled at how differently she moved here in her own home from at school. There was none of the prowling, the rolling of her hips that dragged everyone's gaze with her. On our way up the stairs she said cheerfully, 'You mustn't worry about him,' although I hadn't said a word. She'd noticed, which had me feeling grateful but exposed. I wished she hadn't seen me there, tongue-tied; I wished she'd seen me braver. 'He's protective of me,' she said. 'It's just if he doesn't know someone.'

But I'm me, I thought. Not someone. And I'm only a girl.

'That's just men, isn't it,' she said. 'Protective. It's natural, it's their instinct,' and with a squeeze of my arm, 'Luckily for us.'

She always spoke of his arrival in the life of her family as a stroke of luck, but so far nothing I had seen of him seemed to fit with that. And I realised that so often what she said seemed to hang in the air unconnected to anything, like radio interference.

It was a relief to be up the stairs beyond his reach but then I forgot all about him because ahead of us, on the main landing, stowed rather haphazardly in a corner, was a doll's house. Or was it? It was on a scale so big that it almost disqualified itself; it denied the fundamental principle of a doll's house, made a mockery of being a miniature. Sarah-Jayne was saying something about it having been moved to safety because of a leak in the outhouse roof. She didn't sound interested – for her, it was merely in the way – and then she was dismissing it as having been her mum's ('It's ancient, it's probably about a hundred years old or something'). She could see I was entranced, though. Opening its façade for me, she warned me not to expect much: everything was jumbled up, she said, and a fair few of the contents still in a box somewhere in the outhouse. 'Bits and pieces,' she said, 'like teapots,' and, true, in every one of its rooms the furnishings were upended and strewn around as if there had been a calamity, a ransacking. Toppled and heaped were armchairs, benches, tables, beds, lamps, a piano, and a statuesque bath like the one I had glimpsed in this very house.

I got cautiously to my knees as if the house might take fright at my approach, but my gaze raced everywhere at once, gleeful and greedy, in pursuit of each and every detail. A dog basket, a tennis racket, a rifle, a soap dish the size of my little fingernail, a dustpan and brush, a boxed board game, candlesticks, books, an iron, a chopping board, a rolling pin, a swede. Nothing had been overlooked, nothing was too humdrum or mundane. My eye anticipated every detail in the instant that the house offered it up. My attention scrambled through the rooms, almost tripping over itself to race ahead of the house in seeking various items. There were objects I didn't even know I was looking for but then there they were (a jewellery box) and I felt as if I myself had magicked them up. It was as if the house was playing tricks on me, but with my complicity: it was a bit like being tickled.

All the paraphernalia of domestic life was reflected back at me, even if it was nothing like my own because at home we had no hatstand, piano stool, needlework basket. It was all as steady as a ticking clock, all correct, very proper, every eventuality catered for. Nothing making a bid for attention but just standing (or in fact mostly lying) quietly to attention. Mustered, I thought, was the word.

The house as a whole I recognised in some fundamental sense although it was unlike any I had ever known with the exception perhaps of the one I was at that moment inside. Despite the mayhem in the rooms, I could make perfect sense of them from attic rooms to scullery, from nursery to parlour. I knew all this from *Upstairs, Downstairs* and *Peter Pan*. I knew that if I could somehow be conjured into there, I'd be gazing through tall windows over the moonlit, fog-enrobed rooftops of London.

Sarah-Jayne knelt down beside me and said I should feel free to touch but then as soon as I did, reaching inside to right the piano, she sounded bored. 'We're not going to play with it, are we?' she despaired. 'What are you supposed to do with it all?'

I knew what she meant, I could see how it left her cold: those gloomy, staid rooms with their antimacassars (the word came to me from nowhere). A distinct lack of Sweet posters on those walls. For a wild moment, I came close to suggesting she give it to me. I wouldn't have meant it in all seriousness – I did know this was an heirloom – but still in a fairy-tale world she might have said yes. *This old thing!* She might have said it was clutter and they'd done with it and needed to have a clear-out now they were on the move again, and I'd be doing them a favour. She could have said, *It's yours*, and then I'd be taking it away to safety.

She was so close to me that the scent of her shampoo hummed in my nose. What did it mean that she was, in truth, Lorna's daughter? Even remembering the fact of it had me feel as if I were sneaking a sideways glance at her, to try to catch her out. But it made no difference who had given birth to her, I told myself: she was who she was. And here she was, beside me on the landing, beneath the skylight which gave a glow to her forearms so that I had the oddest urge to lay my fingertips on that cool skin and press, to test for give and to make a mark.

To break what had become a small silence, I sat back on my heels and observed how there was no doll's house in the nursery; I guessed she'd like that, and she did. 'Yeah,' she said, 'and you know what else this house could do with? A pool.' We could get a bowl, she said, and I said we should use a ruler for the diving board, and then we were laughing at the absurdity of it, the notion that a volume of water was enough to make a pool.

Amid all the jumbled furnishings there were a few figures: a man in a brown suit, prostrate in the parlour; a tweedy woman with hair that looked to have been made from cotton wool, supine, gawping at the cellar ceiling. *Aftermath* was the word I couldn't quite banish from my mind. I took hold of them, to find they weren't as realistic as everything else in the house; they were interlopers from a different workshop, rudimentary beneath their stiff clothing, a peg-like construction that meant at least that the woman didn't have to worry about hairy legs.

'Who are these?'

She took the man from me, and held him up to disparage him. 'Well, this is the mister of the house,' she said vaguely, sounding unconvinced. 'He's ... ' she was inviting a contribution although she went first, 'Alfred.'

'Archibald,' was my offering, and she seemed to think I'd gone one better. So, Archibald he was.

And then she made a grab for the woman. 'And this ... '

'Beryl?' I ventured

A shriek of laughter. 'Madge?'

Done, as far I was concerned: 'Oh, definitely Madge.'

'Or Gladys,' and yes Gladys was good, but, 'Enid?'

A squeal of delight, and Enid she was. 'Meet Archibald and Enid,' she proclaimed, but then bashed the two figures together and ground them into each other, saying in a high, strangulated voice which was supposed to be Enid's, 'Oh get off, you beast!'

And I laughed in spite of myself, because the voice

was funny, but then she chucked them back into the house with a contempt that had me flinch, and said, 'She's frigid.'

Well, she looked more than warm enough to me, in that tweedy regalia.

Getting to her feet, she said, 'Max always says "You women are your own worst enemies",' and now I laughed for the sake of politeness, because it sounded as if it was supposed be funny, although I couldn't see it and anyway I couldn't care less what that man said. Then she said, 'Imagine if a spider got in there! They could saddle it up and ride it around.'

'Don't,' was all I could manage, panicked by my own panic, the swiftness of its descent and its magnitude.

She nudged me, to bring me back to myself: 'Don't worry! Because remember – Sonny to the rescue!' And with that, she proposed we go to the outhouse to see if we could find the other stuff, the bits and pieces and the other figures. 'We've got nothing else to do,' she said, somehow making it into a badge of honour: we'd rattle around and do as we damn well pleased.

If it had sounded a breeze, the reality as we stood in the doorway of the outhouse was sobering. In front of us were boxes piled high and higgledy-piggledy and in every state of disrepair. The opposite of how things were in the vicarage. In its disarray it resembled the interior of the doll's house, but everything in the doll's house was clean, only needing some tidying, whereas the jumble in here was filthy. The top flap of the grimy window was rusted open and swaying dejectedly in the draught were cobwebs nothing like the delicate ice-white lattices of storybook illustrations but more the stuff of dungeons, fabric-thick swathes freighted with grime. They looked to have been abandoned by the spiders themselves although I wasn't going to bank on that.

Everything inside me insisted that we didn't take so much as a step in there, that it wasn't safe. Even Sarah-Jayne was taken aback. 'God,' she murmured, faced with the scale of our task, but then turned it into a challenge: 'Right . . . '

'Let's leave it,' I said, so lightly as to imply that it was beneath us to be rummaging around in there. Peg-leg Enid and Archibald would just have to make do without a teapot.

My reticence only increased her resolve, though: 'No, no, it'll take two ticks.'

I hung back, silently sifting objections and excuses as she ploughed forward, poking about in various boxes and crates. And then, conversationally, over her shoulder, 'Max keeps his magazines somewhere in here.'

Horse and Hound, I thought. He liked hunting. I'd seen *Horse and Hound* in Smith's.

'Nude ladies,' she said cheerfully, peering into an old straw bag. 'A secret stash.' She caught my gaze and rolled her eyes, smug and scornful, *Boys will be boys*, and I knew to rustle up something similar in return. But nude ladies in magazines? Why? Was this something like Sunny Smiles? Was there some kind of trading? And *how* would they be nude in magazines? *Captured* was the word that came to mind, as I'd seen in captions: *A barn owl captured in flight at dusk*. And were they lined up? Like in our Brownie pack photos – *Cheeeeese!* – but without their clothes on? Or were they parading, as in

245

Miss World? For a second I wondered if she had actually meant Miss World: no clothes but swimming costumes instead, with a sash. She had said nude, though, and she knew what that meant: Sarah-Jayne wasn't someone to make a mistake about that.

She was saying, 'It is a bit weird when you first see them.'

In the corner of my eye she picked up a bicycle pump, scrutinised it, chucked it further back into the jumble. Acting nonchalant, it seemed to me.

'But you just kind of have to keep on looking,' she said. 'You can't not look.'

I was making sure not to look at *her*, wishing she'd stop; if I didn't look at her and said nothing back, then maybe she'd dry up. But on she went, like that fabled radio of hers that chuntered on into the dark:

'It's like when you overhear something – and you know you shouldn't, but you can't stop listening. You know what I mean?'

Well, little did she know just how recently I had experienced exactly that. Or did she perhaps somehow know? Was that what this was about?

'But then, when you're looking, it gets more normal, and really' – she turned around to face me, reclined a little against a tower of boxes – 'it *is* normal, isn't it. Max says people lie all the time about everything, pretending they're polite – all *la-di-dah* and *hell-air-how-do-you-do* – but really everyone's thinking all the time about everyone else without their clothes on.' She smiled that smile. 'That's just human nature.'

My idea of hell, I thought. At church there was a very old, faded painting on the wall that Mr Hadleigh said was of people going to hell. If you looked closely you could see bare bottoms; the people were being bared, it seemed, as they went there. 'Just ordinary people,' Mr Hadleigh had said of them as if that were a good thing: 'Butcher, baker, candlestick maker.'

But *was* everyone always thinking about everyone else being bare? *I* wasn't. Was *she*? She, who wrapped her towel so tightly around her in the changing rooms.

'Men, I mean,' she corrected herself. 'Boys. Not *every-*one.' She laughed. 'Oh, and not *old* men, obviously, like my dad or Mr Hadleigh.'

That was something of a relief; Mrs Hadleigh's pyjamas came to mind.

'*They*'re just thinking about ... ' She cast around, waving a hand as if conducting me, and I came up with 'Biscuits.'

Yes, that was more like it, and now we could laugh together. Inside, though, I was shaking, because Sonny was a man or a boy – I wasn't sure which – and did that mean he was thinking about everyone being nude? In our house?

Sarah-Jayne, now on tiptoe to delve into a box, went on, 'They have urges – men and boys. They just do. It's natural. They can't help themselves. It's awful for them, really, if you think about it.' She flashed me one of her smiles. 'But, well, we love them really, don't we.'

Mum had said that Sonny needed help, *poor kid*, but that had seemed to be about him being far away from home.

'Anyway,' Sarah-Jayne sighed, 'those magazines are going to be well hidden; I don't think we're going to find them.'

I had to get out of there, I thought, and turned towards the door in the instant she crowed jubilantly, '*This*, though, is Max's!' which had me turn back to be confronted by the barrel of a rifle, and then my hands were up and I'd slammed back into the workbench, my heart at a stop as if I had actually been shot.

She sighed, bored, as she lowered it: 'Oh, I know, I know,' and rolling her eyes she recited, '"Never point a gun at anyone." That's what Max always says.'

My heart was groping in my chest for a breath.

'Although *he* does,' she added. 'Messing about, trying to make me scared.' A deliberately flat-eyed smile. 'He's so funny like that.'

I'd caught myself wrongly on the bench and my tail-bone was blaring pain. 'Does it work?' I asked of the gun.

She shrugged. 'Of course it works.' She'd misunder-stood: I was asking if it was loaded.

Rabbits, birds.

But she'd already lost interest, propped it against the wall: like the bicycle pump, it was discarded.

Suddenly I was overwhelmed by weariness and my back was throbbing and how had any of this happened – how had I got myself in here? This hellhole of spiders and nudes and guns, when, unimaginably, a mere few steps away across the gravel was that lovely house with its pink room and peachy stairs.

I had to get out. I had to go back.

Speak up, Mum would say. Stand up for yourself.

Boo, goose.

'Let's go,' I managed, hoping I'd sounded casual, contriving to look bored as if the outhouse had failed to be sufficiently amusing for us. To back it up, I added,

248

'There might be spiders in here,' although I was beginning to think they might be the least of my problems.

She came over, wiping her hands down her jeans, 'Oh, you and your spiders,' and with a playful lunge teasingly ran her fingertips up my arm, and what should have been a laugh came out as a scream. I snatched it back into a show of mortification, pressing my palms to my chest to steady my heart, *Silly me!* and she, having screamed at my scream, as spooked as I was, clutched my arm, in stitches. And so we clung to each other, grabbing each other and fending each other off all at once.

And that was when we heard footsteps outside on the gravel. Tightening her grip, Sarah-Jayne urged, 'Listen.' Our screams had done it; someone had been alerted to our presence. So, now we had an actual foe, and, from the sounds of it, a big one, heavy-footed, and somehow that was even funnier: our helplessness, trapped in there, was ridiculous, and hilarious, and then before I knew it she'd relinquished me for the gun and whirled to aim at the door as it opened and there in the line of fire was the man, Max. He sucked in all the air then bawled it back out of that redly wet hair-fringed mouth: 'PUT THAT DOWN!'

She didn't so much as lower it. Instead, as if she had been for waiting for this, she did a coquettish act of being offended, pouting, head cocked, as she appealed, 'Ma-ax!'

No, I wanted to yell, but she had a gun and although it wasn't aimed at me nothing now would induce me to make a sound. He, though, pinioned her with his tiny, ferocious eyes and roared again, 'PUT IT DOWN!'

But he, too, I could see, was terrified, which, peculiarly, made him in turn even more terrifying. And then came a complication too far: a voice from the house, reedy, oblivious, 'Max! Max?'

Sarah-Jayne gave no sign of hearing it; everything of her was trained on him. She parodied contrition, with a bulbous bottom lip and hangdog eyes as she told him, sing-song, 'I'm not gonna *hurt* you!' *Diddums*. 'We're just having *fun*!'

My skin crawled.

Again, from somewhere near the house: 'Max?' It was Lorna, in all innocence. Her call registered in his eyes on a purely animal level, as a pulse, a beat. But from Sarah-Jayne there was still no sign that she had heard. It took all she had to hold – to aim – that gun.

I knew I should say something. Just *Sarah-Jayne*, just a reminder, to bring her back down to earth. I was the one to do it, standing to the side as I was, not locked into this, whatever it was, as they both were.

But he was the one to break the spell, hissing, '*That* is *not* for *kids*,' at which she shrieked with delight as if this were a joke between them and then did lower the rifle, a little, if only to get a clearer look at him.

She asked him, 'Who are you calling a kid?'

And then as I stood there as dumb as if a hand were over my mouth he took a chance, lunged, made a grab for the gun, but she was quicker, jerking it free of his reach in an alarming arc. I thought I had screamed but neither of them had reacted and there was nothing of any scream left in the air.

'*Max*,' she remonstrated. *Hands off*. 'Uh-uh.' *No you don't*.

I saw that she was shaking, though, perhaps from the weight of the weapon, perhaps from the chill.

Outside were footsteps on the gravel. Max chanced a glance at the grimy window and it was a hunted look; he was cornered. He didn't want Lorna in here: she was no part of this. To Sarah-Jayne, he spat the words, 'Put that back and get yourself into the house.'

'Or what?' She tilted her chin in defiance but he'd already gone, banging back through the door; and outside, in a different incarnation, he was heading off Lorna, his actual words inaudible to us but the tone recognisably conciliatory. He gave a good act of being surprised, as if they'd bumped into each other. Hell-air, I thought, la-di-dah, and I'd have given anything to join them, crunching about on the gravel and making pleas-antries. Outside, under the open sky. Safety in numbers. I trusted Sarah-Jayne even less than I did him. He was, after all, a grown-up. And she had a gun. The inside of my head was thumping and hissing like an untuned radio and I didn't dare look at her.

Then a lift in Lorna's tone indicated she was off back to the house; in my mind's eye, those orange toenails were jaunty among the gravel stones. Sarah-Jayne and I listened hard for Max's intention, for any clue as to what we might still be in for. His footsteps were slower than hers, with none of her sprightliness, but they too were diminishing: he was moving away, although not, it seemed, with her in the direction of the house.

So we weren't yet out of the woods.

There was a cautious quality to his tread – I had the sense he was still under observation, if only disinterest-edly, from the house, and that was probably enough, would at least bring us time. We were probably safe for now. He wasn't, it seemed, going to come back through that door just now. Mercifully, he was moving away from us, if slowly, and, I judged, in the direction of the pool.

After a dozen or so of his paces she put the gun down. She didn't, though, meet my eye. Her cheeks were mottled as if she'd been smacked in the face, and there was a trace, I thought, of the half-smile and the tilt of the head but she held herself unnervingly still, a sign for me to look away, to spare her. I thought of Mr Hadleigh's run-over boy, how he'd stared us down, daring us to pity him.

Outside was the lumbering man-tread. To break the excruciating silence between us, to try to make light of it, I reached past her and snatched up the rifle, hefted it inexpertly to the window, in which I saw a smear – unmistakably him – beside the pool, on the edge of the deep end. And maybe for a fraction of a second I did want to bring him down, to swat him from the face of the earth, but really, honestly, it was just a joke, it was merely for a moment of levity that I poked the barrel of that gun through the open flap as if taking aim; and everything would have been fine had she not recovered herself, rebounded, springing behind me like a cork released from a bottle and letting rip through the open flap a gleeful, ear-splitting, startling 'MAX!' so that as if at her command he spun around to find himself in my sights.

22

Back at home that afternoon I acted as if I'd been nowhere in particular and up to nothing, in terror that Sarah-Jayne had told on me and any minute her parents would be banging on our door. It was true I'd pulled the trigger – but that gun should never have been loaded. The kickback had been as much of a shock as the blast and for a run of heartbeats I'd known nothing but the pain in my shoulder and the ringing in my ears, until Sarah-Jayne had relieved me of the gun and told me, calmly, to go. She'd be the one best to face her family, she meant – sprinting as they undoubtedly already were across the gravel, the grass. And I knew exactly how to make myself scarce at speed and unseen: around the back of the outhouse, through the gap in the hedge.

I had a dreadful night but morning held the promise of Sarah-Jayne smirking across the classroom and whispering to me at break time of the trouble she was in for having given her family such a fright. We might even dare to laugh together, I thought, about how close we'd come to disaster. But I arrived at school to find her absent. For the others, she was simply sick, soon to be back, but I had no idea what to make of that empty chair of hers and I saw from Mr Hadleigh's frown when he took the register that he was none the wiser.

It was Mum who told me. She was unpacking shopping when I got home; she'd had to resort to the local shop, which made her cross. 'You heard?' She slammed a tin of ravioli into the cupboard. 'Accident at the vicarage,' she said into its depths, shunting tins, taking stock. 'Flash Harry.'

The brooding bulk last glimpsed on the poolside the instant the rifle had leapt to life and booted me back from the window.

Closing the cupboard, she turned to me. 'Wee 'un took a pot shot at him, so Peggy says. Can you believe that?' She was aghast: 'Can you believe a wee 'un running around up there with a gun?'

A lucky escape for him, because that bullet had gone anywhere but the direction of my aim.

She shrugged. 'And he dodged, I guess. Ducked. Slipped. Smack down into that pool and cracked his head clean open.'

The next morning, then Wednesday and Thursday, she tried to persuade me back to school, but I was shaking and shivering in my bed and in the end she declared it a summer chill and resigned herself to my being home on the Friday. I knew better than to breathe a word to her of what had happened; I'd learned that to take my troubles to my mother was only ever to make it worse for myself. On the Saturday we couldn't go to the fete, she said, because, after my week off, that wouldn't look right; and that afternoon, on her way to the shop for a compensatory pack of Iced Gems for me, she saw a removal van at the vicarage. 'So, they're off,' she told me. *Pff!* 'And I can't say I blame them, after that.' She wrinkled her nose, enacted a shudder.

I was back at school the following Monday but by then Sarah-Jayne's absence was no longer a novelty and anyway everyone knew the Todds were gone for good and why: the nasty accident that had befallen that man. No one mentioned a gun. We were nearing the end of term, which was the conclusion of our entire time at primary school and Sarah-Jayne had been a negligible part of that, so she wasn't missed over the next few busy weeks from the leavers' service, the prizegiving, the special lunch; and when we left for the final time through the school gate, it was almost as if she'd never been. And if anyone knew the extent of that man's injuries, they never said so in my hearing and to this day I have no idea if he survived.

Clearing Mum's flat, I started small, with her knick-knacks. (Whoever would have thought it of her? But perhaps there's only so much holding out a person can do against the tide of knick-knacks and in the end they come for us all.) It's a nice flat; she was comfortable in middle age and later life. For the final decade or so of her working life she was full-time bookkeeper at a children's nursery – ironic, given her opinion of other people's children, or perhaps ideal in that from behind a firmly closed door she ruthlessly invoiced parents for the privilege of offloading their little dears.

Then and afterwards in her retirement she never lacked for company. There were workmates and she was friendly with neighbours and locals and, seemingly, every last staff member of the nearby shops, including the gawky Saturday kids. At her funeral, people of all ages were lining up to tell me what a good laugh she was.

She stayed living alone. Once she was free of me, she might well have had men friends – attractive, vivacious and independent as she was – but the only one I ever knew was Geoff. They met when she was in her forties and he in his fifties (well preserved, she said of him, as if he were a bog person). He was something in newspapers, she said (sales, I think). Long divorced with two grown-up sons and a smattering of grandchildren. A nice man.

'Going about', Mum called it: that's what she and Geoff did, and as far as Malta, impressively, several times a year, for a decade or more until he died unexpectedly – shockingly – of pneumonia. And after that, in her words, she didn't bother.

Some years back, on the phone, she remarked to me that she'd never really had a friend, not once she was grown up. No one, she said, to whom she could – and she paused, considered – tell things.

What things?

I didn't have a sense, though, that she had in mind any particular confidences; it was more, I think, that she understood that this was how modern friendships were supposed to be. To no one in all these years have I felt a need to confess a hand in that incident at the vicarage. What happened was between Sarah-Jayne and that man as surely as if Sarah-Jayne had been the one to pull the trigger. It was her rage, shot across the lawn, that had him dive for cover.

I'd always considered my mother to be her own worst enemy, with only herself to blame for the lack of friends, but when I came off the phone, that time, I thought how I should be kinder. Because it was all right for me: I'd had it easy. My world has been so much bigger than hers was ever able to be and none of that was my own doing. I was born a late-stage boomer, with a life of free higher education and job opportunities and city-living mine for the taking. I'd had so many opportunities for friendships to flourish. Mum was widowed at twenty-four, with an infant, in the mid sixties, in the sticks, without a qualification to her name and no family to call on. At twenty-four – in the eighties – I was studying for a master's and lolling around in coffee shops sipping cappuccinos.

Those families that we visited, rarely, back when I was small, the Pams and Mikes with their Nicolas and Joannes: were they friends of Mum's? Sitting around in gardens, laughing. Were they friends from before my dad died, or perhaps from before she married, when she had worked in offices in London? If so, what had happened?

Och, life, she'd no doubt have said, had I asked.

Those young couples were moving on, by then, to second babies, third, and bigger houses. Whereas Mum and I were stuck. Mum must have seemed to them both very young – single, with one child – and, as a widow, old before her time.

I wonder, now, what happened to that kid, Sonny. He was there, and then he wasn't: he came to our house on and off, and then, after a time, he hadn't been for a while, and eventually he wasn't ever there again.

Funny to think he was a few years younger then than my own son now. Mum always kept her grandson at arm's length ('You've grown' delivered like an accusation). Even when he was small – perhaps particularly when he was small – she was awkward around him and in turn he, perplexed, was dutiful and respectful, anxious to keep on the right side of her, and my heart clenched to see it. During her visits, I consciously quashed all endearments: she wouldn't have stood to hear any 'sweetie' or 'poppet'.

She baffled him, on her visits, with what sounded to him like questions but weren't. When the first cup of tea was handed to her, *Your dad's a lovely fella, eh? Your mum's a lucky lady. You gonna take after him, are you, eh?* Then when the cake was produced, we'd get *Your mum makes a good cake, eh? Didn't learn that from me! Never had the time; don't know how folk find the time* but two minutes later *It's all work and no play with you people.*

(Which people?)

She seemed to fear that something would be asked of her. 'I've done my bit,' she took every opportunity to broadcast: child-rearing, she meant. She was careful to say it with a chuckle, making light of it, performing a little act: a grandma who was defiantly different. And we three in turn would smile and nod as we knew to do, and give her her due because, yes, she certainly had done her bit. No arguing with that. Once when she saw me taking my son's temperature, she gestured to the thermometer and boasted how, at home when I was a kid, we'd never had one. And I did as she expected, smiling and clucking, indulgent and admiring, when really – it occurs to me now – I could have asked her, gently, if parenting would have been easier if we had.

I do know, now, of course, what she meant by the work of child-rearing: a labour of love was all she had meant. And the job of parenting, as she understood it, was to raise a child to be strong, and the way to make me strong, she thought, was to make me scared.

Don't trust people.

(Which people?)

Don't believe anything anyone tells you.

(Anything?)

Aspirations of kindness, thoughtfulness, quiet confidence, which I might wish for my son, were a luxury, although, to be fair, strength might well have encompassed some of those qualities and possibly, had I asked, she'd have endorsed them. I don't recall her ever mentioning happiness. Survival, for her, was everything.

I've been lucky, I've led a sheltered life and to this day no one else has ever looked at me the way that man did when Sarah-Jayne swung around the newel post and called down the stairs to him. He knew before I did that I could see through him. Which meant I was in his way. I know better than to voice this to any living soul, but my hope has always been that he didn't recover from his fall.

I've moved now to sifting through my mother's documents and I have in my possession that photo of the mystery man. There were no longer any Green Shield Stamps for him to be buried beneath; I rescued him from the even more ignominious habitat of the drawer of recycled envelopes. I am less sure, now – not sure at all, in fact – that he is my dad. He could be anyone. I don't know what to do with him, this faded, old-fashioned, unknown man. He reminds me of how little I know, and that it's now too late to ask. I can't throw him away but nor do I feel inclined to put him on display as, when I was young, I had pledged to do. I suppose he'll end up hidden away again, but this time in my house.

Their marriage certificate was in an envelope in a pile of expired insurance policies and instructions for defunct appliances. I've slipped her death certificate in with it. I'll do the same with his, if I find it.

Acknowledgements

With thanks for support, advice and good cheer to: my agent, Antony Topping, and my editor, Clare Smith; David Kendall and Vincent Kendall Dunn; Matt Bates; Claire Syrett; Sam Scott; Katherine Clements; Victoria Gosling. Thanks to the staff at Curtis Brown Creative and Advanced Studies in England for keeping me in work, and to the students from whom, over the years, I have learned so much. This novel was begun during a residency, for which heartfelt thanks to Ashtree House's welcoming owners Stephen and Judy Penny, and to Julia Copus for arranging and facilitating it. And this feels, to me, an appropriate point to acknowledge and express my deep gratitude for the encouragement at the start of my writing life from Basil Edwards, Malcolm Bradbury and Jonathan Warner.